TENURE

Library and Archives Canada Cataloguing in Publication

Title: Tenure / Kieran Egan.

Names: Egan, Kieran, author.

Identifiers: Canadiana (print) 20200405616 | Canadiana (ebook) 20200405659 | ISBN 9781774390306 (softcover) | ISBN 9781774390313 (EPUB)

Classification: LCC PS8609.G36 T46 2021 | DDC C813/.6—dc23

Editor for the Press: Doug Barbour
Cover and interior design: Michel Vrana
Cover image: Composite of images from iStockphoto
Author photo credit: Greg Ehlers

 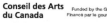

NeWest Press acknowledges the Canada Council for the Arts, the Alberta Foundation for the Arts, and the Edmonton Arts Council for support of our publishing program. We acknowledge the financial support of the Government of Canada through the Canada Book Fund for our publishing activities.

NeWest Press wishes to acknowledge that the land on which we operate is Treaty 6 territory and a traditional meeting ground and home for many Indigenous Peoples, including Cree, Saulteaux, Niitsitapi (Blackfoot), Métis, and Nakota Sioux.

NeWest Press
#201, 8540-109 Street
Edmonton, Alberta T6G 1E6
www.newestpress.com

No bison were harmed in the making of this book.

Printed and bound in Canada

1 2 3 4 5 23 22 21

To Susanna,
whose tenure was nothing like this.

TENURE

a Novel

Kieran Egan

NeWest Press

CHAPTER 1

AS MARK MORATA PRESSED HIS FOOT DOWN, THE NEW Tesla silently accelerated up the hill, easing him back into the seat. This was his favourite stretch of road: the coastal mountains towering up on the left, the cedar-clad islands speckling the sea to the right. Mid-morning, mid-week, a sunny spring day, just a few cars heading the other direction, north to Whistler, where fresh snow on the higher runs was drawing to the ski-slopes those who could be free from work. He had wined and dined and flattered and subtly threatened the beautiful Thai twins who were miraculously effective at conveying his cocaine to the party animals needing a further high after skiing. A satisfactory couple of days. Nothing on the road ahead and in his mirror only the Honda he had swept by moments before.

A thump under the car, subdued by the massive batteries. Had he run over something? An animal, a stone he hadn't seen? A spurt of yellow and black smoke briefly filled the rear window. The car veered left then right, then straightened. He wrenched the wheel to follow the curve of the road ahead, with no effect.

"Mierda!"

No brakes either. He crossed the yellow lines, into any traffic that might come round the bend ahead, drifting unstoppably towards the rock-face at the side of the road, splattering loose stones on the hard shoulder.

He pulled himself away from the door as the mountainside began to scratch then tear at the car. He tightened his grip on the steering wheel, turning it uselessly. The scraping noise of metal against rock was made worse by the snapping and cracking of the shrubs that had found niches in the mountainside. Holding his breath, the muscles of his hands, arms, and shoulders began to lock. The car juddered as it was bounced from one outcropping of rock to the next. He might at any point be thrown across the road and over the cliff down to the sea. The cliffs were not high, but were enough for a fall to be fatal.

A rounded chunk of the mountain came towards him, slamming the door by his elbow with a tearing boom, and the Tesla lurched back over the shoulder of loose stones onto the road. It gathered speed going downhill, wheels now astride the central yellow lines. There was a straight run for maybe a hundred metres and then the road curved sharply to the left. Still no cars coming towards him, but if he continued straight, the Tesla would be over the cliff before it was halfway round the curve.

He caught a flashing glimpse of the Honda he had overtaken accelerating to get between the Tesla and the fall over the cliff. Close to the bend, the Honda turned against the right front side of the Tesla, trying to force it to follow the curve away from the fall to the water. The panels of the two cars crashed against each other. The tires of the Honda shrieked as it turned harder into the Tesla. Mark was horrified that his much heavier car would carry the Honda and its driver over the cliff as well. But the screaming wheels of the Honda found some traction, and the two cars began to move slowly, strainingly left, till the Tesla's wheels were again over the centre lines.

The road curved more sharply left up ahead, and the weight of the Tesla could not be turned that much while moving so fast. Mark waved at the driver to pull away, let the Tesla go! As the bend approached, the Honda leaned harder into the Tesla. But its wheels began to lose their grip and the two cars slid towards the edge, their panels screaming like metal banshees.

Ahead, there was a picnic area with a gravel entrance—some hope, if they could only stay on the road till they reached it. The wide slipway leading up to trees and picnic tables was in sight. But the two cars were being pushed with a terrible tearing sound onto the hard shoulder, and now losing more traction on the loose stones.

A ridge of shrubs and bushes crowned a low rise between the squealing cars and the cliff. The Honda's right wheels bounced against the root-packed earth of the rise as the heavier car forced it closer and closer to the edge, tearing into the bushes. The sturdier bushes kicked the Honda back, battering it harder into the Tesla. Mark could do nothing as the Honda jumped and crashed between the bushes on one side and the Tesla on the other. The Honda driver was clearly trying to brake, but he was entangled with the Tesla, being dragged at clattering, frightening speed. The front of the Honda rose up. It was going was over the edge!

Bushes flashed by Mark, and his front wheels hit something hard and bounced. He was free of the Honda, and on four wheels. Then slowing as he climbed the deep gravel of the picnic slipway.

Behind him, he was relieved to see, the Honda also hit the slipway, veering to and fro as it skidded through the gravel. The Honda's brakes began to slow the car as it slalomed towards the trees to Mark's right. The Tesla, heavier and brakeless, kept rolling towards the low bracken and smaller trees at the southern end of the picnic area. Mark gripped the wheel even tighter as the car rolled majestically into the bracken, bounced a little as it tumbled into the rough drainage ditch, then slammed into the small trees and came to a stop with breaking glass, a crunch of metal, and the ·air bags exploding out to cushion him.

Mark took a deep breath, then quickly disentangled himself from the collapsing air bags and climbed out of the car. He shrugged off the danger and fear and smiled grimly; it was like his earlier days in the drug business before his recent power and eminence had insulated him from everyday violence. He walked past the bushes at the edge of the picnic area, and looked down into the shocked face of his saviour, who had managed to drive across to check if Mark was all right. They stood in uncertain silence for a moment. Odd, after the noise and eruption of terror into their lives, that no one was in the picnic area to witness their almost deadly drama.

"You saved my life!" Mark said.

"Oh ... glad to be there. What happened? There was a spurt of smoke. Your brakes and steering both go?"

"Yes. Your name? If I may, because I am in your debt."

"Geoffrey Pybus. Geoff."

Mark held out his hand. "I am Marcos Gomez Morata. Please call me Mark. I Canadianized myself." He smiled. "Yes, both brakes and steering. Something, a kind of quiet explosion, and then I could do nothing."

They inspected the crumpled panels from front to rear of the Honda. The wheels seemed surprisingly undamaged.

"Are you going down to Vancouver?" Mark asked.

"Yes."

"Can you give me a lift, please? I have to get to the city."

"Of course. Yes, of course. If the car is okay."

Geoff Pybus stood holding onto his open door, expecting or perhaps hoping to talk for a few minutes. Mark delayed a moment, assuming that his new friend's heart was still pumping fast. Geoff seemed a little faint, perhaps dazed that his peaceful morning drive had brought him in minutes so close to death—had he known the risk, would he have done it? Mark stood by the passenger door, looking down the road towards Vancouver, letting Geoff's heart calm down.

But Mark had business to deal with and, after some minutes, smiled as he opened the passenger door and climbed in. He had particular business with whomever had put the malfunctioning bomb under his car. Geoff followed and slowly eased back behind the wheel.

How to repay the debt of a man who had nearly killed himself saving one's life? Geoff slowly drove the Honda back onto the highway towards the city, attentively listening for unfamiliar noises and any unevenness in the car's ride. His door was rattling badly, but seemed to be holding.

"How are you feeling?" Mark asked.

"A bit shaken, I guess. But fine."

"Good. I owe you my life. I won't forget what you did." Mark tried to lighten the conversation by saying, "But you have taken on a burden of responsibility for my life, of course. And for all that I do and all the further effects of my actions, lo, even unto the end of time."

Mark smiled at Geoff, who smiled uncertainly back. Perhaps still too much in shock for quirky humour.

"Now, the matter of my debt. You will of course permit me to pay for the repair of your car. Or, better, you will permit me to buy you a new car."

"Oh, the repair of this will be adequate, thank you. But I do have insurance."

"I will not hear of it. Really, this is anyway quite old."

Mark recognized this as a mistake from Geoff's brief frown.

"I'm sorry, that was hardly gracious. Perhaps about six years old, and well looked after, it seems."

"No, really. Perhaps it's my Protestant upbringing. I can't accept a material reward for … what happened. It would be like saying that's how much I value your life. You've offered to pay for the car to be fixed, which will be expensive enough. And I have the reward of the satisfaction that I saved your life. Except that you would likely have been fine without my ... intervention."

"But then my debt to you is forever. That is ungenerous of you. My Catholic upbringing, no doubt. There is generosity in receiving as well as in giving. Perhaps you would like a new house? Please, don't smile. I am a wealthy man, I would hardly notice the cost."

"But, I like our house. It's a shabby stucco box built in the 1920s, but it is the house our children grew up in. Its walls and doors are not simply another house to them; they are their home; a part of the fabric of their lives. I think it is important to have such stabilities, don't you?"

"Indeed, yes."

"I think you have had the misfortune to have been saved—if that's what happened—by a happy man. Well, a generally contented one. Or, well, by one whose condition would not be improved by being richer. I like my home, my car. I even like my wife and children. I have enough money. A manageable mortgage. My job pays me well enough and gives me time for leisure, and my wife's job ..." Geoff paused and smiled. "Now there's something we need."

"What is?"

"You could get my wife tenure," said Geoff with a quick laugh.

"Of course. But what is a tenure?"

"No, no. Sorry, I'm only joking. Tenure isn't the kind of thing you can get for someone. She teaches at the university ... It's a contract ... Just a joke. You are from South America?"

"Colombia. I lived some time in Chile."

"May I say that your English is excellent?"

"Ah, thank you. A little old fashioned, I discover. I learned it mostly in Chile, studying English literature at university in Santiago. Perhaps too many Victorian writers."

Mark would have Frank, his general fixer, find out about tenure, about Pybus's wife, about what he would have to do to ensure she got this tenure, without Geoffrey or the wife knowing.

There must have been a small bomb under the car, which had failed to detonate properly. He had been known for infinite caution, so it was worrying that someone had been able to locate his car in Whistler. Could it have been a chance sighting by one of his competitors' people or did he have an unreliable employee, and, if so, who? If Kanehara had wanted him dead he would be dead. Likelier was Jimmy Phan and his enthusiastic but unreliable Vietnamese gang. Mark's chest tightened as he reflected on the affront to his dignity. If his people determined that Jimmy Phan was indeed the culprit, Mark would put in place a simple strategy for closing him down, which he probably should have done months ago when Phan and the Vietnamese began trying to squeeze into Mark's territories.

Mark and Geoffrey Pybus chatted amiably on the drive into Vancouver, the one thinking how to tell his wife about the damage to the car and the other plotting bloody mayhem and to deliver whatever tenure was to his saviour's wife. He had easily made the decision. Mark anticipated some brief intervention in the university, some threats and bribes, while his new shipment of Peruvian cocaine, which was at this hour was scheduled to be leaving Pacasmayo harbour en route to San Francisco, began the process of being turned into billions. He loved the magic of changing the leaves of the coca plants into money; he was a master of this new alchemy.

Before he turned his mind back to Jimmy Phan he felt a brief but quickly dismissed notion that maybe this tenure business might involve him in more than he casually expected.

CHAPTER 2

A COUPLE OF DAYS LATER MARK TURNED RIGHT OUT OF the elevator in the English department, offended by the stark concrete walls and cheap, worn carpeting. The institutional buildings he most frequented were exclusive banks and luxury hotels, and neither of them had public areas like this hallway. He made his way round a group of half a dozen animated male and female students leaning over each other trying to read a paper, shouting and laughing, with a casual physical intimacy that he envied.

"Hi. Can I help you?" A pleasant young receptionist smiled up from her chair in front of a computer screen.

"I wish to see Professor William Simpson."

"I'm not sure he's in today. Let me see." She flicked over some pages at the side of her desk, while Mark registered with some surprise that professors of the university could simply choose to come in to work or not. "Ah, sorry, yes he is. Office hours this afternoon. Did you have an appointment?"

"No. Where is he now?"

"He might be in his office. He's not teaching. I could ring through for you."

"Thank you."

"Who can I say wants to see him?"

"My name is … Simpson too."

She tapped her phone and, looking up doubtfully, asked, "A relation?"

"No. Coincidence."

She nodded and looked down, then spoke into the phone, "Dr. Simpson, I have a … a Dr. Simpson here who wishes to see you. Can you see him now…? No … That's right … I don't know." She covered the mouthpiece. "Can I ask what it pertains to?"

"No. I will tell him. Where is his room?"

She held a hand out towards him, as though to restrain him. "Can I send him up, Dr. Simpson? He'll … Yes. I'll …"

As she put the phone down, it rang again. She grimaced, a hand over it, the other pointing back into the corridor.

"Up the stairs, there, two flights. 516."

"Thank you."

He walked quickly up the concrete stairs, touching the false beard that he had applied to augment his natural moustache. It seemed firm. Even so rudimentary a disguise made him feel a little more secure. And he enjoyed the silliness of the unnecessary pretence.

"Come!" shouted a high male voice in response to his knock. He reached for the handle, but it was opened inward.

A young Asian woman stood smiling at him, dark eyes, long straight glossy dark hair.

"Dr. Simpson, I presume. Permit me to introduce Dr. Simpson." She pulled the door fully open and stood to one side. A tall, thin man, perhaps forty-five, with greying long hair in a ponytail, and a grey, trimmed, and pointed beard gave his rather bland face a slight Mephistophelean tinge. He looked up at Mark, smiling, and then eased himself up from his chair and extended a hand. It was clear that he had evaluated his visitor before offering this courtesy. The young woman and Simpson had been laughing; there was a persisting jollity in the room, and also a barely suppressed sexual

frisson. Mark shook hands and sat as bidden on the cheap chair
tucked in between the desk and the door.

The angular professor exchanged an ardent look with the young
woman, which irritated Mark by somehow making him complicit
in its platitude. Mark glanced up at her as she twirled on a heel
around the edge of the door, flaring her skirt and laughing lightly.
As she looked at Mark, her smile wavered somewhat. She fluttered
her fingers at Simpson as she went out, leaving the door open. Mark
reached out a foot and kicked it closed.

The professor looked a little surprised, but kept his cheerful
smile in place as he turned towards Mark.

"Well, so you are a Simpson too. Do you know if ..."

"No. I just said that to the receptionist without thinking. No,
my name doesn't matter."

"I don't understand."

"I was told that you are the chairman of the tenure committee."

"Chair," Simpson said curtly, stroking his beard in a strangely
self-congratulatory way.

"I beg your pardon?"

"I am the chair of the committee. 'chairman' is sexist usage.
Sometimes the chair is a woman. Increasingly." He said this rather
primly, with a further satisfied stroke. And he seemed to have picked
up something near an English accent, or an English way of talking.

"But you are not a woman."

"We need a term that can be applied equally. The nature of the
task is gender-irrelevant, so one must have a gender-neutral name for
it; that's all. Look, I don't understand what you want. Who are you?"

Mark looked at him directly and intently.

"I mean ... is there any reason for anonymity?"

"Only my preference. The nature of my business is person-
irrelevant. I have had no contact with Canadian universities before
and it has become important for me to learn more about the system
of tenure. Who better to tell me than the chair of the committee."

"But I am only the chair of our departmental committee. Perhaps you should meet the chair of the university tenure committee."

"But it is the English department I am interested in, not any other."

"Any case that we deal with is not decided by us. We make a recommendation. Then it goes to our department chair, who makes an independent decision. There is a senior university committee that cases go to after our deliberations, and they make a further independent decision."

"It seems unduly complicated to deal with personnel decisions."

"Oh, democracy gone mad, dear fellow. Absolutely bonkers. Then there is the vice-president academic, then the president, and the Board of Governors. Each case gets a separate review at each stage. Think of the person-hours that go into each decision; makes no sense at all."

"But your committee makes the first decision, or recommendation, on people in your department?"

"Yes. Look, I've got a few copies somewhere here." He slid open a file drawer in his desk. "Copies of the university regulations governing tenure, I mean. You can have one. Save you a lot of time, trying to remember all this arcane stuff."

"Thank you," said Mark, folding and slipping the sheets into a pocket. "My interest is limited to a particular case. That of Professor Pybus."

Simpson seemed reluctant to look into Mark's large brown eyes, but managed to, with a hesitant defiance.

"Clearly you don't understand. I can't talk about a current tenure case with anyone outside the committee."

Mark contemplated the shifting eyes in front of him. He would be unable to trust this Simpson to do anything more than make coffee in his organization.

"I wish to deal with the Pybus case."

"I'm sorry. I must ask you to leave." Simpson looked petulant and offended. He picked up one of the sheets of paper from his desk, along with an expensive-looking gold fountain pen. "I have work to do. These aren't my office hours, you know. I have ... important papers to work on." A couple of quick strokes.

Mark was a specialist in influencing people to conform to his will. Occasionally his instincts dictated actions that considerably distressed his otherwise fastidious personal behaviour. He half-stood, coughed forward saliva, and carefully leaned over and spat it onto the papers in front of Simpson. The academic looked down in horror, and then across at Mark. He reached for his phone, which was on the side of the desk by Mark. As Simpson picked up the receiver and began to press buttons, Mark took hold of the cord and ripped the jack out of the wall. Simpson began to stand, half-tripped, and fell backwards into his chair. Mark casually lifted the gun from its holster under his left arm.

"Sit down, Simpson."

The professor's eyes were riveted on the gun, as though he had never seen one before. Mark realized this was quite possibly the case. From his jacket pocket he lifted out the silencer and ostentatiously screwed it onto the barrel. Simpson slumped further back into his chair.

"Ah, we live in interesting times, Professor. Everyone should have a reliable gun." He lowered the gun in the direction of the professor's crotch. "If I were to shoot you in the knee or somewhere, it would make little noise. Your neighbours would think maybe you had farted."

"What ... what do you ... want?"

"I want Professor Pybus to get tenure."

"Why? I mean ... What do I mean? I mean this is no way ... I can't give her tenure."

"You are chair of your committee. You must have influence."

"No. Not at all. I prefer not to vote. I like to guide the committee, concerning procedures. I expedite their deliberations. If all goes well decisions should be unanimous. I don't need to vote."

"What is happening with Professor Pybus's case?" Mark pointed the gun again towards Simpson's crotch. Simpson continued to speak very fast, looking at the gun.

"I can't ..." Then hurriedly looking at Mark's face, "Perhaps in general terms. Hers is a rare case. Her teaching is outstanding. The best student evaluations I've ever seen. Any of us has. Students worship her. She's clearly very bright too. What she has published is high quality. But she has published very little. Very little. Just three articles, and two of those were written before she was on track here. They were written a couple of years earlier, when she was a sessional instructor for us. So they can't really be counted. She lists a book manuscript, but as it is unpublished, and possibly unpublishable, and as there has been no review or interest in it from a publisher, then it too cannot be considered to have any weight in the decision."

"Is her teaching not enough?"

"No. There are three criteria. Teaching, research, and service. Service is only a small part—committees, talks to groups outside the university, that kind of thing. She has done a lot of this, but it doesn't count for much when it comes to tenure."

"Why did she do it then?"

"Everyone is expected to do something. She just didn't learn how to say 'no' when people asked her to do things. She was Arts advisor. That's being available to advise students on their programs. Very time consuming."

"Did she ask to do this?"

"No. She should have said 'no' again, but didn't. She also took on an overload of committee work. All done with exemplary dedication and thoroughness. Really, it's a very sad, very difficult case."

"But you say her teaching and service are outstanding. Can they not make up for the lack of publication?"

"No. You can't compensate for lack of published research. It's true we're giving more attention to teaching, but we can't count it in place of research. That is central to our job. We make knowledge."

"But you will."

"Em ... will what?"

"You will count her other work as making up for the lack of research published."

"There's no point. What I say isn't decisive. Even if I tried to argue her case, the other members of the committee would think I'd gone mad. I'm afraid it doesn't look good for her."

"You will support her, Professor Simpson, and vote for her. The other members of the committee will go along with you, I assure you. Do you understand?"

"Universities don't work like that. The merits of the case dictate the result. It is a simple rational procedure. If I voted in favour of tenure in a case like this ... it's inconceivable."

"All right, Simpson. I am leaving now. When your committee votes on Professor Pybus, you will vote for tenure. Or I will kill you. Do you understand?"

As Mark stood up, the professor tried to say something, but seemed unable to think of anything to say, or unable to say whatever he was thinking. As Mark began to unscrew the silencer, Simpson managed to say in a tight, high voice, "I don't understand."

"What you have to understand, Simpson, is what to do. Nothing else concerns you. I will tell you that this matter is important to me. It touches my honour. If you do anything except what I have told you, it will dishonour me. I value my honour very highly. Much more highly than your life. Do you understand what you must do, Simpson?" Mark slid the gun into the holster, and dropped the silencer in his pocket. Talking about honour was absurd, of course, but it was a cliché that Mark calculated would do the job with Simpson.

Simpson sat staring at him, as though unable to quite grasp what was going on.

"Well? Can I count on you, Simpson?" Mark took a couple of steps towards him and leaned down to look him in the eyes.

A pause. "Yes," quietly. "Yes."

"You might feel inclined to tell someone about my visit, or even phone the police, after I leave. But please bear in mind that, as we say, I know where you live. If I get even the slightest hint that you have told someone about this brief visit, you will very profoundly regret it. Do I make myself clear?"

Simpson nodded, struggling with a guttural sound that was close to "Yes."

Closing the door behind him, Mark felt disgusted, at himself more than at Simpson. It was humiliating to compel the behaviour of such people. What would happen to his reputation if this got out? Some of his mentors would at least have used the silenced gun to splatter a testicle to keep Simpson's memory sharp.

Mark returned to his replacement Tesla in a parking space outside the bookstore. He paused before flicking it into reverse. His own car was now facing extensive repairs, and maybe it should be considered a write-off. The small bomb failed to explode properly for some reason. He was intrigued to realize how vivid the sudden shock had made his memory, even of the events that preceded it. But he was alive and the normal routines of his drug business were being slightly adjusted by his self-imposed duty to ensure that a woman he'd never met received tenure in her job at this university.

Was he becoming complacent, or even bored with the details that needed his attention if he was to stay alive and on top of the business? Mark's heart gave another pause, and a quick leap, then a patter of rapid beats before settling down again. He began to

count slowly: "One"—pause—"two"—pause—"three"—pause—
"four"—pause—"five"—pause—"six" ... Breathing deeply, he
pulled off the road into one of the capacious parking areas beside
the sea at Spanish Banks. Looking at the mountains across English
Bay he tried to relax the tension in his chest that seemed an increasing and unwelcome companion.

CHAPTER 3

MARK WAITED IN THE NITOBE GARDEN FOR OLWEN Greenwood, his unsuspecting target. The day was dark but the drizzle that had just begun was the first hint of the forecasted rain. The gold back of a foot-long koi moved under the surface of the pond—or was it a lake? What was the rule that distinguished one from the other? How little we know.

Again, damn it, his heart paused then quickly galloped and lurched for three or four seconds before hitting its normal rhythm. Perhaps just tension from too closely monitoring that major shipment of cocaine from his new source in Peru. The gold koi's back breached the water for a moment, before it dived low into the green depths.

According to the briefing file Frank had prepared for him, Greenwood arrived around 12:30 each day. Still about five minutes to go, but here she came. Head down inside the hood of her waterproof coat, she walked as though her hips were made of glass, shoulders bent, as though trying to fit into as small a space as possible.

As she hesitantly approached the covered rest area, Mark turned sideways, eyes down at the file, to be as non-threatening a presence as a six-foot-four-inch man with a dark moustache could be to a mild and apparently fearful woman. He hoped she wouldn't avoid her favourite place because he was there and decide to eat her lunch elsewhere. If she did, he would follow her, of course, but that might make their coming transaction a little more difficult.

She edged crabwise into the rest area, looking at him with what seemed a mixture of fear and distaste. Olwen Greenwood sat and immediately pulled from her bag two plastic bowls. She opened them on the seat beside her, and began scooping the white globular contents of one on top of the yellowish contents of the other, delving back into the bag for a transparent sachet of what looked like mixed nuts and seeds. She shook them onto the bowl of mush on the seat beside her, then reached back into the bag for a newspaper, followed by a bottle of mineral water. Battling the paper as though fighting some recalcitrant animal, she located the section she wanted to read, slapping the crumpled mess onto her knees. She took a spoon from her bag, picked up the plastic bowl and began stirring the white and yellow and nutty materials together till they looked like something retrieved from a vomitorium. She raised a spoonful towards her mouth, hurriedly putting it down again with a suppressed groan. With her free hand she plucked from around her top teeth a comprehensively sized clear plastic and metal retainer and put it onto the rough and, Mark thought, none-too-clean seat beside her.

"Looks delicious," Mark hazarded as an opening.

She glanced up at him as though she was considering whether to make a run for it. But she had clearly invested too much effort in laying out her lunch. Below her large eyes, made a little alarming by magnifying lenses, her face seemed to recede down and back to a small chin that almost imperceptibly rested in a large and loose neck. Olwen Greenwood was not a beauty. She fixed him with a glare that seemed to assess uncertainly what his intention and meaning might be.

"My own invention," she said with a surprisingly clear and almost musical voice. "Cottage cheese and crushed pineapple, with nuts, seeds, and dried berries."

So that's what Frank's note about "terrific voice" meant. Mark had assumed she must be a singer. It was low, almost husky, yet clear and, he wanted to say, sweet. Eyes closed, one would expect such a voice to come from a goddess.

"Most nutritious too."

"Yes." Greenwood nodded, still eyeing him uncertainly, then, as he said nothing further, bobbed her head down to read the paper on her knee. She spooned the goo into her mouth.

Mark waited a few minutes, glancing through the file Frank had prepared. As she scraped the bowl clean, he began to recite quietly:

"Born, Montreal 1972. Excelled at swimming and gymnastics at school. Scholarship to McGill University. Graduated with a 4-point average in English honours in 1994. Masters degree in philosophy, with a thesis on Aristotle's *Poetics*. Ph.D., specializing in twentieth-century American theatre, from Stanford University. First job at the University of Texas at Austin. Accepted an associate professorship here, with tenure, in 2004. Three books; two on theatre. Most recently *Theatre and Theory* published by Harvard University Press. Widely and favourably reviewed. Subsequently promoted to full professor in 2011. Taking medication for depression, and physical therapy for back pain due, it is assumed, to a fall from the parallel bars in the final year of high school. Began orthodontic treatment last year ..."

"What ... Are you reading this? I'm at something of a loss to account for what's going on here. Those are facts about me you were reading. No doubt another of my potential biographers seeking an interview?"

"Forgive me, Dr. Greenwood. A clumsy way of introducing a topic I wanted to discuss with you. May I say that you have an extraordinarily beautiful voice?"

"People tell me they can listen to it by the hour. Which means they don't care about what I say; they just like the sound. But perhaps I may be allowed to use my beautiful voice to ask you what you're playing at."

"I had a colleague prepare some files for me on people involved with an issue that concerns me. You are among these people. But I must confess, the information in your file helps me less than in most of the other cases."

"Always nice to be considered a 'case,' of course. What am I a case of?"

"A case of tenure committee."

"I would have preferred a biographer. When one can make little sense of one's own life, or not much like the sense one can make, it would be so engaging to have a dark, handsome man, with a luxuriant moustache, delve energetically into the case. But it's the tenure committee. So, you are interested in someone else's biography. Whose?"

"Susan Pybus's."

"Funny world, isn't it? I wouldn't have predicted that. So, what's to be done about Susan?"

"I have an interest in her getting tenure, so I would like you to vote for her."

"Do you have a good reason for her to be given tenure?"

"Yes, I think so."

"Well, that's good enough for me. All right."

Mark paused, surprised.

"I hadn't anticipated it would be so easy."

"Clearly the person who composed the file missed out important information."

"But would you tell me why you are so ready to change your vote?"

"You said the reason for doing so was good. Should I doubt you?"

"I'd have thought you might want more information or evidence."

"One either trusts someone or one doesn't—though there are, I'll grant, dreary cases where it takes events to make the decision for one. I trust you. Perhaps it's the facial hair, or the voice—overly correct English with a South American accent. I don't really know why I allowed myself to be talked into sitting on that damn committee. I am also rather partial to large brown eyes. A very good brown, in my opinion. I suppose such judgements are simply matters of opinion. Probably, when I think about it, the world might be marginally better if Susan got tenure rather than turfed out. She's one of the few people in that unlikely conglomeration of lost souls we call the English department who actually seems to like reading and teaching. Do you want to tell me the reason why you think she should get tenure?"

"There must be people who love you just for the sound of your voice."

"Alas, it doesn't seem to work like that. Faces or bodies can be enough for weak-minded men—which I calculate at roughly ninety-five per cent of the subspecies—but not voices. Women are more susceptible in that regard, but I'm not susceptible to them, in the amatory sense. Maybe I should switch; it might be less generally dispiriting. I assume your observation means you'd rather not tell me why you want her to have tenure."

"I'm not sure you would approve."

"A good reason, but one of which I mightn't approve? Perhaps we need to discuss the meaning of 'good.' I generally approve the good—indeed, there are some philosophers who argue that that's all we mean by 'good'—things we approve of. So your uncertainty about my approving this good reason raises doubt-incurring questions. And yet I decided to trust you. What's a girl to do?"

Olwen Greenwood began to gather together the accoutrements of her lunch, tossed them loosely into her bag, crushing the paper in on top of them. She lifted the retainer from the seat beside her, pushed it into her mouth, and stood up.

"It's ..." She removed the retainer again. "It's been a smallish but not entirely inconsiderable pleasure speaking with you. I will vote for Susan's tenure, and trust that good will come of it."

She put the retainer back in her mouth and, a little to Mark's distress, shook his hand with slightly damp fingers. But instead of walking away, she stood still for a moment then returned to where she had been sitting. Removing the retainer again, and putting it back on the seat, she sighed.

"I had thought I could leave it all deliciously incomplete. You know, they—'they' being anonymous academics who do things out of our line of vision—they have done experiments by reading stories to people and asking them later what they remember. One discovery was that unfinished stories are remembered much more precisely, and over a much longer time span, than completed stories. We crave the sense of an ending, and denied it, just crave. Crave meaning, I suppose. I had thought what a delicious time I might have reflecting on this meeting, and constructing wonderfully implausible scenarios to make sense of it. Material for endless sleepless nights. But, I'm afraid I crave explanation."

"As do I," said Mark. "I can't make sense of why you agreed so easily. I don't think trusting me is sufficient. And I'm not sure I can trust you."

"Really? I didn't mean that part. Well, I suppose I shouldn't have said that—about the reason being I trust you. In fact, I simply thought it might be safer for me. Now that you seem quite reasonable, I should say that I really can't change my mind about my negative vote on Susan's tenure."

Mark paused, entirely surprised again, uncertain what to do next. "I think, then, we need to discuss the matter further. Perhaps I can persuade you."

"No, I don't think so. You can try, of course. But first it's you for the confessional. I want to know why you should care about Susan's tenure. I don't want to know everything, as that would be too prosaic, and deprive me of all potential exegetical pleasure later. Let's have a twenty-question routine. Does your job influence your involvement in this 'case'?"

"Not really."

"Not really? Is it yes or no?"

"The, ah, job is entirely incidental, but if it had not been for my job the precipitating event would not have taken place."

"Well, that's no good. You are allowed to answer yes or no, or you can say that the question is too imprecise to allow an answer. I'll not count that answer, so I still have twenty questions. Well, no, that wouldn't be fair either, would it? I mean I have gained information from your improper response. But, remember now, only yes or no."

"I will try to stick to the rules."

"Very good. Are you sexually entangled, so to speak, with Susan?"

"No."

"I was going to say 'how disappointing,' but on reflection the negative response keeps the mystery alive. How prosaic it might have been had you said 'yes.' And how disappointing for my own hopes of an entanglement. Now, do you stand to gain in some way—let's begin with, financially?"

"No."

"What other ways are there? Aesthetically? No, no. Don't answer that. A silly notion. I don't want to lose one of my questions on that. Are you acting on behalf of some other member ... no, more general ... of someone else?"

"No."

"Has Susan appealed to you for your help?"

"No."

"How long have you known ... no, I have to put it differently. Have you known Susan for more than five years?"

"No."

"More than one year?"

"No."

"More than … a week?"

"No."

"Oh dear, what a waste of questions. Do you know Susan?"

"No."

"You don't know her? This is interesting. How many questions have I had?"

"I thought you were counting."

"How can I count and think of incisive questions at the same time? I think it's about six."

"I think it's more like nine."

"Oh dear. Oh dear. We could split the difference and call it seven."

"It's nine."

"If you insist. Have you ever done anything like this before?"

"No."

"I just can't imagine a plausible scenario. I know—you've invented this entirely implausible situation just to meet me?"

"I would, of course, have done just that if I had known about you. But I'm afraid the answer is no."

"That wasn't a question! Just an inaccurate, as it turns out, or rather as you claim, assertion. Does Susan know you are doing this on her behalf?"

"No."

"Are you doing this because you wish to redress what you see as a wrong?"

"No."

"Eleven."

"Twelve."

"Really?"

"Yes. Thirteen."

"You certainly can't count that one. Was the file you have there prepared by a friend of Susan's?"

"No."

"Do you know Susan's husband, Geoffrey?"

"Yes."

"Ah ha! Are you doing this on Geoffrey's behalf?"

"No."

"Oh. Are you an old friend of Geoffrey's?"

"No."

"Is that fifteen?"

"Sixteen."

"You know Geoffrey, but haven't known him long, and he's, as far as I can see, your only connection to Susan. But he isn't paying you, as you do not stand to gain financially, and the file you have wasn't prepared by a friend of Susan's, which, in my view rules out Geoffrey. Was the file prepared by someone Geoffrey knows?"

"No."

"Good heavens. Just three to go. This is difficult. Are you doing this as a favour to Geoffrey?"

"Yes."

"Yes! Yes as a favour. What kind of favour? Are you sexually entangled with Geoffrey?"

"No."

"No, no, I only meant that as a joke. That doesn't count. I still have two more questions. A favour to Geoffrey. In return for something he did for you?"

"Yes."

"So what did he do for you? I must admit, while I may be getting closer to the answer, this is promising to be much less interesting than it was when I knew so much less. Knowledge can be a great prosaicizer—I suppose there is such a word? So you are repaying a favour to Geoffrey, and it isn't sexual or financial. How dreary.

What else is there to motivate the human heart to action? Last question too."

She sat for a few moments longer, looking hard at Mark, then picked up her retainer and stuck it into her mouth. She held out the damp fingers again, which he shook. Mark couldn't help smiling at the liveliness and wit, for which he had not been prepared by anything in Frank's file nor from the appearance of the seemingly anxious woman who had come around the garden and settled nervously into this shelter.

"I'll just have to live with the mystery, though I fear it won't likely entertain me in the silent deeps of the night. I really should have left earlier. Oh well. A little knowledge is a dreary thing. I do hope we'll meet again."

"But you can't go yet. I have to persuade you to vote for her tenure, and I won't take no for an answer."

She smiled, waved briefly, and began to scurry away.

"I'm afraid you have no choice. Goodbye for now."

"I do have a gun. Are you not concerned I will shoot you?"

"Don't be silly." And away she went onto the gravel path towards the tea house.

Mark watched her retreating figure, torn between anger and laughter. Whatever he was doing here, he wasn't doing well. What would Pablo Escobar have said if he could see this attempt to compel a mild middle-aged English professor to do what he wanted? What would Pablo have done? Blown up her house, killed her parents in front of her, shot her in the knees—before beginning to negotiate. Mark shrugged. Well, let her go. He needed only a majority, and he could be more persuasive with her later if need be. He was angry at the wasted time, but a part of him was amused and felt that the time was not really wasted. He had been entertained, she was an interesting woman, and the pressure in his chest had eased.

But then anger suddenly rose up and came over him like an unstoppable wave. He stood and turned to follow her. He began to run, his feet heavy and harsh on the gravel, then stopped, watching her head out the gate. Sinking down onto the bamboo bench under the sheltering overhang of the tea house, he pushed back with disgust the gun he had begun to reach for, spread his legs out in front, grabbed at the notebook in his pocket, and opened it fiercely.

When he had taken his chest pain to the doctor, and described this clenching fist of tension he could not will to release, the bald and affable Pole in his sterile glass and metal office had said lightheartedly in a hurried and heavily accented voice, "My diagnosis: after many years of work, men in their early forties need variety in their activities. Try building a boat, or harpsichord, take up a hobby, make poetry, join a choir, travel more, cruises, hiking. Not all, ha, ha. The mind narrows into itself, and you're not married, it all leads to a need for escape. It's the body's mind saying you are not giving it enough varied nutrition."

So he had begun to try to write poems, which seemed the easiest of the options Dr. Dyakowski had suggested. He looked at the lines he had been struggling with the previous week. It had started with him searching for something to write about—and that had involved a long time staring at the blank first page, then thinking—he had no idea why—of a dark wood in which he saw a flicker of light. When had that happened? What had the light been? What causes a flicker of light? A bit of metal shining, or broken glass, or a reflection from water, or a moving branch against a pale sky, or an animal's eye. What else? But that had given him his first line—"metal, wet, or bird's eye," which he liked. But it needed some context. So he started with "Something glimmered in the winter wood." But maybe "glittered" or perhaps "flickered."

His impotence before three words made him grimly angry again. "Glitter" was maybe too sharp, and not very wintery-woody. "Flicker" was where he'd started, but "flick" was more an action than something you might see. "Glimmer" wasn't ideal either. And he had been thinking about this for a week. Damn it, how was one to know! It was harder work than he'd imagined.

Something glimmered in the winter woods,
Metal, wet, or bird's eye.

Was that a question? Should he finish the second line with a question mark? Actually, "glittered" maybe sounded better? He wanted to add to the scene, and thought of a bird falling dead from the cold sky into a foot or so of leaves. Too many birds, perhaps?

Maybe poetry wasn't the solution he wanted; it was harder than dealing drugs, and he seemed unable to decide which were the best words. How was one supposed to know when one had got it right? It seemed mostly arbitrary. Though he still liked "metal, wet, or bird's eye."

Maybe try building a boat? Damn stupid woman! Twenty damn questions. Can't change her vote. He flicked over the page viciously, and looked at its accusing blankness. He stuffed the book away; he didn't have any idea what to write. Far from helping solve his chest problem, he felt, striding out of the gate of the Nitobe Garden, that his morning now included two distinct areas of failure.

He should write about what came to his mind unbidden from his past, perhaps. The images from his past were of churches, incense, colour, and the drama of the Mass; of the nights with the donkeys, carrying the coca leaves down from the hills, every part of his mind and body alive for sounds of soldiers, helicopters, betrayal; of Josefina in Santiago, dark, beautiful, bleak-eyed, and unattainable, for whom his heart still ached. We grow into our past more than we grow out of it, Freud had said, but Mark wondered whether he was looking for some escape from the self his past had delivered to him. At school they were encouraged to reflect on such things on the Feast of the Transfiguration, an exercise that didn't mean much at eight, but maybe the priests knew, too, that we grow into our pasts, and we would rediscover what we learned as children, suitably transfigured, when we needed it.

CHAPTER 4

KEIICHI KANEHARA LIVED IN A MODULAR HOUSE IN THE woods near the head of the inlet that formed Vancouver Harbour. From his bedroom he could see across the water to Dollarton, where Malcolm Lowry had written *Under the Volcano*. This pleased Mr. Kanehara.

He was thoughtfully feeding the koi in the pond outside his living room when a chime sounded, indicating that one of his cars was coming up the drive. He returned to the sitting room, drawing the shoji screen, and sat quietly on the tatami. Two shoeless young men entered the room, bowed low, and were invited to sit.

"What have you learned about our friend Marcos Gomez Morata? What is he doing at the university?"

The taller young man seemed reluctant to speak. Kanehara waited, his round face holding an expectant half smile.

"We have interrogated two of the people that we established had spoken with him." The young man stopped abruptly.

"And you have learned?"

"Both the man Simpson and the woman Greenwood held to the same story. They say that he has pressured them to help another woman in the English department in some way. They both denied that there had been any mention of drugs in his discussions with them."

"And how were they to help the other woman? Who is the other woman?"

Bowing again, the young man pulled a piece of paper from an inside pocket.

"They were to help a woman called Susan Pybus. They were to get her something they called tenure. It is security of her position in the university."

"Is Pybus a part of his organization?" Kanehara was disconcerted that his rival might have dimensions to his operation that he was unaware of. Surely Morata could not have concluded that the university provided a sufficiently profitable field of operations? What small-scale, cheaper drugs they used were supplied by lower-level operatives who received them mostly from Mark's downtown outlets, though Kanehara had begun to make inroads into this market niche with little exposure to risk.

"We can find no connection between Pybus and other parts of the South American operations. Please forgive our failure, sir. We cannot understand how this operation works."

"What damage was necessary to gain this information?"

"You said minimum damage. We needed only to create some fear in the two we spoke to. A finger was broken in the case of Simpson, to ensure he was not deceiving us. Greenwood provided confirmation, and was unhurt. We took Simpson to the hospital afterwards. The Pybus house is under surveillance still."

"I regret the finger." Both young men bowed low and remained down. "But it probably was necessary. Thank you. You have left a disk with all your information?"

"With Akira." The young men rose, bowed again, and quickly left the room.

Kanehara sat for some minutes. He moved a hand to the set of buttons hidden between two of the tatami mats.

"Akira."

"Yes, Mr. Kanehara." The voice came from a hidden speaker in the wall.

"It is becoming urgent that I locate Marcos Morata's apartment downtown. Has the tap on Wilkie's phone yielded any results yet?"

"It came online yesterday, sir, and since then there has been no contact from Mr. Morata. I will inform you as soon as I discover anything."

"And, Akira, do an internet search on Dr. Pybus, of the English department, and let me have a summary. And increase our presence in the university. I need to know what Marcos … Mark is planning. I do not like understanding so little of something that touches on my interests."

Kanehara slid open the door, stepped on the irregular flat bluestones set into the gravel and moss, and moved across to the rustic seat above the pond. Mark was a wily opponent, and not easily frightened. Could his activity in the university be some kind of elaborate trap? He would have to move carefully, but he could not afford to ignore the possibility that Mark was onto some new and lucrative market, or perhaps to a new supplier of high-quality local marijuana, or maybe a product of the university's chemistry laboratories. But he was working in the English department, not chemistry. Kanehara would prefer to squeeze him out without too much violence. Mark was also a lover of literature and he should be harmed only if necessary. But harmed if necessary.

Kanehara was unsure how to understand many of Mark's actions. The South American seemed to tease him, giving clues to his address, to indicate he knew Kanehara was spending resources trying to locate it, but the clues always led to dead ends. And now he seemed to have broken Keiichi's computer security, and also seemed aware that he wrote haiku.

He picked up his writing brush, first reading the verse he had written during the previous two days:

NIGHT
The dark air gathers.
The water lily's colour
Fades slowly away.

This morning's work, before he had had to turn to the business of Mark and the university, had yielded:

Grey stones in wet moss
—[the apparent relative strength/permanence of the stone]—
Stone too will crumble.

He read the two finished lines a few times, and reluctantly thought the first was a cliché and the last was trite. Kanehara required silence and calm to write; even the sweep of his calligraphy gave evidence to the degree of his perturbation. And the seven syllables of a second line about the strength of stone that would connect the first line to the last just would not come.

He was disturbed by the haiku that Mark had sent to him. Firstly, because it had arrived from an email address that Akira had been unable to trace, though he had followed it through an anonymizing site in Oslo, which coded packages of emails, sent them to Adelaide, where they were decoded then sent for distribution by a dozen sites in Malaysia. Kanehara felt unaccustomed vulnerability, yet Mark had shown no hostility, and Kanehara wondered whether there was nothing but friendly play in his misleading clues and now the haiku.

Secondly, Kanchara was disturbed because he could not decide if his own haiku were any good, and now he was faced by this example Mark had sent him:

In the winter woods
Something glimmers, a quick flash,
Metal, wet, or bird's eye?

He couldn't decide if this was any good either. It was more, somehow, muscular than those he himself composed, all begun from inspiration in his own restful garden. And he didn't know whether haiku could end with a question.

CHAPTER 5

CAMERON TODD SLIPPED HIS HAND DOWN RUTH Whatshername's back and clenched her juicy buttock with increasing firmness as he kissed her with a finality that he hoped would enable him to escape.

"Phew!" he said appreciatively, pushing the release bar on the door with his other hand. "See you Friday?"

"And no phone calls about having to leave town this time!"

"Not if I can help it."

He stroked her cheek with the back of his hand, gave a slight tug to a hanging lock of her fashionably frizzed dark hair, and strode unstoppably out into the sunshine of his accountant's parking lot. He'd have to start extricating himself from Ruth. Ruth ... one of those Mennonite names, or Slovak ... from the prairies. Something to do with Vienna, she had said. Wiens; that's it. Scorchingly exciting in bed, but a major clinger, hinting at permanence after the third outing.

Tall, dark, sleek, good-looking, obviously intelligent, and fashionably dressed in a casual blazer over slim trousers and a flowered shirt, was how Cameron Todd saw himself, as he moved cheerfully towards his Jaguar, opening the doors as he approached. Frank's file for Mark described him as looking like a salesman of something unreliable, too concerned with projecting an external appearance of human perfection, constantly veneering himself, while excessively concerned to be thought honest, honourable, and reliable in all things. Mark was beginning to recognize skills in Frank he had not previously noticed.

Todd was halfway into his car, swinging down into the driver's seat—too late to stop—when he realized there was someone sitting in the passenger seat.

"What...?!"

"It's okay, Professor Todd. Please sit quietly," Mark said. "I just want to talk to you for a few minutes."

"Who the...? How did you get in?" Todd asked, grabbing for his own door handle as though to get out again.

"Please sit. Hands on the steering wheel. Ah, these electronic entry cars are vulnerable to this device a friend loaned me."

The stranger held up a stubby instrument that looked like a small TV channel changer.

"And what do you want ... It's illegal to break into a car."

"Is it illegal to sit in someone's car? Is it trespass? Perhaps so."

"Perhaps you'd like to tell me what you want." Todd's voice betrayed the fear he was trying hard to hide.

"Well, I'm going your way, so why don't you start the car and drive to the university, taking the route by Spanish Banks."

"I have an appointment I need to get to," Todd said, his hands trembling slightly on the steering wheel.

"Yes. Yes. The tenure committee. That's what I wanted to talk to you about."

Todd paused. Mouth open and glancing round at Mark, he pressed the ignition and the big engine mutedly roared into life.

"My business is very simple, Professor Todd. You are dealing with the case of Dr. Pybus. I have an interest in the case, and my interest requires that Dr. Pybus be given tenure."

Cameron Todd turned to confirm that the seriousness of the voice was not betrayed by the face. Yes, it was serious. The brown eyes turned to look into his. Discomfited by the steady gaze, Todd looked to the front, easing the car through the early afternoon traffic towards the bridge. He was not accustomed to being at a loss for words.

"So you want Susan Pybus to get tenure. Why on earth? Anyway, we're not dealing with her case today." He paused. "She won't get it, you know. Or, I mean, the straw vote ..."

"She will get tenure, Professor. And she will be aided by your voting for her."

"Well, to be perfectly honest, I did actually consider it. To stick it to that shit Simpson. He's the chair. But there's no case to be made. It would be laughed at by the university tenure committee if we sent it forward with a positive vote."

Cameron Todd kept taking his right hand off the wheel to smooth down his dark hair, which seemed already smoothly in place. Perhaps a nervous tic?

"You have only your vote to worry about. Leave me to take care of the university committee."

The car was moving slowly and Todd's jittery eyes and fierce grip on the steering wheel were doing nothing to make the drive comfortable.

"You are too close to that cyclist."

The car lurched left and sped up. "Well, I'd like to oblige you, of course. But ... I mean, it's pointless. My vote ..."

"You will find, when you next deal with her case, that many of your fellow members are also inclined to vote yes. I would like it to go forward to your department head with a significant majority of yes votes."

Todd's foot decreased its pressure on the accelerator again. They were ascending 4th Avenue, and the car slowed almost to a halt.

"For heaven's sake, will you drive more carefully!"

The car leapt forward again and kept a good speed till the next red traffic light.

"I wonder can we start again?" said Todd. "To tell you the truth, I just don't get it."

"It is very simple. You will attend a tenure committee meeting at which a vote will be taken on the case of Susan Pybus. You will vote in favour of tenure."

"And what if I don't?"

"The light is green."

Mark had felt ashamed of using his gun to gain Simpson's easy compliance, but Todd's jumpy condition led him to think that simply showing it might get the business done more quickly. He slid the gun from its shoulder holster, and, holding it out of sight from pedestrians, screwed in the silencer.

"What in God's name is that?"

"This?" Mark laid the gun barrel and silencer on Todd's thigh. "It is a standard Glock 17. If you fail to vote in favour of Dr. Pybus, I will use it to shoot you, to death."

The Jaguar slowed and veered towards the curb, then jerked back to the centre of the lane and sped up.

"You will kill me if I vote against Pybus?"

"You will kill me if you don't drive more carefully."

"Being threatened with death doesn't help my driving."

"Alternatively, I will reward you moderately well for the inconvenience of voting for Dr. Pybus."

Todd stopped the car at the red traffic lights on the hill at Arbutus Street and shifted into park. Mark watched a grey-haired woman leaning across a table in the restaurant at the corner, cutting something on the plate of her mother or older friend, smiling and talking as she did so. Todd slipped from his seat belt, opened the car door, and was out into the street in a couple of seconds. Mark turned to see him running fast to the rear of the car and onto the sidewalk, heading at impressive speed down the hill. What on earth did he think he was doing? Had he thought what he would do next after escaping from his threatening passenger?

Mark laughed at the absurdity of the situation. As the light turned green and cars behind began to honk, he opened his door, decided against giving chase to the speeding Todd, went round to the driver's seat and moved the car ahead, pulling it into the curb halfway down the next block. Then he sighed. This was pathetic. He felt foolish and weary. What in God's name was he doing, chasing some professor around the streets?

Well, he was trying to pay a debt to Geoffrey Pybus for saving his life. So he might as well just keep doing what was required rather than face the psychological consequences of giving up. He picked up Frank's file from the floor of the passenger seat, remembering that the efficient Frank had included all the contact information for the tenure committee members. He checked Todd's address and drove towards it.

Where else would a frightened single academic male run? A girlfriend's? The depths of a coffee shop? Bookstore? He would likely want to get off the street or keep to busy streets. From where he jumped out of the car he could get to his apartment in fifteen minutes or less, and if he was frightened he might prefer to go there by the shortest route. But wouldn't he expect Mark to have his address if he could locate and enter his car? Sixty-forty he would head for his apartment, Mark calculated.

He left the car in the visitor parking space under Todd's apartment block, took Frank's file and the paper bag of hundred-dollar bills from the passenger-side floor, and walked round to the front of the building. An Asian woman was coming out the double doors as he approached and, smiling and imprudent, she held the door open for him. It was a large, impersonal, and moderately glossy entrance, and he wore a tie, which seemed an emblem of trustworthy respectability in such a place. He nodded his thanks and headed for the elevators.

Apartment 504 was protected from the casual thief by a sturdy lock, which took Mark about twenty seconds to spring with his small kit. Locks had entertained him from his earliest years. These large modern door locks presented no challenge at all to the security device addict. He closed the door behind him and walked down the small hallway of Todd's apartment and sat on the sofa, again taking out his gun and screwing on the silencer, in case it might have some persuasive use. He would try not to use it again.

He put the gun on the cushion beside him and pulled out his notebook, looked at the lines he was trying to move in the direction of a poem. He had added a new line: "When you come to the gate at the foot of the hill of childhood." But he couldn't see how it fitted with the lines he already had, or where it had come from.

He was too distracted. Slapping the book closed, he slid the pen into the elastic ring on its cover. The Peruvian shipment was now at sea and heading to the docks in San Francisco. Damn Todd. Damn the whole stupid process. Where would he look for Todd if he didn't turn up here? Trying to write poetry was not a cure for unhappiness but just another way of failing, which only made things worse.

The scratch and click of a key. So he had chosen to come home. The door slammed shut. Mark picked up the gun and turned it towards the small hall from which Todd would emerge.

"Bastard! Bastard! Bastard!" Todd said energetically.

The scuffle was the noise of him removing his shoes and putting on slippers.

"Ah, welcome home, Professor Todd."

Todd stood, silent and scared, then began to turn, looked at the gun aimed at his legs, took a step, stopped.

"Now, sit there, Todd. Yes, that chair. Yes, sit. Here, incidentally, is a small bag I had brought with me. I was about to give it to you when you clearly remembered another appointment earlier. Oh, and I've left your car in the visitor parking under the building."

"Right. Right. What's this?"

"I thought I should give you a small payment for your trouble, and the trouble of voting for Dr. Pybus."

"A bribe?"

"Yes. You can have a bribe as well as the threat."

Todd looked in the bag, and leaned down, his hand slowly grasping and lifting one of the thick wads of bills. He inspected it, mouth slightly open, then looked into the bag to see how many others there were.

"My God! How much is in there?"

"Enough. A friend of mine used to call it the *plata o plomo* principle. Silver or lead; take the bribe or a bullet. Your choice, though I'd have thought, in the circumstances, that it's what they call a no-brainer."

"Well, to tell you the truth, I'll be happy to oblige you, but I think you are wasting your money." Cameron Todd seemed to be regaining some of his buoyancy. "I suppose you could bribe and threaten the committee, and the chair, but once it gets into the tangle of university committees, then the president's office …"

"Can you assure me that you will vote for Dr. Pybus?"

"Yes," Todd said quietly.

"That's all you need to worry about. If you change your mind, I will know about it, and you will regret it. I gather your area of research is the metaphysical poets?"

"What?" Todd slicked back his Valentino-style hair again, surely unfashionably oiled, thought Mark. "Yes, yes. I teach the metaphysicals."

As he unscrewed the silencer, Mark said, "I ask only because in my student years I was a great lover of Donne's poetry. I should maybe see if I could audit your class. What is your research?"

"Well, to be honest, I've published most on Donne's 'The Courtier's Library.' It's a satirical library catalogue that Donne put together. The catalogue pretends to be a list of book titles a courtier can mention in his conversations to seem more learned than he is. It was probably written between the summer of 1603 and autumn 1604."

"Not his poetry?"

"Everyone and his dog's written about his poetry. Not a lot on the Courtier's Library. I did my Ph.D. thesis on it, and then, really lucky, some guy poking around in Westminster Abbey—I mean a guy who worked there, not a tourist—found a copy, which had variants, and not in Donne's writing. I got a couple of articles out of that and a grant to visit London for a few weeks."

Mark slipped the silencer in his pocket, holstered the gun, and pulled the cell phone from its pouch on his belt.

"What brought you to do a Ph.D. on the Courtier's Library rather than on his poetry?"

"Same reason. Scads of stuff on the poetry. When I was starting my Ph.D., I looked around at the professors who were best at getting their students jobs, and the guy who was streets ahead did the metaphysical poets. I quickly worked out that hardly anyone had dealt with the Courtier's Library, and there's only about six pages of it, so it seemed a good bet. Then got the job here straight from the Ph.D. I don't mean it to seem opportunistic. But I really didn't get Donne's poetry, and his later stuff was just weirdly religious."

Mark tried not to look astonished, especially as Todd had cheerfully described this evidence of his ingenuity dealing with the academic world as something he clearly felt merited admiration.

"How astute of you, Professor Todd." Mark stood and hit the button on his cell phone for a taxi. "You won't forget how you are to vote in the case of someone likely less astute than yourself, will you?"

At ease now, and pleased with himself and his very profitable morning, Todd smiled and nodded. Mark walked to the door of the apartment, took the elevator to the street, ambled to the park opposite, and sat in the bleachers behind the baseball diamond for the few minutes till the taxi arrived, somehow unable to grasp what the sleek-headed and apparently empty-headed Todd had told him. And this salesman of something unreliable, as Frank had neatly described him, had been ready to dismiss Susan Pybus from his scholarly company.

He gave up and turned instead to trying to think of a sentence that would connect the children at the end of the field of childhood, or at the foot of the hill of childhood, or whatever the line would end up as, with something flickering in the winter woods. Maybe it might be better to work on two separate poems. And maybe he'd read Donne again for inspiration.

Geoffrey Pybus had risked his life when Mark's car had lost its brakes and steering. If Kanehara or Phan had been able to get to his car, they could have put a simple bomb under it and been sure to kill him. Why the timer? And why, if it had worked as intended, did they think they could afford to treat him so contemptuously? Phan and the Vietnamese had begun to secure their own lines of cocaine supply. Perhaps they were announcing their new confidence. They had much to learn and the lessons, he would ensure, would be painful.

He felt pleasure in the prospect of action and revenge, but he recognized something less satisfactory underneath the pleasure. He had initially thought it was just boredom—the operation running too smoothly, too easily, ludicrously profitably. Life with the telephone and shifting investments was no match for the years of constantly rerouting supplies, dodging police, soldiers, and secret service agents, occasionally killing and being shot at. He increasingly felt that nothing now was a match for those early years, travelling at night, under the stars with just the pack animals' feet and those of his comrades sounding on narrow paths through the highlands of Colombia. Or under the clouds, in the heavy rains, wondering if someone might have betrayed them. The intensity of listening for every smallest sound that didn't fit, as the beasts breathed and snuffled and plodded uncaringly on.

He was wearily amused every time he thought of himself as what the newspapers called a drug lord. But he did rule a considerable operation. He had secure supplies from Colombia, and had recently completed building a bigger system that would bring in even larger quantities of superior cocaine from Peru. He distributed an increasingly small proportion locally, and shipped much greater amounts east and to the States, in addition to the European lines of supply that came through Kaliningrad. The Peruvian bags would go first to California, at top prices, and then to Denver for detailed distribution by the Dominican gangs, who had the most reliable network. And while the struggles to create and maintain this magnificent money-generating machine remained an enjoyable challenge, even though he was able to keep it pumping with increasingly little effort, he was finding in his mind this unidentified malaise. He was reluctant to think it was connected with subterranean concerns about what his life had become, and reluctant to think that those concerns might be connected with his disturbed and disturbing heart.

The drug business had taken him from the slums. When he had become too well known, too energetically pursued by the police, his boss had indulgently sent him off to university in Santiago. There he had, unexpectedly, learned to delight in English writers. But he missed the excitement and sleeping under the bush that had smelled like incense in the sun. He had loved church, for its drama in a drab place, when he was young, and its feast to the senses, the colours in the glass and vestments, the dramatic stories of saints, the singing, the smell of incense. Perhaps that was why he had always chosen when possible to sleep under the incense-smelling thorn bush. It had once saved his life. After helicopters had been heard, he and his comrades had tethered the pack animals under the cover of broad-leafed trees, and decided to catch up on sleep after a long trek through the previous night. The rest of his comrades had thrown blankets down near the mules, but he had walked back half a mile to a small hedge of incense bushes. They had been betrayed. Everyone was killed, including the mules. The clatter of heavy machine guns and the roaring of helicopter blades down the hill had woken him. Such a cataclysm of American-supplied gunfire, after which he had huddled with his arms around his knees, while bits of leaves and powder and cloth packaging drifted down on the path in front of him. And the smell of sulphurous smoke and helicopter fuel overwhelmed that of the incense bushes, and blood had spattered so far up the hill that he had red spots on his shirt.

But in those days the turbulence had been outside him, not within. Drugs had been dangerous but the only business available for the energetic and ambitious. Now he was finding it harder to resist this self-interrogation that awaited him whenever the action of his life paused.

CHAPTER

6

"THANK YOU FOR FITTING ME IN, IAN. I JUST HAD A SMALL question about this tenure business. And I didn't want to see William Simpson at this delicate stage, and didn't know who else to ask. And as it will all come to you next anyway as department chair, well, I thought I'd drop it onto you."

"No problem, Susan. Any time. But I think Sally mentioned I have Hilary coming in a few minutes, so ... well, sorry ... if it can be brief?" Ian Carbonell leaned forward onto his desk, patently full of attention, patently for no more than a few minutes.

Susan Pybus opened her light-brown leather folder. She was nervous. Carbonell was physically imposing, and whenever possible imposed himself physically, never quite in a way that one could object to, certainly never with any overt sexual intent, but his big frame, still powerful despite the accumulation of flesh around it, and his striking head, now more florid and heavy than classically handsome as it had been a decade or so earlier, were usually placed too close, and always loomed domineeringly, over women in particular. She felt, too, that he was unsympathetic to her case and was quite looking forward to informing her with expressions of his deepest personal regret that she was not to be granted tenure.

"I have had a letter from Shirley Jenkins, in Boulder, University of Colorado. She's very well known in the nineteenth-century fiction field. Two books from Yale University Press. Both very well received. She's editing a book on nineteenth-century women writers and asks if I would be interested in contributing," she looked down at the letter in her folder, "on any of the Brontës."

Carbonell looked at the greying head as she looked down. She was a good-looking woman. She never wore makeup, but was somehow entirely feminine, which seemed to endear her to large numbers of female graduate students who took her as an ideal role model, and irritated Carbonell because she seemed totally uninfluencable by all the means he used to get his way. Even the fact that she was an untenured assistant professor did not prevent her contradicting him in department meetings. He distrusted her apparently uncompromising rectitude. It was like having a saint on a bank's board of governors, admirable but a hindrance to the way business needed to be done.

"That's good."

"Yes. What I want to know is whether I should ask to have this added to my file and considered. It indicates something of my reputation that Shirley Jenkins would issue such an invitation, don't you think? But I suppose the fact that it is an invited paper for a book rather than a refereed paper in a journal will make it count for less in the eyes of the tenure committee?"

"Well, as you know, Susan, peer review is always preferred. As far as the committee knows, and certainly the university committee to whom your file will go after me, Shirley Jenkins could be an old friend of yours, trying to do you a favour. Of course"—he raised a hand as though she was going to object, even though she had made no sign that she was—"I know that isn't the case. But I'm afraid invited articles do count for less in the eyes of a tenure committee. And, again, this is hardly written yet, is it? But, all that said, my judgement would be that it can certainly do no harm to add a copy of the letter to your file and may do some good if someone might be wavering about their vote. Send it to Bill, with

a covering note detailing the things you've just mentioned to me."
He looked at his watch.

"Thank you for the guidance, Ian." She stood and smiled briefly,
in a distracted way.

"Anything about the book?" he asked.

"No. I'm afraid not a word. Nothing at all since the letter
acknowledging they had received it."

"Pity. Unfortunately the committee can't weigh a manuscript
that has elicited no interest, no peer review or evaluation." He
tried to sound regretful, but he considered Susan Pybus's long-
hatched book manuscript one of those hopeless, unpublishable
ventures that too many academics had at the bottom of desk
drawers. Decades later, they would haul them out and make students read the dreary stuff.

"It seems not fair to say it has elicited no interest. It simply
hasn't had reviews yet."

"Yes. Of course. That's what I meant, of course. Sorry."

He stood, too, feeling slightly more comfortable so high above
her, where her direct appraising eye was a little further away. She
had a disconcerting way of looking at him so that he saw himself
through her eyes. Tom O'Shea had said much the same about her;
she made you feel you were looking in an unflattering mirror. She
knew this tenure process was not likely to go well, and he couldn't
help feeling some sympathy, recalling hopes of his own that were
disappointed—perhaps in his mind because he was expecting
Hilary soon.

"I know I keep making pessimistic sounds, Susan. But you are
an entirely plausible faculty member. I mean, it would not be weird
to have you as a tenured member of the department, if I might put
it that way. Your work is better than that of a number of people
who are already tenured. It may well work out."

She turned at the unexpected warmth in his voice. He smiled.
Susan was aware that Carbonell was capable of genuine charm

and kindness, just that he seemed usually driven by motives that submerged them or displayed merely a pretence of the real characteristics. Odd to see a charming man so often unconvincingly pretending to be charming, but she was pleased to see the real charm had not been submerged completely, whatever he would prefer to happen about her tenure. She smiled back, remembering the definition of charm as that aspect of a personality that expects the answer yes before a question has been posed.

She had taken up less than five minutes, so as she closed the door behind her he sat down to look through the list of faculty who had applied to offer honours seminars next year. Always a lot. An honours seminar meant they could teach in the area of their current research, the seminars would have the best of the students, and the classes would be smaller. In the old days the chair had simply handed out these plums to his friends, but now he had to give enough to the feminist lobby to keep them from his door, the pre-tenure group to keep them from complaining to the dean, and those he hated most to show how even-handed he was. His friends and supporters were the only ones he was able to offend.

His secretary, Sally, phoned to say that Hilary Lockett had arrived. He passed a comb through his thick blond and grey hair, feeling the quiff with his fingers, pushing it forward and up a little. He was only too aware that his early Apollo-like good looks were sinking under accumulating weight and years, and he realized increasingly that he tended to sit slightly hunched so that he pushed his face forward and up a little to minimize the lines and sag. In fact he'd lowered his office chair a little to make this less obvious, and wondered whether, for Hilary's visit, he might have wisely slipped it down a further notch.

Hilary seemed always to sweep into rooms with a kind of challenge. She had for years been one of the few women in the upper ranks of the department; she was tall, blond, and strikingly handsome. Now approaching fifty, she was slim, large-breasted, wide-mouthed, and the lines on her strong face were slight and somehow flattering. After a few moments close to her he invariably felt the beginnings of an erection; he felt it already. This was an atavistic response to memories of their affair seventeen or eighteen years ago. It had begun when she first arrived, already separated from her first husband, a weedy physicist who washed rarely. How she ever became mixed up with him Ian had never been able to understand.

For two months they had made love almost daily. The one part of the whole business he recalled with any pride was his organizing it so that his tolerant wife—his first tolerant wife—had had no suspicions. Then one day as he arrived already engorged in anticipation at her Kitsilano apartment, she opened the door fully dressed, unlike her usual dangerous swinging of it open while naked. He had a number of times tried to dissuade her, suggesting he might be a delivery boy or the electricity man; also he preferred to undress her. But she had just laughed and persisted, in that reckless way, as though half hoping it might be a stranger some days. Hilary had not let him in, told him she had found someone better: "So there we are," she had said, smilingly dismissing him.

But he still could not see her without recalling that long naked body and her generous passion, and the memory had its inevitable effect. Despite much sexual experience, he found the old cliché entirely apposite: he had never known it could be like that. She had since treated him as though nothing had ever happened between them; a daily humiliation over many years. In the old days, when he still tried to mention it, make some reference to what had been the clear highlight of his sexual, and romantic, life, she had looked vaguely at him, slightly perplexed, as though perhaps he was making it up.

She swung the door open. "Ian, something very odd is going on."

Her eyes seemed to be becoming greyer with the years, from the clear blue, becoming a kind of smoky blue that he found even more alluring. Perhaps she was wearing tinted contact lenses. She had an extraordinarily interesting and beautiful face. His old question about why she had never married again, after the two short-lived experiments in her early twenties, floated by as he tried to come to grips with what she had said.

"With what?" Something odd? When isn't something odd going on in the department?

"The tenure committee. I realize our deliberations are supposed to be confidential, but you do get a report in the end, and as head I think you should be aware that something very peculiar is going on."

She had a disconcerting habit of stopping when one expected the point to be clarified, and somehow challenging her listener to respond as though she had already delivered her message.

"Yes, Hilary. And what is going on?"

"It's about Susan Pybus. I just passed her. I suppose she had been in here making her case?" Ian could not work out why Hilary should be so hostile to Susan. They were about the same age, and every advantage was with the tenured full-professor Hilary, except perhaps she too was a victim of the unflattering mirror. And who knew what she saw in it.

"Just asking some advice."

"Today Simpson insisted we take a straw vote on her case—which was odd in itself. We've all been through the file, of course, but we were putting off votes till next week when we're promised the remaining referees' letters. Todd insisted on having his vote in favour of Susan recorded for the report that would go forward with the file, and Simpson said he had changed his mind as well."

"Maybe they have simply changed their minds—if you could call them that? Even been persuaded by arguments on the other side."

"There haven't been arguments on the other side. Look, everyone thinks she's very worthy and all that, an excellent teacher, but she hasn't done the research. Well, there's that putative book manuscript no one's seen and no publisher seems interested in. She just hasn't published enough. Now look, I don't want to rehash all the arguments of the committee."

She said this accusingly, as though he had improperly solicited them.

"Everyone would like to say yes to her, but the publications just aren't there. Even if we say yes, it'd be turned back at the university level, or by the vice-president academic. And then we'd have a black eye as well." She ended on the usual challenging note. He realized, not for the first time, that if she wasn't so sexually alluring, he probably wouldn't like her at all; but he applied quite different criteria for liking men than for liking women.

"I'm not clear why you are so convinced something odd is going on. Or what you think I can or should do."

"Simpson has been one of the most dismissive of Susan's case up to now. And suddenly, with no argument but a few strokes of his absurd beard, he votes in favour of her. I think that's quite sinister."

"You can't mean that Susan Pybus is seducing Simpson."

"That is the only form of influence you can imagine, I suppose. No, of course I don't think Susan Pybus is seducing Simpson. Good God, Ian, you're hopeless."

"No doubt. So what sinistral forms do you imagine?"

"Mary Chou ... you know her? Graduate student, seems to have been around since the Old Testament. She asked me the other day if I'd met the other Professor Simpson."

"The who?"

"Quite. She described him as a big dark-bearded man she'd met as she left Simpson's office last week. She thought nothing of it, till she remembered seeing the same person talking with Greenwood in the Nitobe Garden. Made a bit vaguer as she said she wasn't sure he had a beard in the garden."

"How do you know it ...What's so odd about that? My dear Hilary"—it still added a thrill when he could use endearments however formally couched—"the sinistral element isn't coming through. Did Olwen Greenwood change her vote as well?"

"Well, no. But there was something weird about the way it took her a while to get her hand up with the negative votes. Mary had no doubt that the man she saw visiting Simpson was the same one she saw in the Nitobe Garden talking with Olwen, despite the beard uncertainty. She said—that is, Mary said—there was something … something chilling about him. And that she wondered if the visiting Simpson was related to William. I've talked with her again today, eliciting as much detail as she could remember, and it certainly seems the same man who talked with both of them."

"So you are suggesting that someone is going round the department trying to influence the members of the tenure committee to change their votes about the Pybus case?"

"I'm not suggesting anything so precise. But I'm glad you immediately drew such a conclusion, however bizarre it seems."

Ian sat back, conscious of a momentary advantage. She wanted his acquiescence, felt uncomfortable suggesting so extraordinary a possibility as coercion of a tenure committee by an outsider, and so was looking at him with her most challenging glare. He found this moment of her vulnerability exciting, and glanced quickly over her white-bloused upper body, with desperately suppressed longing.

"When is the final vote?"

"It could come as early as Tuesday next. That's the next scheduled meeting, but we still are waiting on two of her reference letters, as I said. Simpson has phoned and they both promised they would fax them. Why people can't write a simple reference letter in a month and a half defeats me."

"I'm not sure what I can do. Send a memo around alerting people? That would be alarmist, and this person you have seen could be about entirely legitimate business. He could be a publisher's rep. and the two sightings pure coincidence."

"Mary said he was introduced as *Doctor* Simpson."

"A misunderstanding possibly. One of the secretaries making a mistake phoning up? Who knows? Certainly too little information to take any precipitous action. Leave it with me, Hilary. I'll have a word with the dean. Also we might informally alert people. Tell anyone you see to give me a call if they see this person again. Will you phone each member of the tenure committee, except Simpson and Greenwood of course, and tell them to be wary? I hope this is nothing, but you were right to bring it to my attention." Oh, bad, bad move.

"There's no need to be patronizing. Of course I was right. Good heavens ... really!"

As she strode to the door, he watched the movement of her buttocks. Something pulled at his memory. Not her body long ago and naked; something he had read recently. Ah, that damned pamphlet from the Women's Centre on harassment; the detailed section on how visual attention to the sexual characteristics of women's bodies constituted a form of harassment had surprised him. The precise characterization of "lascivious looking" exactly described how he had always looked at women, how he was looking at Hilary as she closed the door behind her. How else was one supposed to look at women, for goodness' sake? What else is as pleasant to look at? That policy document was no doubt written by a committee of overweight lesbians in the Women's Centre, and passed by gutless and clueless male administrators. They all seemed to live under the bizarre illusion that their policy documents could rewrite six million years of evolution.

CHAPTER

7

HILARY LOCKETT ALLOWED HERSELF A NUMBER OF INDUL-
gences. Indeed she occasionally reflected with some satisfaction
that her life was increasingly filled with little else. And she was
engaged in the constant challenge of whittling away at those
regrettable features of her life that still intruded on her indulgences.
Prominent among those regrettable features were her colleagues,
meetings at the university, students, especially having to read students' papers, and almost all aspects of her job apart from her own
research. Despite this, she was an intellectual—which meant only
that she took her greatest pleasures from intellectual things. She
was a woman of many strong appetites: sensual, gustatorial, aes-
thetic, athletic, spiritual, but above all, though only just above the
sensual, she was an intellectual. She also, to the bewilderment of
many of her colleagues, had a small passion for ballroom dancing.
But this was Friday afternoon; the *Times Literary Supplement* had
arrived, and she was at her favourite table in the Pan Pacific Hotel's
upstairs dining lounge. Before her on the crisply white-clothed
table was a large pot of tea and an assortment of small German
cakes. She had just opened her *TLS*. She turned the chair to her
left so that it faced her, and the screen of her titanium Apple laptop
computer glowed on its seat, waiting for her to enter any notes or
ideas that might come to her mind as she read.

"It doesn't get any better than this," she muttered to herself.

Hilary Lockett's intellectual interests were boundless, some would say wholly undiscriminating. She would read reviews of books about medieval Persian pottery with as much fascination as articles about modern Norwegian politics or nineteenth-century Argentinean poetry or theological disputes among Shinto sects or the history of cricket in Jamaica. She was astonished that anything as purely intellectually excellent as the *TLS* could be published week after week.

She poured the first cup of a special Darjeeling tea she had discovered the Hotel kept for VIP visitors, and could be persuaded to provide to the discriminating few who asked for it insistently enough. She lifted her fork and made a generous slice through the small mocha cake. As she raised the sweet richness to her mouth, a large, good-looking man sat down opposite her, and smiled. He carried a copy of the *TLS* she hadn't yet seen, and put down on the table a computer exactly like her own.

"Forgive my asking," she said. "But how is it that you have a more recent *TLS* than I have? I've just got this week's in the mail."

"Ah, I have a friend bring me a copy from London as soon as it is available. He travels to and fro a lot." Mark had been interested to discover that Frank, in his scenario for this afternoon's meeting with Dr. Lockett, had known this; clearly his employees gossiped about him.

"Ha."

She looked around at the number of empty tables, while forking in the mocha slice. Normally she would simply ask an intruder to move, or get the waiter to move him. But she was torn between wanting her privacy in order to get on with her Friday intellectual delights and the possibility that this intruder might lead to serious sensual pleasure. He had obviously seen her and intended to force himself on her attention. She returned her eyes to the review of a book about spies at the court of England's Elizabeth I, interested in how the stranger would make his move, and what move he would make. The *TLS* and identical computer, she regretted, gave him too easy a line of approach. She took a sip of tea.

The Eastern European waiter approached the table.

"What can I get you, sir?"

"I think some cakes, such as the lady has. And I understand you have a fine golden Darjeeling tea. A pot of which I would like."

"So the same as your lady friend."

"Ah ...yes," said Mark. "The same as my lady friend."

Hilary felt at a distinct disadvantage. Normally she would have enjoyed dealing with such impertinent presumptuousness, but didn't know what to make of the *TLS*, the identical computer, and now the order for her favourite tea. What was going on? She took a slice of the walnut cheesecake, chewing meditatively.

Irritated, she realized that she had not understood a word of the previous paragraph, while, instead of following up with one or other of the more obvious approaches open to him, her visitor had folded open his *TLS* and seemed to be reading intently. They read in silence for the five minutes it took the waiter to bring Mark's tea and cakes.

"Thank you."

She had read the whole review twice now and had little idea of what it said. Hilary was growing increasingly irritated, and felt the need to take back control of the situation.

"Don't you think it odd that we should both have the *TLS*, an Apple computer, ask for the same tea, be here at the same time. Pushing coincidence a bit far, don't you think?"

"We do have different issues of the *TLS*. And I'm male and you are female. I'm taller than you and you are older than me ... There are so many differences; why dwell on the very few things we have in common?"

Hilary looked at the brown eyes opposite threateningly. But, unusually, it was she who wavered. There was something disquieting about him. She took a drink of tea, as he poured a cup from his pot.

"Would you care to give your best explanation of the coincidences?" she asked. "And I'd guess the spread in our ages is no more than five years, and I'm sure most people would assume from looking at us that you are five years older than me."

"Oh, ten years older at least, I'm sure. My best explanation of the coincidences? I can't. I do not believe this set of similarities could be a matter of coincidence. The odds against are astronomical, even allowing for the different issue of the *TLS*."

Then he began to read again. Hilary returned to the mocha cake, feeling in need of comfort and a reliable ally in this somewhat irregular conversation. He was clearly playing some kind of game, but what and why? And the elaborate contrivances—what could justify them? He had more or less admitted they weren't coincidental. As a pickup strategy, this one was certainly interesting, but the work required was out of all proportion. She turned the page of her *TLS*, giving up on the spies for now, sipped her tea, and returned to reading—about the relationship between capitalism and the development of standardized time and calendars—leaving him to make the next move. She decided she would be in a stronger position counter-punching, rather than leading and letting him monkey around. Her irritation at the interruption to her Friday afternoon routine with the *TLS* gave way to a furtive pleasure as she realized this was a game, and, even though she hadn't a clue about the rules, the personal and intellectual challenge from a good-looking stranger was readily engaging. The bout over tea and cakes began to take on a slight sexual frisson. Which is how she liked her games.

They continued in silence for ten minutes. They poured further cups of tea, forks clinked against plates as small pieces of cake were cut, pages were turned noisily, the waiter was informed that neither of them wanted more of anything, at intervals both of them turned to their computers and the soft clicking of keys made each of them wonder what the other might be writing. Hilary considered various lines she might use to break the silence: What game are we playing?—I'd like to play my part as well as possible, or, I'd be at less of a disadvantage if I knew. Do you come here often? What's the verdict on the new Schopenhauer book?—I see his picture is on your front page. How about a quick fuck? She had used the last to good disturbing effect a few times in the past.

"Excuse me," Mark said.

Hilary looked up in surprise. Had she said it aloud? He was pointing with his fork to the mocha cake on his plate.

"I wondered whether you might like this last cake. I've had more than I should."

"There's no point having less than more than one should, I tend to think. But another one of those would mean another quarter hour in the gym tomorrow, so I'll pass, thanks. You should ask for a doggy bag."

"But if you were to accept the cake, I could then ask a small favour in return without feeling too guilty."

"For a mocha cake, it had better be a small favour."

She liked his easy smile and good teeth.

"Is this elaborate farce of the computer, the tea, and the *TLS* all part of getting me to do you some favour? Or is the favour separate from the backdrop?"

"Ah, I should explain. I wanted to meet you, but I have a colleague who made the arrangements. I have been discovering in him, much to my surprise, a theatre director manqué. All this"—he opened his large hands indicating the table, computer, and *TLS*, and grimaced—"is a result of my perhaps indulging him too much."

"So what is the favour? And who are you, et cetera, et cetera?"

"I want to persuade you to vote for the tenure of Susan Pybus."

"Oh so that's who you are. You had a beard—what happened to that? And why, for God's sake? Susan Pybus! Do me a favour!"

Hilary considered, briefly, getting up and walking away. That this handsome man was pitching for Susan Pybus, though, suggested puzzles too interesting to leave unsolved because of offended propriety.

"I'm afraid you would likely find my reasons boring."

"How could they be boring? I'd expected something quite exciting after all this staging. So you've been going round the tenure committee one by one persuading each one to vote for Susan. What have you been offering them?"

"Oh, little things. To not kill their children or burn down their houses or erase their hard drives. That kind of thing. Send them on cruises. Actually, I have only recently begun, so I haven't exercised the range of inducements open to me. I should make it clear, though, as we begin negotiations, that I will accept no other result but your positive vote for Dr. Pybus."

Hilary paused. She could pretend to be affronted, and see how he would deal with that. Perhaps get up in a huff. How would he restrain her? Would he try? But the game was engaged at last. If she threatened to leave, he might let her go, and that would be an afternoon's potential entertainment down the drain.

"But what if what I require to deliver my positive vote is something you find yourself unable or reluctant to give me?"

"We will just have to find some other way."

"But there must be a point at which what I require is maybe just a little inconvenient, or a little distasteful, for you, but not enough for you to refuse. I mean, if I say I'll do it for no reward, you'd be happy, and probably my asking for ten dollars would be fine. But if I asked for a million dollars, that would not be fine. So there must be a point between ten and a million which you would ..."

"I understand the principle. What do you have in mind?"

Hilary felt irritated at being wrong-footed again, but also noted for possible future use in the verbal battle that he was sensitive to being underestimated.

"Well, nothing at the moment. That's what we have to explore. Maybe I'll have that mocha cake after all. Some more tea? I need to go to the toilet. Please order me another pot of Darjeeling."

Hilary returned as the pot arrived at the table along with a new plate of cakes. She had checked that her teeth were clear of cake debris—nothing worse than discovering one's most alluring smiles were being delivered with a dark chunk of chocolate cake waving at one's victim.

"I thought we might both need reinforcements," he said. "Perhaps we might share the fresh pot and cakes?"

"How nice." Hilary closed her computer, folded her *TLS*, and slipped both into her briefcase. "What do you do, by the way? I had assumed the computer and *TLS* were tools of your trade, as they are of mine, and so I had assumed you must be an English professor, at some other university or one of the colleges. But if they are merely props for this scene you were to play, I suppose you could be anything."

"The *TLS* and the computer are mine—my colleague who plans these scenarios works with what materials he knows are to hand—but I do not teach English, nor do I teach anything else at a college or university."

"Am I to guess your occupation, or are you going to tell me?"

"Because your knowing my occupation might make my present task somewhat easier, and any threats more plausible, I should tell you—implausible though it may seem—that I run a large organization that imports and distributes cocaine. I am a drug lord, as the media insist on putting it."

Hilary felt that she was consistently losing control of the conversation and needed to be energetic in regaining the initiative. But she approved of a man, especially a foreigner, who knew that the word "media" was plural.

"You're right about the implausible part. And I hadn't realized that threats were also on the agenda. I thought we were to discuss what positive inducements you could offer me. Though I suppose threats are cheaper."

"The money isn't important. Let us, indeed, restrict our discussion to rewards."

"I'm not sure I can believe anything you say. Have you seen *The Draughtsman's Contract*?"

Mark shook his head.

"It's a Peter Greenaway movie. Set in the late seventeenth century. A woman wants to have the most famous painter of houses— the exterior of the house in its setting—paint her husband's house. She wants to give it to the husband as a gift. There was a craze for such painted Prospects, and the most famous 'draughtsmen' could command huge fees. The woman couldn't afford this particular draughtsman's fees, but desperately wanted the painting, so signed a contract, one of whose provisions permitted the draughtsman access to her body for sexual purposes at any time during the month that the contract was in existence. Or, at least, that's what I remember of the story. It ended badly for all concerned, as I recall. So, what about a deal whereby I deliver my positive vote in return for sexual services over a period to be negotiated and a frequency to be negotiated, that will allow for the frailty of the male in these regards, especially an aging one?"

"I had thought of universities as places of intellectual endeavour, but I seem to find them riddled with fevered and uncontrolled sex and a passion for money, on a small-scale. The answer to your question is no."

"No need to be so self-righteous. I was just exploring the range of possibilities. You'd indicated that money was no problem; I was just beginning to see what else might be on the agenda. So, sex is off. How about dancing? Do you dance? I sometimes need a partner for ballroom dancing."

"I don't dance."

"Well, this is becoming increasingly unenticing. Perhaps it would be more interesting if I refused to change my vote, and we could discuss the various tortures you might inflict on me to change my mind."

"Yes, I'm sorry. This hasn't gone well. I was not prepared for your suggestions."

He reached into his jacket pocket and took out a chequebook and pen.

"This is appallingly crude, but may I offer you $20,000. Not as a bribe, but as a consolation for not having to face the threats and tortures I would otherwise resort to?"

"I like the subtlety. And I was just beginning to enjoy the conversation. You're only trying to quit because you were beginning to lose. Okay. $20,000 is fine. Pity about the sex."

"You are a beautiful woman, Dr. Lockett, and I am an inexperienced man. I would be a great disappointment to you."

"Most men are."

"Now if I had just come into the dining room, pulled out my wallet, and offered you $20,000 for your vote, would you have said yes straightaway?"

"No."

"So I can report to Frank that his stage-setting was significant in our getting relatively painlessly to this satisfactory, though not ideally satisfactory, conclusion?"

"Yes. I suppose the hidden Frank's screenplay was somehow complicit in the successful result, arid though it is. Would you like me to hold out for more? After all, I can't with good conscience vote for Susan Pybus."

"Why not?"

"'Good conscience' is not the phrase to use, of course. Susan is such a dreary goody two-shoes. Well, I don't know. I have spent some time trying not to think about why I don't like her. I mean I hardly know her, oddly enough. And the hostility is unmotivated by anything she has ever said or done, and so powerfully visceral that I don't want to explore it. I have found such things tell one more than one wants to know about oneself."

"You sit here alone, and clearly get your greatest pleasures alone."

"Yes. I don't like human beings much. I would rather have been ... oh, a vole. I think Oscar got it right when he said, 'I sometimes think God overestimated His abilities when He made humans.' And I don't think we need a psychoanalytic session. You are a nice drug lord, no doubt, and I would really like $20,000, and if voting for Susan is what it takes, that's what I call easy money. And how dare you say I get my greatest pleasures alone!"

"It is what Frank has written in your file."

"Fuck Frank."

"I'm sorry. I didn't intend to irritate you."

"Oh, don't take any notice. One peaceful Friday afternoon down the tubes, and we don't have too many. I thought I had sacrificed my pleasure with the *TLS* to a pleasant game. But that has been a disappointment too. And now I've only got $20,000 to show for it."

"What will you do with the money?

"No idea. You have any recommendations? Stock tips?"

"Clear a week early next month and go to Verona."

Hilary smiled at this seriously offered suggestion.

"Will you come with me? I'll pay."

"You don't want me to, of course. My fault, or Frank's, for the realizations our tea has brought us to. And we can't start again now."

Mark handed Hilary the cheque. She looked at it a moment, tore it into small pieces, and threw them across the table at him. At last, the initiative was entirely hers.

"And of course I won't change my vote."

She stood and walked imperiously across to the exit. She took her coat from the rack by the white-roped entrance to the restaurant, and looked back towards Mark unsmilingly.

And he had thought the world of drugs was ruthless. He sat back, wearied by the emotional currents of their conversation leading in the end to his sense of helplessness and suppressed rage at failing again to compel a positive vote for Pybus's tenure. And a bit late, and public, to use the gun for persuasion.

Hilary stood a moment, waiting for the fool to respond, to come after her, even to signal something. What was wrong with him? Of course he could have her vote. She couldn't stand here longer. Annoyed, she moved towards the stairs. He was just sitting there. How had she miscalculated? She couldn't turn round again. Should she go back and say she'd do it for $30,000? She surely hadn't sacrificed $20,000 just to take control of a conversation! Surely he'd come after her? Each step down made her angrier. Entering the car park, she looked round, but he wasn't there. And, she admitted to herself, she found him curiously attractive, even if a bit disquieting. She tried to assure herself that he'd certainly try again, perhaps with some better inducement. Men are useless.

As his slow and too familiar anger was mounting, Mark wrenched his notebook from his jacket pocket and opened at the page he had worked on last night. It was poetry or smashed teapots, he reckoned. He had woken that morning with an image of a brutal captain, facing mutiny, yet his dream had finished oddly hopeful or bright in a tangle of emotions. But he hadn't the energy to do anything with the notes now.

He had been unusually incautious in mentioning Verona. He looked up and out the window across the harbour, thinking of his visit last year when he had deposited twenty-three million dollars in the Antonveneta bank, profits from the supply of drugs and services to a branch of the Neapolitan Camorra crime conglomerate.

Leaving the money in Italy had been only in part a whimsical decision. He had accounts in a few countries; useful to have nest eggs in
case something goes wrong. Perhaps it had been the whimsicality
of the visit that kept it so vividly in his mind. Sitting in Piazza Bra
reading a book, with espresso and ginger biscuits, luxuriating in
the late afternoon warmth and the success of his side-enterprise
with the distasteful Camorra captains, he had felt exultant. His
briefcase had held papers as authentic as the Camorra could forge.
It had taken three days—during which even Mark's cold audacity
had begun to waver—for the forgeries to be found satisfactory by
the bank's lawyers and investigators. The papers established his
account in the bank, indicating the source of the money as sales
to three Italian companies, two in Milan and one in Verona, of
large-scale imports of exotic executive toys and also fish products
from two of Mark's companies in Santiago.

The movement of his unbalanced table each time he picked up
his cup had caused his equally ill-balanced briefcase to fall against
the back of a chair at the next table, at which had sat a woman
reading a journal of some kind. He had apologized, at which she
smiled, and Mark, bewildered, found himself looking at Josefina. It
was not her, of course, but so like her that Josefina's presence, and
her perfume, befuddled him for a moment. It had been like those
dreams he had not had for a few years now, in which her presence
was so completely vivid that he woke turning towards her so happy
that she was with him again, only for it all to decay in a second, as
that previous life and its possibilities had decayed when he had
been called back to Bogotá. And he had gone, and she had refused
to wait for him, and he would not take her with him to the risky,
tricky, fast-footed, quick-minded daily life he nevertheless still loved.

The likeness had been disturbing; it was Josefina as she might
well look now. They had chatted for a few minutes about the
pleasant warmth, their work—his, briefly, as a businessman and
hers, at greater length, as an autobody designer for, implausibly,

Toyota. He had found himself stuttering, bewildered, for moments wishing desperately that it could be Josefina and not this Veronese auto-designer. He had somewhat distractedly played his part in the conversation.

Then she had left, indicating regret, saying that she had an appointment. As she had stood and smiled down at him, and paused, apparently puzzled, he realized that she was a striking beauty. She stood for the second as though she felt something was wrong. And perhaps it was. He was neither gay nor married but was so completely delighted by the immaculate success of his deal with the Camorra that part of him just wanted her to go away so he could return to luxuriating in how he has stitched it all together; from the first contact with that lawyer in Chicago, to using the reliable Antonio Ruis and his group as envoys to the Camorra, to setting out the conditions for the deal with the unsavoury and unsanitary Camorra captains, to the diversion of three hundred short-ton sacks of powder from Cartagena to Gioia Tauro in Calabria to Naples, to his careful brazenness in the three meetings with the bank's managers and lawyers. The whole had been stitched together like a perfect song, and he had wanted to play it again in his head. But he had also wondered why the delight in his ingenuity, forging and consummating the deal, displaced what for most men would have been the greater pleasure of the Josefina-like beauty's company. He did not think of himself as a cold man. Nor, he had reflected, was it that he did not appreciate her charm and beauty, but somehow her being so like Josefina confused him; it was as though she was improperly impersonating the woman for whom he would have forgotten the Camorra and his triumph to sweep into his arms. He had felt deceived and disappointed beyond reason, and regretted that he had been unthinkingly unkind to the Toyota employee.

But now he swept together the pieces of the cheque Hilary Lockett had thrown at him, and put them in his computer bag. The tightness in his chest had eased, even though he had not earlier noticed it gradually gripping him. And the damn poem needed a sense of the captain's humour, which was part of last night's dream but sat ill with the brutality:

'More sea, Seymour!' I wave them off.

That's a bit unclear, but he couldn't see how to make it fit otherwise. Though it was unclear, he calculated that a reader would be able to form an adequate image from "I wave them off," whether they imagined him waving with his hat or just a hand.

The tea was cold, Kanehara would be closing in, the Peruvian cocaine would be landing in a couple of days, and within the next few days he had to deal seriously with Jimmy Phan and the Vietnamese and start putting them out of business. Maybe that was where the images and emotions in his dream and now poem had come from last night. The action with the Vietnamese, which he looked forward to, would take place on the cold waters of English Bay.

He called for the bill, put on his coat, and reflected that one possible world, in which he would spend a week in Verona with Hilary Lockett, was lost to him and all the infinite connections from their visit that would have ramified through the rest of human history, though more likely diminishing like a dropped stone that tides and winds would eradicate. Working on poor Seymour's fate had indeed suppressed his rage to manageable degrees, for now. Another "No" vote. Pablo would be sneering in contempt.

CHAPTER 3

SUSAN PYBUS WAS CLEARING LAST YEAR'S MULCH LEAVES off the emerging iris against the side fence, standing back every few minutes to assess the effect. Satisfied, she strolled towards the rear of the garden wondering what to do about two heathers that were being crowded out by the St. John's wort. As she gathered a trowel and small fork, she noticed a man leaning on the fence by the garden gate.

"Geoff," she called softly to her husband who was measuring for the support posts of the tea house that would complete his Japanese garden project at the back. When he turned, she nodded towards the stranger leaning over the fence. Geoff clicked his tape measure shut and ambled back towards the gate.

"Good afternoon!" the stranger greeted him.

"Good afternoon."

"A good afternoon for gardening. Overcast, but not dark and no rain in sight." The stranger was Asian, with a round and tanned face, casually but expensively dressed in a striped jacket and light-blue jeans, floppy collared shirt with no tie. Somehow what one might expect on the Promenade des Anglais in Nice on an early summer evening rather than at their garden gate. Geoff was unsure how to ask him what he wanted without it sounding rude or brusque.

"Yes."

"Allow me to introduce myself, Dr. Pybus. And explain my presence here, for which I apologize."

Geoff made a deprecating gesture. "No, please, you ..."

"I mean I apologize for coming without contacting you first and seeking permission. But I was passing and thought I'd take my chance. We have a friend in common, Mr. Marcos Morata, who told me of your garden project. I am from Japan, as perhaps you guess by now." The stranger smiled broadly. "I have a long interest in Zen-style gardens, and maybe I might see yours. My name: Keiichi Kanehara," he said and bowed.

"Of course, I would be delighted to have some expert advice. I really don't know what I'm doing. I didn't know Mr. Morata knew about it."

"Ah, Marcos always seems to know more than you assume."

The two men walked to the back of the garden while Susan stood beside the cherry tree watching them. They stopped by the low wall around the pond and leaned forward to look down at the goldfish looking up at them, expecting to be fed.

"The garden is good. I like the placing of the stones in the moss garden here. If I may? It is too bold of me ..."

"No, no. Please, I would value any suggestions or criticism. I do feel it is a bit cluttered at the moment. The problem of the beginner, wanting to fill all the spaces. Not realizing that spaces are sometimes best left as spaces."

"Yes. So. These are what?"

"Estrella gold—they are a form of heather. Evergreen, with small white flowers in the spring."

"Perhaps you might place them further back, or remove them. Too high here at the front. Too much in the moss, you see." He swept his hand as though across an uninterrupted stretch of moss. "And that small rhododendron, I would also move. Let the moss to flow around the stones. The stones are good. Perhaps this is too white and too prominent, but perhaps not. It is a sentinel."

"That's where it stopped when I dragged it when digging the pond, with a come-along. You don't argue with a ton of granite when it decides to settle."

"You can put yogurt on it in the spring. That will make the lichen to grow on it, or perhaps moss. Will subdue its whiteness."

They walked around the garden, Keiichi asking questions and giving advice, which Geoff found nearly always excellent. Susan seemed busy, but watched uneasily from her shrubbery. The two men came across the ground on which the tea house was to be built, and Geoff was showing his plans to Keiichi.

"I have a tea house something like this in my garden. It is not far away." He stopped, and looked round at Geoff. "Would you care to visit my garden?"

"I'd very much like to see it. When would be suitable?"

They had come close to where Susan was standing. Keiichi looked from one of them to the other, raised his hands in the air with a broad smile and said:

"Now. Let us go now! What is the phrase in English—no time is the present? No ..."

"No time like the present?" suggested Geoff.

"Yes! So. You will come. I have a phone." He reached into his pocket and pulled out a gold iPhone. "I will have tea ready for you. You will come? I insist you come! I am proud of my garden." He smiled broadly again.

Geoff looked round to Susan.

"Well, it would be interesting. Susan? What do you think?"

"I'm not sure. I had ... I'm not sure it would be good today."

"Yes. Yes. It would be good today," said Keiichi. "Please. I would enjoy to show you my garden. I think you would learn much from the tea house structure. We could be back in an hour. Tea. I show the garden. We return. An hour."

"Perhaps I might come. My wife has things to do here today. Is that all right, Susan?"

"No. I mean ... I think we should go some other day. I think you, too ... Don't you have papers to mark later?"

"An hour would be fine. I'd be interested to see another garden."

Geoff could see that Susan was clearly distressed for some reason. She was distrustful of the friendly visitor, who was pressing buttons on his phone.

"Please, let us go now. Both of you will like to see the garden I think."

Keiichi had presumably dialled, but then let the phone hang in a hand by his side. Within a minute a black stretch BMW limousine nosed up the drive. Two young men stepped out of the rear door and came into the garden. Two women also emerged from the car and stood by its opened doors.

"Please, let us go now," said Keiichi.

Geoff looked around at Susan, and then at the young men coming towards them. Something was wrong. This was not a casual invitation.

"Your wife's instincts are better, Dr. Pybus. Now, I insist you come and visit my garden."

One of the young men discreetly removed a gun from inside his jacket, holding it close to his body so that it would not be visible to prying neighbours. Geoff and Susan were ushered towards the car, Susan putting her tools on the lawn as she walked to the gate.

"I'm afraid this is impossible," said Susan. "Our children are at a neighbouring party. They will be home in an hour or so. We must be here."

"Don't worry. These young ladies will be here to greet them and explain that you have had to go to visit a sick friend. You will phone them. All will be well," said Keiichi.

"No. I won't go. I'll scream."

"Please, Dr. Pybus. If you scream, we will shoot your husband in the leg. Now, get into the car. I am not going to debate with you."

Geoff looked at the two young men, both of whom now had guns on display. There was another man at the wheel of the car, and Kanehara. It was hopeless. He realized suddenly, bizarrely, that they were being kidnapped. Which made no sense at all, to either of them.

CHAPTER 9

"THEY'RE LATE."

Mark looked at his watch.

"I don't like it," Alan Wilkie said.

Alan and Mark were each looking through powerful binoculars at the *Orient Pearl* tanker sitting in English Bay, from which the Vietnamese gang was to receive a shipment of cocaine, negotiated in China three months earlier by Jimmy Phan. They stood in the main cabin of Mark's powerboat, a little back from the windows, whose curtains were drawn enough to give them a view out and to restrict the view of anyone looking back at the boat.

"Here they come!"

Mark spun from his examination of the upper deck to the rear of the tanker at water level. Slowly moving along the side of the metal city was one of the medium-sized transporters used to ferry crew from ships to shore. The *Orient Pearl* had gone through its clearance, and the customs and excise men had been on board for a couple of hours. Those crew not needed until the time for unloading the tanker, which could be days away, were on their way to the city for R&R after weeks at sea.

"There's the drop!" Alan called.

From a porthole in the tanker, what looked like a large rucksack was squeezed and fell towards the transporter below. Someone on the deck of the smaller boat caught the falling bundle. Immediately the transporter picked up speed and headed towards the harbour.

Because the transporter was running five minutes late, Mark's course was taking him too far to the west. He spoke into the microphone in the wall beside the window, to Andy Curry who was in the Captain's seat above them.

"Andy. Curve around to the north. The drizzle is cutting down visibility. We need to be able to see where they dump it."

The boat began a slow curve. Mark and Alan kept the transporter carefully in sight.

"Why haven't they dropped it?" Alan muttered. "They're goin' too far in. Hey, that's the laddie! There she goes!"

Both of them saw one of the sailors lean over the side of the transporter, holding the rucksack. As he straightened and turned, the rucksack slipped over the side, hitting the water with a splash that was immediately swallowed in the boat's wake.

"Andy, keep the present speed and take us about fifty feet to the west of where their transporter is now, then keep heading north."

"Don't you want to pick it up, Mr. Morata?" Alan asked.

"No. It's only about twenty kilos. We might have a chance to pick it up later. I'm more eager to remove their supply. I don't mind them peddling whatever they can from their various grow-ops, but I don't want them moving in on Asian-supplied cocaine. I'm more concerned to show whoever supplies them that they can't be relied upon."

"We could take 'em out now, and get the powder. Isn't that why you brought out the three boats? Look at that! They're using a bloody white balloon marker! They'd better pick it up fast or they'll be inviting visits from everyone and his dog."

"Alan, can you go across to the other window and watch out for their pickup boat?"

"D'ye remember when we used to do these water drops, Mr. Morata? Ten, a dozen years back. Pretty crude, eh? Hard to believe these guys are still at it. Do you know where this stuff's come from?"

"Myanmar. The fields are about a hundred kilometres east of Mandalay. These gangs have no access to any other supplies. The Chinese are getting theirs from the same area. Goes northeast, then overland for some way across the old Silk Road. Not so romantic any more. Old trucks most of the way. Via Xi'an, and they take it out through Shanghai."

"You know a lot about their supply lines."

"But not enough. Which is mainly why we're here. I need to find out exactly who receives it in Xi'an and who carries it from there to the coast. It changes carriers there, and that's where it would be most convenient to be able to move it to our carriers instead. I'm keeping Kanehara on his toes, or treading on them."

"Here's our lad comin'," said Alan.

Mark crossed the cabin and studied the powerboat coming in from the mouth of the bay.

"Can you tell how many are on board?"

"Can't see. Could be a pile of them in the cabin. They've got their curtains drawn like ours."

Mark looked for signs of movement on the other powerboat as its raised bow carved a spreading arrow through the choppy water towards the bobbing white balloon.

"Can you see another boat covering them? They'll be coming out from the harbour or from the Inlet. Andy," Mark called, "head round as though you're going under Burrard Bridge. Keep about this pace."

Mark flipped open his cell phone and hit one of the buttons. Wilkie's son was steering another powerboat nearby.

"Dave, can you see another boat on your side? It should be moving out towards us now. It'll keep coming towards us, and pass close to that white balloon they dropped. Did you see it?"

"See it? Everyone in Vancouver could have seen it. Discreet ain't the word for these guys."

"Be ready. If there isn't a second boat, we might try moving in on both sides as they make the pickup."

Mark's boat passed by the balloon, and kept moving. No doubt their passing so close to the drop would have had the Vietnamese in panic for a few minutes, now relieved no doubt, but likely watching with suspicion.

"Okay, Alan. Just beyond that barge. There's their number two, that black job, coming in slowly."

"I see it. Yeah, that's them."

"Dave, there's a second boat. We'll let their pickup boat take the powder. Call Larry and the two of you can follow the black Seafarer. You'll find Jimmy Phan is on board. I want him to tell you who handles the transfer in Xi'an. In detail. Names, places, quantities, equipment. Got that? Larry can do the interrogation."

"Xi'an. Right. I'm sure Larry'll be able to get him to chat to us."

"The black boat will probably hang around till the pickup boat is clear, and then come back towards you and Larry in the inlet. Follow them in, and make sure they see that your boat and Larry's outnumber them and carry much greater firepower. Then persuade them to go up to our dock. Get Larry to invite Mr. Phan onto one of our boats, and chase the others away. You could frighten them a bit. And Larry can ask the questions in his usual way."

Larry Grace was nearly as big as Mark, and his handsome face had suffered scaring from a serious car accident about eight or nine years ago. Like many of Mark's employees, he worked part-time on single-contracts per job, like this one, with a moderate retainer paid monthly. Larry's main ambition was to become a psychiatric nurse, and he was currently taking courses towards his degree at UBC. Mark had been amused to discover that the fact that Larry was big, and Black, and scarred, and spoke softly with his lilting Jamaican accent, made the gentle Mr. Grace quite terrifying to Phan and his gang.

"Okay, Mr. Morata. I'll hear from you later."

"Look at that," said Alan. "They're just goin' straight in for it. Not your most cautious bunch, eh?"

Through the binoculars, Mark watched the boat slow as it came towards the balloon. A man in dark blue leaned over the side with a grappling hook and, straining, pulled the balloon and its attached rucksack from the water. As soon as it was on deck the boat surged forward turning towards the harbour entrance under the Lions Gate Bridge. Mark raised his phone and pressed a button.

"Harbour police?" A pause. "I realize this is probably nothing. But I'm out on English Bay and saw someone from one of the transports from a tanker drop something into the water. It had a balloon attached. Then a powerboat just went by and picked it up. The powerboat is heading around Stanley Park for the harbour entrance. The boat is a Pershing 45, white with a green stripe. Its name is *Eight Success Eight*."

He cut the connection.

"Andy, I don't want to lose them if the police miss. Can you keep them in sight but stay well back? If there's no police presence once we are under the bridge, close in on them fast."

Mark and Alan put on yellow waterproof coats and went out onto the deck. As the boat picked up speed, the wind was a little more than refreshing. They followed the spray of the Vietnamese boat around the treed and rocky edge of Stanley Park, closed in a little as they sped past Second Beach, and stayed a steady distance back as they turned past Siwash Rock towards the iron span of the Lions Gate Bridge.

Mark was relieved to see a police helicopter hovering high above the Vietnamese boat as it passed under the bridge. Clearly they had it identified, and a couple of harbour police speedboats were closing in on it.

"Andy. Take us around and back to the Burrard docks."

Mark smiled and apologized to Alan for the lack of action.

"It's okay, you know. I can take it or leave it."

But Mark's control of the cocaine supply was strengthened by this little non-adventure. The idea that he could leave behind the serious pleasures of the drug business, its fascinating risks and organizational challenges, and its massive rewards, seemed absurd at moments like this. Unlike Alan, he was not sure he could take it or leave it.

CHAPTER 10

MARK LEANED AGAINST THE SAWN END OF AN ENORMOUS sea- and weather-ravaged log on the beach at the west end of Spanish Banks. He started to count the hundreds of yearly growth rings exposed by its loggers. Just past the knuckle on his thumb measured out the length of his life so far. Each red-brown ring was formed as branches and leaves waved in past rainstorms or through quiet sunny days while birds' dark eyes searched for insects. He was sweating heavily, as had been his intention, or at least had been Frank's intention setting the stage for confronting the next tenure committee member. He was beginning to wonder whether Frank had also been surprised to discover his latent dramaturgical talent and was maybe abusing this opportunity to explore a possible new career as playwright while also enjoying the mischief of making his employer suffer.

But Mark had achieved this moist and heavy-breathing exhaustion more quickly than he had expected. He was out of shape; which was a mild description for how soon he had found his limbs howling for him to stop the torture of running. It was, he reflected, a long time since he had done regular exercise. Three, four years since those laughter-filled and grunting games of squash he used to play twice a week with Vicente.

He looked at the ribbed and pitted wood by his hand, and was overwhelmed suddenly with regret at Vicente's quitting, and the harsh words. It had happened in the time marked by one of those rings under his finger. The costs of doing business, he had thought in anger at the time. But now, he wondered ... What did he wonder? Too much was happening too quickly somehow. Not in his business, or even this faintly absurd adventure of getting the Pybus woman tenure, but somehow within him. Perhaps, in time ... He forced himself to complete the thought that he would earlier have suppressed: that the business was not worth a good friendship.

Just before they broke up, Vicente's daughter Isabelle had been born, and his twin boys were to begin kindergarten next September, and the bright and miraculous Sarah, whose godfather Mark was, would be starting grade two. Mark had felt like part of the family, and realized that he had lost more than one good friend. Vicente had said to him, that rainy day driving down to Seattle to recruit new mules, "We can still almost forgive ourselves ... the world we came from ... We can tell ourselves we were almost innocent boys. But we are now men, Marcos. It is spoiling our souls."

Mark had not been ready to listen then. It was still too much fun, and the rewards after the hard years were coming too easily. But now Vicente's voice was echoing with greater insistence.

And what was he to make of this further shock; that his body was aging? Of course bodies age, but he had never before found his body would not easily do what he required of it. He had always been strong and fit, and had, people joked, infinite stamina. He had thought of his body in the terms used by the Franciscan fathers: as brother donkey, whose job was tirelessly and unobtrusively to carry the soul. Mark felt that his soul must be getting increasingly burdensome; and brother donkey was beginning to show the strain of bearing it. Perhaps it was consciousness of aging that was at the root of his recent perturbations? A message sent along the bones and muscles, up the nerves and sinews, tightening his chest, whispering to the brain daily until he finally heard it. Everything is relative, they say, but not this—age shall weary us all, and wreck our bodies.

The path along Spanish Banks by the sea was sprinkled with runners. He could see them for miles back, multicoloured, occasionally a couple together, one or two pushing three-wheeled strollers with an ecstatic baby smiling into the breeze rushing by its face.

Among the sweating and panting bodies is that of Kenneth Gissing, who should, if Frank's file is accurate, come along soon, to find Mark leaning against the log, of uncounted rings, which Gissing was accustomed to use for his post-run stretching.

And here he came, sweating profusely. A small man, greying, flamboyant quantities of hair held back with a red elastic headband, grey face, darkly lined under the eyes, and a heavy walrus moustache. No doubt he'd look less ravaged after a shower and rest. Small demons clearly drove him on. Gissing stopped and drooped forward, hands locked above his knees, seeming at something of a loss.

Mark stood back from the log. Gissing nodded as he moved up against the giant base of the cedar stranded at the top of the sandy beach. The log would have escaped from a boom that broke up in a storm maybe years before. It would have floated about in the water, perhaps for a few weeks or months, and then been deposited on the sand, and carried up to this high-water mark either by a hundred tides or by the city engineers who placed the logs for sunbathers to rest against.

"We'd better live forever after all this, eh?" Mark said to Gissing.

"Yeah. At least forever," Gissing gasped.

Mark left him to his stretching and ambled across the gravel path to the wide stretch of grass between the car park and the beach, avoiding decapitation by an errant Frisbee, whose Apollo-bodied owner laughingly apologized. He settled himself in the Tesla, and flipped through Frank's file on Gissing while waiting. Frank's extensive notes suggested he had spent a lot of time studying Gissing, and had turned up a genuine exotic. The hair and the moustache were carefully styled to mirror those of his hero, the

Victorian novelist, George Gissing, to whom Kenneth's whole
academic life had been devoted. Frank had discovered that as an
undergraduate Kenneth had changed his last name from Gardiner
to Gissing, as an extreme form of homage. Kenneth never overtly
claimed to be descended from George, but he did nothing to discourage the assumption of such a connection, and had gone to
some trouble to hide the earlier name change. As far as Mark could
see, Kenneth had spent his life reading and writing about George.

Gissing, the professor no less than the author, was unquestionably industrious. He had been married while in graduate school,
but the marriage broke up shortly thereafter. His first job was his
present job. He had been living with one of his ex-graduate students, who had been teaching English at a local college for eight
years. Mark counted about twenty-five articles on George Gissing
and five books, in Frank's abbreviation of his CV. How did one
compare lives? Kenneth Gissing had been engaged in reading and
writing about this long dead man while Mark had battled competitors for market share—which was the odd way he now represented
to himself those years of killing and nearly being killed. Gissing
would find a comparison with a drug lord no doubt offensive. Well,
here he came, loping across the grass to his Jetta, which was parked
next to Mark's Tesla. How odd that the head under that bobbing
mass of hair should be carrying so much knowledge about an
Englishman who died more than a century ago.

Gissing nodded a brief acknowledgement to Mark while opening the rear door of the Jetta. After towelling his neck and face, and
applying some cream to it, he pulled off the headband and engaged
in lengthy and careful combing of his wavy hair, then a quick flash
through the moustache. He stepped into a pair of good dark trousers, and belted them with an old-style snake fastener. Where Mark
had pulled on a sweater as he cooled off, Gissing carefully tied and
fasted a silk cravat around his neck and slid on what looked like
a velvet jacket, of a rich plum colour. He did indeed look like a

miniature version of the Victorian novelist. Gissing climbed into the driver's seat, fastened the seat belt and turned the key. The engine made a choking sound, but did not start. He tried again, letting the engine turn over for ten seconds or so. Then tried yet again. It refused to spark into life.

Mark got out of his Tesla and wandered around to the front of Gissing's car, indicating that he should release the hood. With the hood raised between them, Mark fiddled around for a few moments undoing Frank's earlier handiwork by reattaching the lead to the ignition coil and removing the small insulating pad from the distributor cap. He moved to the side of the hood and turned his hand. Gissing tried again, and the Jetta burst into life.

"Hey, thanks," said Gissing, half standing by his half open door. "What was the trouble?"

Gissing clearly decided that politeness required him to come around to the engine and look down at its mysterious clutter of metal and wire objects.

"You'd somehow got something stuck in the distributor, and a wire was loose, shorting it."

"You know a lot about cars?"

"No, no. Just played around with engines a bit."

Gissing's face suddenly registered surprize, looking past Mark's shoulder, and then broke into a delighted smile.

"Elisabeth!" he shouted.

Mark turned as a woman jogged towards them at an impressive pace, blond hair tied back with a black headband, black running outfit. Mark almost gasped.

"Can't stop, Ken," she waved. Then she saw Mark, seemed to half pause in her stride, nodded quickly, and was past them like a stately athletic goddess.

"Elisabeth Norland," Gissing said, almost to himself, looking after her as she powered her way towards the university. Mark glanced at Gissing as he watched her diminishing figure for a moment in silence. His face showed an innocent unrequitable longing; while Mark was pleased that she was on the list of tenure committee members he was due to meet. There might be rewards he hadn't anticipated from this tenure business, and he might want to pay special attention to Frank's scenario in her case, and insist on revisions if it might not show him at his best.

"Well," said Gissing dragging his eyes away from Norland, "I'm really grateful. I guess there's nothing … I mean, really, thanks a lot."

Mark had hoped Gissing would make it easier. He wasn't fitting into Frank's screenplay, in which he was to ask whether there was something he could do for Mark in return, which was the appropriate response of the terminally insecure. He nearly had—so Frank got points for that—but he had balked, perhaps because the glamorous jogger had unhinged his mind briefly. As Gissing slid down into his seat and began to stretch the seat belt across his body again, Mark moved around to the closing car door. Gissing stopped pulling it closed, looking up at Mark. So much for Frank's scenario.

"There is, in fact, something you might do for me in return."

"Oh?" A slight look of alarm spread across Gissing's face, quickly covered with a smile.

"This might seem an odd question," Mark said seriously," but would you like a new desk?"

"A new … What kind of desk?"

"It's bleached oak. More a workstation really. It has a recess below the desk for a computer keyboard, and a sliding tray that would carry the keyboard under the desk. There is also a sliding component for one of those thin screens that can be pushed to the back of the desk when not in use. Shelving on both sides, with locking cabinets to ground level, with drawers for pens, pencils, and iPad stand, and so on. Locking storage for CDs, DVDs, and slots for memory sticks, and auxiliary components. There's another module for a flat-bed scanner, and one for a printer. Beautifully made. I've got just the one I have no use for. In fact, I don't have space for it and I need to get rid of it. You'd be doing me a favour."

"Is the desk ... is the height ..."

"It's slightly higher than average, to accommodate the various modules and the under-the-desk keyboard tray. And I do also have an off-white leather chair to go with it, adjustable in various dimensions."

Gissing looked at Mark, unable to sort out what to say. Mark had described for him his ideal desk. Gissing, Frank had somehow discovered, was exotic in more than the one dimension; another was maybe the less rare fetish for office furniture. He loved nothing better than wandering around the more expensive furnishing shops' office departments. It seemed to be almost a libidinal fascination. Gissing drooled over office furniture catalogues. Frank's homework had turned up this harmless weakness, and the fact that Gissing had described a less elaborate version of such a desk in a memo to his head of department. Frank noted that Carbonell had, with his usual noises of deep personal regret, turned down Gissing's request.

"I don't understand. Is this what you are asking me to do for you in return? Take a desk, and chair? Where is it? I mean ... Do you want something from me in return?"

"Yes, I would like you to do a little something in return."

"I've got it! I know who you are! You're ... This about tenure for Susan Pybus, isn't it?" Gissing flicked the heavy lock of greying hair from his forehead.

"Yes. How perspicacious of you, Dr. Gissing! You should know that many other members of the committee will be voting in favour of her tenure. Your voting against would therefore have no effect, except that you will not in that case get the desk I just described. What do you think you will do, in these circumstances?"

"Does the desk have any security devices?"

"'The drawers and the screen slot are both secured by a Sentris security system. The very best."

"So I read."

"Difficult choices, I know. But I think you might consider, as many of your colleagues have, that Dr. Pybus contributes most valuably to the work of the department and to the education of her many students, and that her research, while hardly to be compared with your own remarkable productivity, is, according to those who know it best, of a high quality."

"True. I haven't been one of those who was firmly against her tenure. As anyone would tell you, I only reluctantly went along with the majority in the straw vote. And I would favour another Victorianist in the department. How soon ... could the desk...?"

Frank had added a supplementary line to follow up if necessary, but Gissing had raised it himself. A further Victorianist was keenly desired by Gissing so that he could off-load onto a newcomer the burden of teaching the entry-level courses and more than half of the Masters and Ph.D. students, whose theses and dissertations, when about authors and topics that were not George Gissing, he found dreary, consuming the time he could spend on his own research into his hero.

"Tomorrow, if that would suit you. I will have it installed at any time you wish."

"Splendid, splendid! Not the morning. I have ... Tomorrow afternoon? I should give you directions to my office, and arrange that the door be opened."

"Yes. Don't worry. I do know the location, but leaving the room open would be most helpful. We will even take away the old desk. We will also box all the items in your old desk and leave them on the new one, unless, of course, you will have an opportunity to do that yourself."

"No, no, I won't. I'll be off-campus in the morning. Well, I suppose you could do it in the morning, if that would be easier for you. I'd forgotten my appointment for a minute. You caught me off guard, I fear."

"So all will be done by the time you next go to your office. Perhaps you might write a definitive work about George Gissing on the new desk. I'd be delighted to have made this tiny contribution to the great impact such a work could have. I assume a great-great-grandfather or some such relation?"

Gissing smiled and said, "Something like that."

"Please remember to vote for Dr. Pybus. If I find out you failed to do so, the punishment will be quite disproportionate to the small reward you are to receive."

Gissing looked up in momentary surprise, then pulled the door closed, fitted his seat belt, and backed out fast, then accelerated onto the road towards the university. Mark stood back, a little ashamed. Well, another "Yes" vote, he noted wryly. The men seemed easier than the women.

He needed four positive votes to carry the recommendation for tenure forward to Ian Carbonell. He now had Simpson, Todd, and Gissing. He would be more comfortable with a one-vote insurance by adding both the remaining committee members, Colebrook and, he thought with pleasurable anticipation, Norland. If those two turn out to be adamantly opposed, he felt that Olwen Greenwood or Hilary Lockett could be induced to change their votes. And yet, there was something about this whole business that was disturbing him. Could he rely on any of them to vote as they had promised?

Was his increasing uncertainty where last night's lines for a poem had come from? He took out his notebook. Maybe he could rework it as a haiku that he could send to Keiichi Kanehara. If he went in that direction, maybe he could play with the lines he had begun to add before being interrupted by a phone call from Alan? God was "disturbed by images of naked creatures, pale as death, brown like chestnuts, and some of ebony." The images were an attempt to make sense of a dream he had woken from. In the few minutes he had to spare, he had shaped the interrupted lines in the direction of a haiku, but he still had to shave some syllables away before he could send it to the meticulous Keiichi:

Gods dream of naked men,
Pale as death, brown like chestnuts,
And gleaming ebony.

CHAPTER 11

"MRS. WILKIE. HELLO. IS ALAN THERE?"

"Oh, aye, Mr. Morata. Alan is. He'll be right glad you got his message. He says it's urgent, and hasn't known how to get in touch, apart from leaving the message. He says no one knows where you are. Just a minute now."

"Thank you, Mrs. Wilkie."

Mark had his feet up on the coffee table, looking over to the North Shore Mountains, listening to the sounds of distant shouts and hurrying feet in the Wilkie household across town. He was careful to pay Alan Wilkie enough to ensure gratitude, and for random holidays in Hawaii. He had offered to buy for them a bigger and gleaming house on the west side, but Mrs. Wilkie had turned it down saying they were happy in their east side community and a fancy new place would make them uncomfortable. Geoffrey Pybus had also been alert to the disruptions of such changes. And indeed where the Wilkies were now was paradise enough after where they had come from in Glasgow. Mark's attempts to sort out people's lives seemed to be what was meant by playing God, but in his teens it had become clear to him that God was not doing a satisfactory job with most people, so why not? The atheism that had overtaken him in university relieved the presumptuousness. And, he had reluctantly to admit to himself, playing God did serve to relieve loneliness. Perhaps God's initial motivation too.

"Augh, Mr. Morata. Thank God, you phoned." Alan Wilkie's voice sounded atypically edgy. "Somethin' came up while we were takin' care of those Vietnamese fellas. No, nothin' you need worry about. They're taken care of. No, it was somethin' one of them said. Bit fanatical some of these lads, if you know what I mean. Anyway, we set about havin' a chat with them like. To cut a long story short, it looks like they got somethin' from one o' Kanehara's lads that you've got some operation out at the university. They'll be looking for you there. Especially after our work this week. You'll want to be careful, if you've got both Kanehara and the Vietnamese after you out there. Is it something we can handle for you, Mr. Morata?"

"No. No. Thank you, Alan. That is most helpful. I will take precautions. This is just a small thing I am having to deal with myself. I am very grateful. I will be in touch soon. Is everything well? The family is well?"

"Aye. Everyone's fine, thanks."

"And Mrs. Wilkie continues to recover?"

"Aye, she does that. She's already put back all the weight she lost, and a bit more."

"Good. Thank you, Alan. Oh, one final thing. I'd like to keep Kanehara off-balance. It helps to divert his mind from what I am actually doing. Can you drop him another clue to where I am living downtown, maybe misdirect him to one of the high-rises on Pacific? Send it to one of his yakuza whose phones we've broken."

"Okay. But you know I think there's a danger in these games. Too much electronic traffic. And the poems. Easy to trip."

"I think we are secure for now. But I hear your concern, for which I am grateful. And thanks for the reminder, I'll forward a poem to send too."

Mark put down the phone, stood up, and looked out at the tankers waiting in the bay. Off to his right he could see the sleek white bulk of one of the first cruise ships of the season heading out towards the Inside Passage to Alaska. So … more careful. He would visit the remaining members of the tenure committee at their homes or somewhere away from the university. Frank can find out their addresses and schedules and suggest a new set of confrontations with them. But he might have to go to the university again, perhaps a few times. He felt some irritation that what he had assumed was the easy task of persuading mild academics to vote as he wished might require more effort than he really had time for. And he should not show his gun again. Bribes first, and only then, if necessary, threats.

Both Kanehara's formidable organization and the less well-organized but more vicious Jimmy Phan and his Vietnamese gang now knew he was doing something at the university. Well, they would be spending time and resources fruitlessly, but they could cause him some problems if he wasn't careful.

He had begun by thinking that dealing with this tenure committee might offer a pleasant distraction, isolated from the routine dangers of his business life, but now it was being absorbed into the familiar and tiresome world of infinite circumspection. Also, as he learned more about this tenure's strange operations, he began wondering how Susan Pybus felt about it. What must it be like, to be his age, as she was, worried about keeping her job while caring for her three children? Maybe indeed it was best for her to have secure and sympathetic work. Her children would leave home, and her job with young students would likely be a consolation, and give her other rewards.

What was he doing? Kanehara was hunting him, he knew, and he should be spending his ingenuity on more comprehensively leading Kanehara astray not wrestling with poems. But the distraction of the university was doing double duty, repaying his debt to Geoff Pybus and keeping the Peruvian network and its first shipment completely off Kanehara's radar. He should decide on a poem to send Kanehara, and to unsettle him by further reinforcing the fact that Mark's organization had broken whatever further security he had put in place on his computer system.

CHAPTER 12

MARK SAT UNCOMFORTABLY IN THE ANGLICAN CATH-
edral on Burrard Street. Though it was more than twenty years
since he might have considered himself a Catholic, the Church of
his boyhood still provided the paradigm of what religion was and
what churches ought to be and do. The Anglican cathedral seemed
to him like an attempt to copy a real church, in which the most
important features had been forgotten. There was no sanctuary
lamp, no hint of that smell of ingrained incense and candle wax,
no vividly carved Stations of the Cross, and it seemed somehow
a friendly social organization, lacking the sense of the numinous
and the fear of hell that had suffused his boyhood, and nearly made
him a priest instead of a drug lord.

He was uncomfortable on other grounds too. That morning
he had received a phone message from the Panamanian ship, the
Santa Barbara, closing in on San Francisco. The captain reported
unauthorized phone calls made by a Filipino deck engineer to and
from a number in Palo Alto, which had included docking times of
the ship and the destination in the city to which the drugs were to
be moved, and the route they were to follow. The deck engineer had
been interrogated energetically and had delivered information about
his phone contact and their plans with regard to the drugs, before
he had been persuaded to leave the ship in high seas. A report of
this tragic accident had been sent to the coast guard station in San

Francisco and to the ship's owners. The Filipino deck engineer had uncertain information about the extent of the gang that was planning to hijack Mark's drug shipment, but his impression had been that it was quite a small group of no more than eight or nine men.

Mark's phone vibrated with an incoming text message, telling him that Carolina Lopez was ready on an encrypted line for his call. The religious service seemed to be coming towards a close, even though it was quite unlike the pattern of the Mass of his youth, and Mark slipped out as inconspicuously as he could. Standing in a cool breeze outside the doors of the cathedral, he hit the connect icon and held the phone to his ear. The Lopez brothers and sister offered efficient muscle, mostly Mexican, for a decent price. Carolina, the sister, was smart and her brothers were brutal but smart enough to recognize her talents. She handled the office, they directed operations. They spoke in Spanish.

"Mr. Morata. I gather you have a need for some labour services?" she said in a high singsong voice that might have fronted a dental office.

"I do. You were most efficient about four years ago, you may recall, with a problem of lost property of mine in Los Angeles."

"I remember and have just checked out our satisfactory arrangement on my computer. How can I help you?"

The traffic was heavy at the main city intersection outside the cathedral, and Mark leaned to the side to hear better.

"I have a fairly urgent request, I'm afraid. I would have liked to give you more notice, but I need thirty men to prevent a planned theft of my property from the docks at San Francisco. The thieves may number as many as ten, but I am not certain. We have good data about their timing and likely places of attack. First, I need to know whether you can meet my labour needs, and the cost. If these are satisfactory, I will have a colleague contact you to arrange strategic details."

He heard the distant tapping of computer keys, an irritated sigh, paper being moved.

"I can procure for you, Mr. Morata, twelve of our own people supplemented by eighteen others subcontracted from a colleague whose people in the past have proved competent. You catch me at a busy time, I'm afraid. Our people come at our usual price, available on the website you are familiar with—I regret that inflation has increased the costs a little since our previous arrangement—but I can manage a discount for the others. The full total for the labour costs of the job will be no more than three hundred and twenty thousand American dollars. Any other expenses or equipment will be added to this, of course, and once I know more details I will be able to give a more precise number."

"Around three twenty is fine. I do not anticipate a need for equipment or complications, but am happy to pay for whatever you run into. My colleague in San Francisco will be in touch with you about the details. Our purpose is the elimination of the thieves and ideally our arrangements with our property can go forward just as it is once they are out of the way. The elimination may only require their incapacity to perform their roles with regard to my property, though their leader in Palo Alto might need a more permanent incapacitating. I would also require that he provide information about how and from whom he learned about my shipment."

"We will discuss all the details with your colleague here and I will send a costing for the elaborated plan. My suspicion, guessing who these people likely are, is that your request for thirty personnel is excessive, and a careful analysis of the actual details may result in some savings to you."

"Thank you again, Ms. Lopez. I know I can rely on you."

"A pleasure to again do business with you."

Already the worshippers, or whatever he should call them, were dribbling out of the church, and the—what was he?—priest, vicar, canon, dean, prebend? He'd heard so many terms, but the man who had celebrated at the service and given the sermon was now standing opposite him at the broad doors of the cathedral, greeting parishioners as they emerged. While Mark was muttering the final pleasantries to Carolina Lopez, he realized that the woman in the off-white raincoat who had passed him was his target for the morning.

"Dr. Norland!"

The tall blond woman turned and smiled. Mark slipped the phone into his pocket and ran towards her down the cathedral steps, stopping in surprise as they came face to face. She was familiar from his first vivid encounter as she jogged past Kenneth Gissing and himself on Spanish Banks. She was as strikingly lovely now as then. His heart skipped a beat again, and he felt a moment of breathlessness. The patient face with a slight smile now left him bewildered, scrambling to remember Frank's scenario. Maybe she was used to men responding like this to her.

"I just wanted to thank you for your Prayers of the People. It is so rarely that one hears such eloquent and sincere prayers in church these days, and so beautifully spoken. I'm sorry," said Mark. "I don't mean to praise them for the wrong reasons. It's just that I found them quite … spiritually enriching."

"Didn't I see you with Kenneth Gissing on Spanish Banks a few days ago?"

"Yes."

"You are a friend of his?"

"No, a chance meeting. I was helping him with his car."

Mark meant what he had said about the prayers, even though he was simply following Frank's suggested opening gambit for their meeting.

"Thank you for the comment about the prayers. Do you attend regularly? I don't think I've seen you here before."

She held his eye fearlessly. Perhaps one of the privileges of imperious beauty. Her clear blue eyes were only a few of inches lower than his own.

"No. This is my first time. I knew your name because we have a friend in common. Well, a friend of yours whose husband I know. Dr. Pybus."

"Susan? Yes, a good friend. How do you know Geoff?"

"It is perhaps a little early, but would you consider it improper if I were to invite you to lunch at the Hotel Vancouver across the road? I had an early start. And I did have a concern about the Pybuses that I wanted to raise with you. Which is, I confess, why I am here. Geoff did me a favour a while ago, and I am looking for a way to repay his kindness."

She hesitated for just a moment. He waited, then hesitantly bowed slightly, raising a hand in the direction of the hotel. They turned together and began to walk towards it. Well, that was the end of Frank's script. Now he was on his own.

"I had planned to lunch there with a friend today," Elisabeth said, "but she just sent a message to say she had a lousy cold and couldn't or shouldn't make it."

"Ah, her misfortune and my good fortune."

They were led to seats at a window looking out on the Sunday traffic. Mark felt a moment of regret that this was not simply a social lunch. They were a plausible couple he thought. She was less than a decade younger than he was—perhaps thirty-four, elegant and attractive, another tall blond beauty, though more sympathetic than Hilary Lockett. Maybe he should have been looking at English departments and cathedrals for partners.

"I understand that Susan is being considered for tenure?"

Elisabeth Norland looked at him in silence for a moment.

"You don't have a beard," she said slowly.

Mark stroked his chin.

"True. Is a beard important?"

"But you are the one, aren't you? Each member of the committee received a warning phone call last week. That a man, whose description you fit except for the beard, was trying to influence the decision."

"Oh really. How interesting. I had requested each of the people I spoke with not to divulge the content of our discussions."

"They didn't. You were seen talking with a couple of them, who abruptly changed their straw votes. Two and two were put together. And guess what they added up to? One. You."

"Oh dear. Yes, I confess. But I think I am an agent of justice in this case. While I am confessing, I'd feel a lot better if I can get everything off my chest before we go any further, and add to my sins the fact that our meeting was planned by a colleague of mine. I suspect he even was responsible for the text message from your friend cancelling your lunch appointment, and he probably sent her one saying much the same from you." He really would have to give Frank a raise. "And," he tapped his chest, "est mea maxima culpa, even the comment about the Prayers of the People was written by him—though I likely wouldn't have used it if I hadn't considered it exactly true."

"Likely?" She arched an eyebrow.

"Well," he laughed, "I might have used it if you had turned out to be someone quite different from the person you are, or seem. I mean … oh dear … Maybe I can offer a general confession for all past sins, and we might be able to begin again?"

"Very Catholic of you," she smiled. "Though you were in an Anglican cathedral. But, I admit, a rather High Church one. Well, I am in a slightly weak position to take the higher moral ground, in that I have been rooting for your success since I heard what you were doing. I had a sneaking suspicion that's what you were about when I saw you with Ken Gissing. Perhaps if I didn't support the conclusion you were persuading my colleagues to reach, I might be leaving you to lunch alone. Perhaps I still should—maybe I still might have to, not believing that a confession removes the guilt of sin. Tell me, what is this all about? Or, better, tell me after we have had a chance to look at what to eat, " she said, leaning over the menu as though short-sighted. "I'm told the fish is good here."

Her thick blond hair was cut to shoulder length, with a neat fringe combed sideways. But he was clearly on probation, so had better try to not give her a reason to head for the door.

They studied the menus till they both set them aside, having made decisions.

"Geoff saved my life a couple of weeks ago. I tried to offer him some kind of reward, but he was uninterested. I learned that his wife receiving tenure would please him. Initially, I intended to make sure she was tenured regardless of the merits of her case. But, as I have learned about tenure and about her, I think a system that prevents her getting tenure is unjust. So, I go about my nefarious plan with a somewhat easy conscience."

"How did Geoff save your life?"

Mark began to describe the circumstances of his runaway car, interrupted by the hovering waiter. She chose the Arctic char and he the salmon.

"So," she said seriously, "I found it easy to cheer you on when you were presumably working your way through the committee, but I'm not sure how to feel now that I'm the one to be coerced."

The large room was quiet, with maybe a dozen other diners chatting and eating, and his companion was … well, quite exciting. He felt his chest relax as he considered his situation. But he had no idea what to say next. She saved him the trouble.

"Well, it won't be too hard to compel me. I had initially spoken for Susan on the committee. I have read her book in typescript, and know her work. I think she is first-rate, a real scholar—unlike some of the journalists and shoe salesmen that constitute our department. She is slow perhaps, but works with care and is making significant contributions to literary scholarship. I think her book will change people's perceptions of Victorian women's fiction. Not, you may think, something that matters much in the world."

Mark waved a hand, to indicate that he was on the side of Victorian women's fiction and a fervent believer in changing perceptions of it.

"But our culture shapes our consciousness," she continued, "which shapes our sense of who we are and what we think we should do. Most people think they decide for themselves what to do in the world, but they are really just the slaves of dead scribblers, even though they have no idea who is pulling their strings or that they have string being pulled."

Mark looked steadily at her. It sounded like a piece from one of her lectures.

"Well, you must think that's just part of one of my lectures, and that's because it is. Sorry. And the 'dead scribbles' is a quote from J.M. Keynes. You have the eye of a stern critic."

"Sorry. I was just thinking about what you were saying."

"Hmm. Well, that's more than most of my students do."

Their food arrived while Mark tried to answer her questions about his background and how long he had lived in BC.

"This Arctic char is delicious," she said. "Also, the lecture I started in on earlier goes on to clarify the image of dead academics being the legislators of current behaviour, but I can see that's not really on the agenda for today."

He began to wonder what was happening to him; her smile actually seemed to increase the light in the room. He followed the tiny movements of her face as she talked; the tiny frowns, the slight smiles, the attractive, unusual small muscles above and to the sides of her top lip.

"Maybe we can begin to create an agenda for some future occasion, when the present less complicated business is out of the way." He had meant it as a question about a future meeting, but either she didn't pick up on that implication, or chose to ignore it.

"I have really lost a lot of sleep about Susan's case. A lot due to the pressures of the committee, and my feeling helpless on it. It was my first time on a tenure committee. I was half-bullied and half-persuaded into going along with the rest of the committee. I have felt ashamed since. If you have managed to sway more than half the committee, I shall happily go along with the new majority. Not, I would like to make clear, because you have compelled me to, but because I had decided I would anyway, though the idea that I might be in with the new majority certainly makes it easier. But what about the senior committee?"

"I think they may be persuaded to see it our way."

"Who are you?"

"Mark Morata." He reached his hand over the table and she shook it firmly. "As I said, I do import/export trade with a few South American countries. Mainly smoked salmon to Chile and Argentina, skilled artefacts in wood—business toys—from Honduras, Colombia, and Brazil. And a few other items." He thought it best to get off his business activities and onto his interest in literature. "My pleasure-reading includes many English writers. Indeed, my honours paper at university in Chile was on the poetry of Philip Larkin. Though I should add that, if I have an idle moment, I will more likely pull from the shelf Bioy Casares or Borges or Gabriela Mistral, or Neruda. So I lay out my insignificant credentials to the English professor."

Elisabeth became gradually aware that, unlike nearly all of her male colleagues, Mark had no twitches or mannerisms—and he sat still, with a slightly disturbing calm, which she found very attractive, even if somewhat daunting, and wondered whether it was so prominent because it determinedly hid something else.

"Perhaps you can get a couple of dessert menus while I go to the loo? It was a long service."

"Of course."

As she walked away he was conscious of his heart pausing, then lurching into rapid beats, then stabilising. This was the third or fourth time in the previous week or so. Maybe he should see the doctor again.

He looked around for a waiter, and not seeing one began to view the other diners. He felt oddly disoriented by Dr. Norland, and by his heart's unfamiliar beating, or perhaps the two were connected? She was not at all what he had anticipated among the set of academics. His fellow diners seemed distantly anonymous. He saw himself sitting, a smallish dark blob, in the large room, which was framed and held in fixed place by metal girders and heavy stone. He imagined the room sideways, and upside down. The massive hotel around him stuck into the sky turning daily with the earth. Mark braced himself against his chair arms, as though he might need stability if the world that was carrying him round juddered a little with a heart murmur. He closed his eyes, trying to imagine all the motions he ought to be able to sense—the smoothly spinning earth, which seasonally swayed to and fro as it sped around the sun, which was on its own headlong rush though gyrations that were shaping our outer ring of the galaxy, which was itself in a chaotic dance, perhaps all headed …

He opened his eyes and pulled out his notebook, thinking whether he might be able to catch the moment's sense of vast fevered movements one would see if only one lengthened the time scale from our momentary human perspective to the bursting of galaxies. "A slight murmur of the earth," he made a note, then "flickering millennia" and an image he might be able to shape later: "our cosmic bonfire vents/a scatter of reeling galaxies/flickering on, flickering out." He stopped, dissatisfied, as always. For a second his anger flared. The shipment in San Francisco was troubling his mind, and these attempts at poetry were hopeless, and now this woman whom he found immediately enchanting—too much was suddenly uncertain. But something different had been in his mind before he began writing, something fleeting, which he had lost. He hunted for the images that had somehow faded away, or hidden themselves. What had he glimpsed? Maybe it would emerge again, perhaps in a different form.

"Did you get the menus?" Elisabeth asked, sitting down.

"Oh, I forgot ... I didn't see the waiter."

"Remind me not to invest in your company." He smiled in response, though she wasn't smiling. She looked at the notebook in his hand.

"Absorbing business?" she asked.

"Ah, something I needed to remember. Nothing important," pocketing his notebook.

She looked around, and the waiter appeared immediately, already carrying menus.

"Do you realize that our eyes invert the images we see?" he asked her, accepting the menus with a nod at the waiter, who was looking at Elisabeth.

"Invert? How?"

"What we see—didn't you learn in high-school physics or biology?—is all upside down. The lenses of our eyes make what is up down and what's down up. Imagine passing through the earth to Australia now. People would seem as though they were hanging off the earth, and the buildings would seem upside down, sticking down into the air. Well, that's how things really are here, we just see it all inverted."

"Really? Actually I don't remember learning anything in high-school science classes. 'Energy,' a few times, I seem to remember, though I can't remember anything about it—I moved schools. And a lot of how great the environment was, and how we basically shouldn't do anything to upset it. Stewards of the environment, they told us. Again and again. But I don't remember being taught that we saw everything upside down. Oh, and the solar system, about three times—but nothing I hadn't already learned from my father. Why do you ask, about seeing upside down? You mean we are really hanging down from the earth by our feet rather than ... well, standing the way we see, seem?"

"I don't know what brought it to mind. I felt disoriented perhaps, and ... I don't know."

"Well, if we are impressing each other with our bigness of mind ... Oh dear. No, no, I didn't mean that's what you were doing ... You look ... No,"—she leaned over and put a hand on his forearm—"It's just that I was going to show off, by saying I do remember learning about evolution. But I was never much interested by all the animal bones and skulls and the obsessive focus on our forebears and the dinosaurs. I became fascinated with what had happened to plants in all those millions of years. In fact, I've been, well, 'haunted' is too strong a word, but haunted by the flowers that came and went and that we cannot now imagine. And the fruits; what delicious tastes and fantastic colours and sizes that left before we arrived, and the trees and grasses. I sometimes feel that the real drama and beauty of the plant-world happened long ago, and we just have some rather dull and enervated bits and pieces left now. Though I do think apples are pretty good, and bananas.

"Anyway, that's me showing off. I didn't mean you were, really. Oh dear." She had left her hand on his arm just for a sweet moment, and now used it to pick up her menu.

"No, you are right of course. I was the show-off. Though, in mitigation, I was distracted. Not my usual conversational gambit, my cosmic routine. Nor forgetting to get menus."

"Well, now we've got them ... Oh dear, I think any of these would do me more damage than good."

She put down the menu and began to fold her napkin.

Mark, copying her, said, "Probably true."

They looked at each other, but seemed both unable to think what to say. Mark put a credit card on the table and caught the waiter's eye.

"Can you ..." she trailed away as he spoke more loudly at the same time.

"But I am pleased that you approve of my little scheme for Susan Pybus."

"Oh, I don't approve of it all. I think it is quite wrong. The ends never justify the means."

Mark looked at her serious face, feeling some alarm.

"But I thought you had said you were delighted and would yourself change your vote."

"True. I am delighted, and I will change my vote because I think I was wrong to have been persuaded to vote negatively in the straw vote in first place. I had, as I said, decided to register what I had assumed would be the only positive vote. That I will now be in the majority delights me for Susan's sake, but I can't condone your use of compulsion. I can do nothing about your scheme, though I feel pleased about its results, but you, of course, can do something, so you are culpable. You must stop it."

"I am ..." What was he?—apart from disturbed by the small frown above the blue eyes that accompanied her surprising criticism and condemnation—"... disturbed."

"You should be. Incidentally, how did you manage to persuade such a diverse group? Boots Colebrook, Slimy Simpson, Georgie-George Gissing, Toad Todd, the Greenwood, and glamorous Hilary."

"I haven't met them all yet. But mainly I used bribery, with a hint of a threat now and then. Your descriptions of them ..."

"Oh, that's just what I call them in my head."

"Well, maybe your descriptions might help me when I meet the rest."

"Please don't tell me any more," she said, raising her hand as she pushed back her chair. That she smiled as she said it gave Mark some relief.

He signed for the lunch, for which she didn't thank him, and they shook hands as they parted outside the hotel.

"I hope you will allow me to contact you again?" Mark asked.

"Well, we didn't sort out all the cosmic stuff, so, yes, I'd like that."

He walked away a happier man.

CHAPTER 13

KATE COLEBROOK KICKED THE DOOR OF HER VW CLOSED
with the metal toe of her Doc Marten boot. It didn't give her any
particular pleasure or relief to do so, but she couldn't bear to close
it like the bourgeois car-fetishists of the upmarket west side street
she lived on. There was a good-sized dent in the door panel now.
The car was mottled with rust and dents, trailing weather stripping,
and the crevasse created by her boot added to its in-your-face chic.

The pile of papers in her dark-blue canvas bag were the products of her first and second year classes. The first year set had lain
in a heap in her office for more than two weeks, and the bloody students were beginning to complain, so she was resentfully bringing
them home to mark, expecting to spend a frantic hour skimming
through them, making random corrections on each. She refused
to let students submit them online, as she hated staring at them on
screen even more than on paper. She pulled a key out of her jeans
pocket, slipped it in the door, and shouted into the hallway inside.

"Hey, Jim! Ya home?"

Silence. What day was it? Wednesday. Where the hell was Jim?

"Meathead!" she shouted up the stairs, dropping the canvas bag
and papers on the floor. Perhaps he was in the garden with the dog?
Kate trudged through the living room, noting today's newspaper
on the back of the sofa and Jim's sweater on top of it.

"Your friend will be out for the next two hours."

Kate jumped and tried unsuccessfully to contain a high squeal at the sound of the male voice. She turned towards it in fear. He was in the back corner of the room, sitting in the good chair she had "liberated" from the faculty lounge one night last year.

Her voice wouldn't work. She thought of what was around her. What could she use to defend herself? She'd slam him in the balls with her Doc Martens. He was still sitting. Could she run?

"Jim is doing a small but well-paid job for a friend of mine. Please sit down. Yes there. Good. I only want to talk. I don't mean any harm."

"That makes you bloody unique. How did you get in?" What a dumb question.

"Locks, and opening them, are a hobby of mine."

"You're foreign. What do you want here?" Shit, she was too scared to think straight.

"Yes. I'm from Colombia. But you too are foreign. Isn't that an English accent? Please sit down. I had something I wanted to ask you. You are Kathryn Colebrook? And you are on the English department tenure committee? I want to talk about one of the cases you are dealing with."

"You want what?" She began to stand up, then sat down again.

"Does neither of you ever tidy or clean this house?"

"You from *Homes and Gardens* then?"

While the professor was appropriately frightened, Mark admired her aggressive conversational style. In the circles he was familiar with, women didn't usually express such verbal bravado, especially when afraid. Nor, he reflected, did men.

"My honour is bound up in ensuring that Susan Pybus is given tenure. I want your assurance that you will vote in favour of her next week. I know that she has not published enough, but you are to conclude that her other work compensates for the few publications."

"You what?" A pause while Kate's jaw hung open in an undignified way. "Are you for real? I mean, or else what? You gonna shoot me if I don't?"

"If necessary. I will also shoot Jim."

"But you don't mean any harm, right?"

"Yes. If you do what I ask, you will be in no danger from me. I might even give you some small reward as a token of my appreciation."

"How small?"

"What would you like?"

"I could just do with a Mediterranean cruise, for two."

"All right."

Kate found herself smiling. While she was threatened and frightened, she had taken him seriously, but as soon as he promised her pleasure she realized it was a charade. Like life in general.

"Okay." She formed a T with her right forearm over her left. "Time out. Nice work. You had me scared shitless there. Whose idea was this? What's the occasion?" She looked around, began pulling the cushions up and looking beneath. "Is someone recording this? Look, I give up, eh? We can stop playing silly buggers. This some gig of Jim's?"

"You were right earlier. No gig. You should be scared shitless."

Kate looked at the man in the shadow of the door. Big guy, moustache. He wasn't playing some trick for Jim. But this couldn't be real.

"Do you mean Susan Pybus has hired you to ..."

"No, Miss Colebrook ..."

"Doctor Colebrook to you." One of her favourite lines to overbearing males, but perhaps a miscalculation in the present situation.

"I am doing this for my own reasons. Mrs. Pybus ... *Doctor* Pybus does not know of my actions. Now, do we understand each other? You will vote in favour of Doctor Pybus's ... you will vote in favour of her tenure. If you do, I will not shoot you or Jim, and I will send you on a Mediterranean cruise."

"Mid-April, after exams."

"If you do not, I will shoot you both. I will not personally kill you. I will have it done. To you, of course, it will not matter. Who does it, I mean."

"Right. Well, so we're done then? That's it? Or was there something else?"

"You haven't yet told me that you will vote 'Yes' for the tenure."

"Oh, that. Sure. No worries. Easy. You got it."

"Is that 'Yes?'"

"Right. Yes. Well, nice of you to have dropped in."

She tried to keep the tremble out of her voice, and failed at the end of the sentence as he stood. God, she hated her cowardice in the face of these big confident bastards. If she had the gun she'd shoot him, shoot him all over, arms and legs and head, and belly, and crotch. God, what was she thinking? Her mind was batting around at the incomprehensibility of what was going on. He seemed to be serious.

"If you mention that I have been here, to anyone, even to your partner, I will kill you. If you fail to turn up to the committee meeting, I will kill you. If you vote against, I will kill you. Do you understand?"

"Do you want to repeat the bit about … no, right, yes. I think I've got it."

He stood up and turned into the hall. She followed slowly, intimidated further by his size, a bulky chunk of meat who was probably more than twice her weight.

"What's this about, then?" she asked. "Who are you? I mean, why?"

"None of these are your business. You have only the one thing to do."

"Right. The one thing. Vote right. Right." She smelled after-shave or something. She looked at him in the light of the glass fan of the door. He was no joker. The kind of face that the world respected, full of authority; the kind of face she hated—the alpha male who assumes he owns the world. Then she remembered vaguely, because she only ever listened to shit-for-brains Simpson vaguely, that there had been warnings about this guy. A typical stupid warning that didn't include what was she supposed to do about him when he showed up.

Kate Colebrook stepped back in fear as the alpha male stopped in the narrow corridor leading towards the front door. He seemed to sigh, then leaned his back against the wall.

"I'm sorry, Dr. Colebrook. Of course this is now your business and you have every right to ask what I am doing. Forgive me."

He was uncomfortable leaning while turning his head round towards her. He pushed himself upright then sat on the third step of the stairs.

"I think I was unduly aggressive towards you. I am sorry. I wouldn't really kill you, of course. Just," he smiled, "a manner of speaking. But the cruise is real. I will do that."

"Yeah … thanks … well, I guess we didn't get off on the right foot, did we?" she said. "Interesting to discover how having some-one threatening to kill you tends to dampen the social niceties. Sorry about the existential angst. Story of my life. Perhaps a Mediterranean cruise would help."

"Why did you come to Canada from England?" he asked.

"Why would anyone stay in England if they could come to Vancouver?"

He smiled, but sat in silence a further moment. He stood up, intending to head for the door, but he was suddenly dizzy and put a hand against the wall. She had taken a quick step back in fear again. His heart seemed to skip a beat, then thumped hard for a few beats. What was wrong with him? She was looking at him expectantly.

"For a while I thought I would become a priest," he said, then paused, worried his heart might lurch again. "I'm ... I find myself unsure, doing something I am unfamiliar with, that I thought would be simple, but is ..." Mark looked down at Kate. She had a round face, framed with dark hair, cut rather like his own, with signs of grey streaks over the ears. Slightly puffy around the eyes, and slightly irregular teeth in a firm and distinguished mouth, that turned down at the thin corners. Whatever else, it was an intelligent, mobile, and unorthodoxly attractive face.

She leaned sideways against the wall, bewildered by this veering conversation, alert and increasingly fearful as her visitor behaved increasingly oddly. She began to wonder if the Mediterranean cruise was a fantasy, and he a nutter of some exotic kind.

The dizziness had passed and his heart seemed steady again. He smiled at her: "I had intended to try to somehow make amends for my earlier behaviour, but I seem unable to do other than make things worse. I should leave. Do remember to vote for Dr. Pybus, and I will remember to send you tickets for the cruise. A ten-day cruise is probably as much as one can take of those things. And I am very serious about the vote." But he made no further move towards the door. He stood half-turned towards it, as though uncertain whether to go or stay. He seemed pale, breathing a bit heavily as he had stood up.

"Did you want a cup of tea?" she asked into the silence. Oh damn—her fear as nothing in the face of her Hampshire country-house upbringing and the inerasable mark of Roedean School.

"Thank you," he smiled.

"Toast, or a biscuit?"

"Whatever you are having."

"Toast it is then. Raspberry jam and marmalade."

Mark followed her into the kitchen, and sat at the round kitchen table as she busied herself with kettle and toaster, clattering cups and saucers.

"You teach modern poetry. Who are your favourites?"

Kate leaned on the counter, looking down into the whiteness of a Minton bone china teacup, beginning to wonder again whether this was some kind of joke. She turned towards him. He had spent half a second too long looking at the scuffed and crumb and stain spattered table surface.

"After teaching them for twenty years, I'm not sure ... You have favourites?"

She pulled out a low drawer, grabbed and neatly spread over the table a crisply laundered cloth.

"Well, I did an honours paper on Philip Larkin ... Do you teach Larkin?"

She paused from putting the cups and milk and sugar on the table and looked at him. "I'm ... I've ..." pointing to the ceiling, "I've just finished an article, about gender and poetry, and why some poets seem to appeal almost exclusively to men and some to women. Not on grounds of 'quality' or 'content'"—she made quick clicking sounds to indicate the ironic quotation marks—"or even their subject matter, and Larkin is one of my examples, of someone whose work appeals very strongly to many men but rarely appeals as strongly to women. I teach some of his poems, some of the simpler ones, 'As Bad as a Mile,' 'First Sight,' and such-like. Well, I've got copies of the article upstairs in my study, if you want one."

"I'd be interested. Thank you. I have noted that you also teach a poetry writing course. Perhaps you have everyone offering you their poems to read."

"No, not so much. I have a colleague who teaches autobiography, and he constantly has to fight off multi-volume works that everyone wants to thrust onto him; bus drivers, dentists, his students. He says everyone seems to be writing their autobiography, even if they call it blogging. No, I don't get asked much, partly because I have a reputation for the nasties, and I say crap is crap. Well, not crap, more like trite, conventional, dreary stuff."

"Oh dear. I think that's what I have begun to write. I started, on an impulse. Well, someone else's impulse. But I can't tell whether what I am writing is rubbish or not. Or whether it is even poetry or not."

"Is it different from everything else you write—notes, emails, reports, well, whatever else you write?"

"Maybe I should enrol in your class. I have begun to write … well I wake up with some idea. Like last night. I had been earlier leaning against a log on the beach at Spanish Banks. So this morning I wrote out what was unlike an email or a note or a report, but I don't know if it is a poem."

Kate had been half turned listening as she poured water into the teapot. Mark looked with foreboding at the rim of the cup she put in front of him. But it was pristinely clean, as, incongruously in the general wreck of the housekeeping, was everything to do with the tea setting. Not even dribbles of jam at the sides of the Moulton jam bowls, spoons decorated on porcelain handles with colourful images of the fruit within.

"Do you remember it?"

"Well, I've got it here." Pulling out his notebook. He paused, embarrassed.

She put a flowered tea cosy round the pot. Noticing his moment's glance at it she said, "My mother used to make them— I've got a drawerful. Why not read it, while the tea steeps?" She nodded towards his notebook.

He looked at the page doubtfully, coughed, and began:

"You can count back your years in wavering rings
on the cross-cut end of a beached cedar.
From the bark inward no more than a thumb's length

of a stump as big as you, marks off your life.
As your finger glides slowly round each ring
you release memories of green summers
and the songs of long-dead birds.
Children stop and listen all the way down to the sea,
elders remember long-ago walking in woodland …

"It's just the way I scribbled it, and it needs work, of course, and I don't know how to end it. But I have many like this; I don't know what to do with them after the first draft."

"Well … there goes the toast. Shall you pour?" She got up and brought the toast to the table in a silver rack quite like his own.

Settled, adding jam to their toast, letting the tea cool, Kate felt bizarrely comfortable.

"So, I'd be inclined to say that what you've got is a good idea for a poem. But, as you suggest, it's largely a slice of prose so far or, where a bit poetic, it's a bit clichéd perhaps, and maybe in danger of a touch of sentimentality at the end, no? What this lacks is … well, what you might try to add is, if you want to work at it, well, try putting it into rhyme. No need to finish up with rhyme, but you need to get out of the chunks of different registers. And while it's a nice idea, it's not an original one, so you need to go for a new and different insight. Think how Larkin works out ways to put some music into the lines, which you don't really have there. You have some nice bits, and now you need to make it all sing the same tune. And maybe read Wikipedia on growth rings, to give you some extra vocabulary perhaps, and further ideas. Can't hurt."

"Mm. Thank you. That's really helpful—at least gives me a direction, which is more useful than me staring at the words after I've scribbled them down. I think I need to take your course."

"Well, registration for the fall course opens in a couple of months." She nodded again at his notebook. "Got others?"

Mark was reluctant to read any of the others, but did. After second cups of tea, and a further round of toast, and a few other poems, he was feeling heavy and a bit battered from the criticisms. She even made a slight grimace at "metal, wet, or bird's eye," while actually saying it might work if it was "set better." Then she stood, collected the cups and dumped them in the sink. He helped carry the jams and toast rack and the plate it sat on to the counter.

"Can I help you wash up?"

"No, thanks. 'Fraid the seminar's got to finish now. Papers to grade, emails to deal with." She looked up at him from the sink. "Writing good poems is mostly hard work. Ten thousand hours to get up to speed, is the new cliché."

She smiled at his serious face. He was taken aback by what she had said and by the surprising sweetness of her smile. He thanked her gravely for the tea and criticism, and they drifted down the corridor to the front door in silence. She waved him off, like 'more-sea Seymour'—she'd liked that bit—and then leaned for a moment with her back to the door. An unusual slice of afternoon.

Had Susan Pybus hired a hitman? It was inconceivable.

"Does not compute!" she shouted; a favourite phrase picked up from students some years back. "It really doesn't," she confided to the stairs. It made no bloody sense at all. Would she change her vote? Vote to keep the female Matthew Arnold on faculty, who kept assuring Kate that maybe they could have a chat about Foucault when Susan had got round to reading more of his work. Her antiquated attitudes enraged Kate, and the fact that so many students admired Pybus enraged her more.

But, of course! Why had she been so slow? Well, because she'd been warned to look out for someone with a beard. That's why Todd and shit-for-brains Simpson had talked about changing their votes! They'd been nobbled by this guy already! What the hell was going on? He might be nuts, but that was even more reason to do what he asked, whether or not she would ever get a Mediterranean cruise out of it for Jim and herself. Poetry, she knew well, was a strange curse that seemed to strike randomly in restricted populations. But this guy was one of the weirdest cases she'd come across. More like a corporate lawyer than a poet, not that she knew many corporate lawyers.

Outside, Mark looked at the much-abused VW among the row of upmarket cars that lined the street. He walked around the block to where he had left his car, noticing little while he looked for rhymes: "rings of wood" produced "good, stood, could, should, make good, Robin Hood, understood." Lots of possibilities, but maybe he should keep "cedar" and change the first line—"reader, bleeder, seeder"—too close—"leader, freed her." Hmm, Kate Colebrook suggested that writing poems wasn't a part-time business; he would have to get serious if that's what he wanted to do. He was feeling more disturbed by her criticisms than he wanted to admit. No one spoke to him like that.

His chest began to tighten as he felt the burden of all the work he would have to do to fix poems he thought were pretty good as they were. And who the hell was she to act as the arbiter of good poetry! Hardly any of the new poets he read rhymed. How can that be the way to make the poems better? He tried to contain his mounting anger—after all he had asked her opinion, and she had given it. But the pompous assumption of certainty about what she was saying! And could he trust her to vote for Pybus? He felt a further plunge of anger and helplessness.

As he climbed into the Tesla he thought how he might improve the opening of the tree rings poem she had criticized.

He pulled out his notebook and wrote quickly, crossed out, tried again:

On the rings of a beached tree high as your head,
You can count back your years,
From the bark inward less than a thumb's length.

Oh dear, "back" and "bark" are no good so close, and further down he had "green" twice. Well, she did say he had to work at them a lot more. The first line, he reflected unhappily, was now a bit obscure, maybe worse than the earlier version.

He pushed the notebook into his pocket, conscious that he had actually been imagining a life of trying to write poems rather than dealing drugs. Astonished, he flicked the Tesla into reverse.

CHAPTER 14

THIS WAS MARK'S AND ELISABETH'S THIRD MEAL
together in as many days: two lunches and this dinner. They had
talked about where they came from, families, what made them
happy—the kind of careful exploration that people might engage
in who were interested in each other. He was, however, afraid
that the incompatibility of their lives would soon come at him
like an express train. His present delight was accompanied by
an undercurrent of recognition that it would soon end. And yet,
he resisted that only too obvious conclusion. Perhaps there was
a way to let her see his life as he himself had seen it. But he knew
this was hopeless because he could no longer see it as he had seen
it before he saw it through her eyes. If he weren't so cheerful, he
would be in despair.

Increasingly preoccupied with his need to tell her some truth
about himself, Mark was distracted as they finished their sorbet.
The kitchen area of this upstairs restaurant was open to the diners,
and the chefs performed with some panache; their flares of fire,
the hissing and clanging pots and pans, the juggling of knives
adding cheer to the low-lighted eating area. Silences were less
embarrassing when one could watch the performance, and when
there was constant background noise.

"You seem a little distracted. Am I beginning to bore you?" Elisabeth smiled.

"Oh no. No. No no," Mark said.

"Ah, can I take that as a negative?"

"Mmm? Ah, yes. I have something to tell you; it's been on my mind. Perhaps ... Would you be willing to come to my apartment after? I can make coffee."

"And I have something I must tell you, too. I would like to see your apartment."

Earlier in the evening, as they had sat down at the table, she had pointed to the area under her nose with eyebrows questioningly raised. He had, on an impulse, cut off his moustache that morning. It felt slightly cold and naked.

"I wondered whether you might approve of the lack of moustache," he said.

"Well, the skin's a bit pallid at the moment, but I'm sure it will look better when it gets a bit of sun, but, on the whole, yes. I think so."

"Hardly the ringing endorsement the great sacrifice was supposed to elicit. But I suppose I can always let it grow again."

"No, no. Really, I think it suits you very well. Give it a month at least before thinking of letting it grow again. It's just a different you I'm meeting. Why did you cut it off?"

"I don't know. I think it may have been a part of exposing my life to you."

She had looked at him, eye to eye, in silence for a moment.

Meal finished, they walked through the West End, talking easily about the rapid changes to the city. Close to his apartment building, they passed one of the city's experiments in "social housing," and under a street light on the paving stones some child had drawn a hopscotch game, the ten squares numbered. Elisabeth burst ahead and began jumping from one foot to two feet to one, turning in the "10" box and skipping back again. Mark smiled at her energy.

"You're not supposed to stand there simpering at my charming sense of fun. You've got to do it too. Come on! Do you know how?"

"Yes, I played it as a boy."

He set off, one foot, jump to two feet, jump to one, two, turn, and back. She clapped as he finished. This diversion hadn't been part of the expected route to his place.

"Not that I'm competitive," she said, "but aren't we supposed to throw a stone or something into the squares? How does that work? I think I could easily beat you—but I can't remember the rules. Do you?" She was hunting around the base of a privet bush picking up a couple of stones. She seemed unaware of the elderly couple walking their dog over the hopscotch squares, looking at these two relative giants warily.

"I've forgotten," said Mark, still hurt by that "simpering," which he thought unjust and unkind. And not cheered by the frowning suspicion of the elderly couple, which brought to life the memory of himself as a boy on the streets of his village where the old women in particular, having survived unsatisfactory husbands, knew that boys had just done something wrong or were about to do something wrong and should be punished for their past and future crimes. They had been right, of course.

"Oddly, we don't play hopscotch much in my business. Don't you have to throw the stones into each square in turn, then do the jumping routine? I think you can't tread on the lines or you lose your turn. And you have to pick up the stones somehow."

"That sounds right. I've got heels, so should get an advantage, though I suppose your big feet are a handicap too. These squares seem to have been drawn for quite small children."

"I don't want to play," he confessed.

"Okay." She sounded disappointed and tossed the stones back into the base of the hedge.

They walked on. Mark was, indeed, charmed by her physical exuberance though her earlier flat statement that she also had something she had to tell him had added to his undercurrent of unease, as he half thought of a dozen unwelcome possibilities. His undercurrent of unease combined with the overcurrent of mournful foreboding at what her response might be to his confession about his drug business. The "simpering" comment reminded him of her suggestion over lunch in the Hotel Vancouver that he had been showing off talking about the inversion of the world delivered to our brain by the lenses in our eyes, and her brusque comment about not investing in his business because he hadn't managed to get the menus. He didn't know what to make of the occasional rough edges to her easy charm. Perhaps he was overly sensitive, or struggling in the silt that had been disturbed from the base of his life.

As though she could hear what he was thinking, she said, "I'm sorry, I shouldn't have said 'simpering.'"

"But you did. And I wasn't."

After a few silent steps she said, "I'm looking for reasons not to like you."

"Why?"

"I'll explain later ... in our agenda for my non-Catholic confession."

"Confession doesn't work without a 'firm purpose of amendment.'"

"Ah, it may have to be a Protestant confession."

"I'm an atheist."

"That's a coincidence. I think I am too ... well, sometimes. I just like the Anglican services. Maybe I feel at home in them from childhood, and I like Anglican communities. No one wants to harm you, and they mean so well," pause, "mostly. I think there's probably quite a lot of atheistic Anglicans for those kinds of reasons."

He took out his key as they approached the old red-brick building. Elisabeth looked up at it with a smile.

"Not at all what I expected."

"Ah, you expected an expensive condominium, all modern materials, tinted glass, metal, and fashionable plants everywhere."

"Yes, I did."

"My other place is like that, but this was nearer."

"Why do you have two places?"

"Actually, I have three. That is a part of what I have to explain."

They took the slow and creaking elevator to the third floor, and walked round the corridor to Mark's apartment. He put the key in the lock, pushed open the door, heard a click he had heard once before, and turning very fast towards Elisabeth, pushed her back against the wall and threw himself in front of her.

She looked at him in sudden alarm, eyes wide. He was inches from her face, looking for one second into a startled blue eye. When the click was not followed by the bomb blast he had expected, he pushed himself away from her and pulled his gun from inside his jacket.

"Stay back! Don't move!"

He edged towards the open door, bent low and, gun leading, pushed quickly into the room. He followed the barrel of the gun around, ran towards the kitchen, then back to kick open the bath-room door. There was a box on the table. The click, he could now see, had come from a simple plastic tool that is used for childproof-ing cupboards, fixed the wrong way round on his door. Opening the door had sprung back the plastic catch and released it to mimic the click one might hear if one had triggered an incendiary bomb. As he approached the box on the table, Elisabeth appeared in the doorway.

"Please get back! Please, just a minute. Into the corridor?"

She withdrew slowly. There was a note on top of the box: "It's okay, Marcos. If I'd wanted to kill you, I could have put a real bomb inside the door. Give me a call. Keiichi." He slipped the note into his pocket and opened the box. It contained three books.

"Elisabeth," he called.

She appeared again in the doorway.

"Sorry, a misunderstanding."

He walked towards her, put his gun away with an embarrassed shrug, and closed the door.

"Please. Shall I take your coat? Do take a seat. There's a nice view over the bay. Coffee?"

"I'm a bit shaken."

"Yes."

"Why did you do that? And the gun?"

"I thought I heard … well, I did hear a click, of a kind that precedes the detonation of a particular small bomb. I feared it was going off, and I was trying to get us out of the way. I have some explaining to do. How do you like your coffee?"

"Do you have decaffeinated? I don't think I need a further jolt."

"Yes, of course. Please. Sit."

He checked the room's temperature gauge, noting the small three at the top right of the panel. The number told him that two others had entered the room since the cleaners, who had been instructed to set the temperature gauge to sixty-four degrees before leaving. That reset the invisible laser tripwire across door and windows, He made the coffee in silence, as they were both engaged with their thoughts. When it was finished he put a tray between them and sat on the sofa opposite her.

"So, yes, I have some explaining to do. I don't know where to begin."

"You have a gun."

"Yes, the gun." He briefly tapped where it sat nestled under his arm.

"Is it licensed?"

Mark looked at her, bewildered.

"Is it licensed?" he said. How could he bridge the gap between what he had to tell her and what her question suggested? His mind went blank. Here he was, running one of the most profitable drug operations in North America, employing more than fifty of the most ruthless characters in the city, moving consistently greater quantities of drugs through Vancouver to the local market and also large shipments east and to the States. Hundreds employed in that operation. Hundreds in South America. He was in the middle of an encroachment from the clever and determined Kanehara organization and his too-eager yakuza, and they were both under siege by Jimmy Phan and Vietnamese gangs in the city. And she wanted to know whether his gun was licensed. He smiled. And then, unable to help himself, began to laugh.

Elisabeth looked affronted, and stiffened, putting her coffee cup down. The mad incongruity of her question overwhelmed Mark's sense of propriety. Was his gun licensed? He laughed harder, until tears began to appear in his eyes. He was gasping, and lay down sideways on the sofa, laughing so hard it hurt his stomach. He couldn't stop. He wanted to stop, but every time he felt he was gaining some control, he thought about whether his gun was licensed, and again curled tighter as the tears poured down his face.

He looked up, blinking hard to see Elisabeth. She too had begun to laugh, hesitantly, and more at Mark's clearly helpless condition than anything she could understand as funny in what had triggered this strange bout. It was a dimension of him that she had not expected. He had seemed so formal and serious in general, and she couldn't decide immediately whether she was simply delighted at this evidence of his sense of humour or concerned that she should feel insulted by what triggered it or worry that maybe that underneath the eminently sane exterior he was actually crazy.

Some moments later, wiping the tears from his face, he said, "No, the gun is not licensed."

"Well, I'm reluctant to say anything else, but you do realize that there is a Canadian Firearms Program for firearms licences and registrations which is overseen by the RCMP, and you might need a registration certificate if it's a restricted kind of gun. I know all this because a friend had to go through it a couple of months ago."

"An academic friend? University life must be becoming more risky."

"No, not an academic; she's a psychoanalyst, and ... well, a topic for another day, perhaps."

"I'd be interested to hear more. And thank you. I must get the gun licensed."

"What was so funny?"

"Please forgive me. I think that to be able to explain, I need to tell you much more about my work. But I'm not sure how to. There are dimensions of it that are ... unusual. Can you give me a few days?"

"What is so mysterious?"

"Oh, no mystery. Please, humour me. Perhaps next week? But you said that you also had something to tell me."

"Yes. I think perhaps it too can wait. Till next week. Actually that would be useful for me, as I will by then have a better sense of what I want to tell you. But we could also meet between now and then, if you care to?"

"I would, indeed. For now, I am interested in what books my friend Keiichi left for me. Would you care to see?" He finished unwrapping the set of three books. "Look, a collection of Hardy's poems."

"Good heavens. That's a first edition," said Elisabeth, astonished again.

"Keiichi is very generous. And this is Akikura's *The Book of Tea*. Clearly he plans to civilize me. And a set of first editions of Larkin's poems. Good heavens, all signed by Larkin. Here's the first Marvell edition of *The Less Deceived*. Signed to Judy Egerton. And a very fine *XX Poems* which Larkin had privately printed in Belfast."

He turned towards her as she leafed carefully though the Hardy.

She looked back at him, smiled quickly, and returned to the book.

They stayed up late, discussing Hardy's poetry, choosing favourite pieces to read to each other. He drove Elisabeth back to her apartment in Kitsilano. They said goodnight quietly, too much unexplained for any further growth in intimacy. Both wondering how to go forward or if they could go forward together after their next week exchange of information.

CHAPTER 15

"AH, GOOD MORNING, PROFESSORS PYBUS. I HOPE YOU breakfasted satisfactorily?" Keiichi Kanehara had prepared the greeting carefully, and was standing and bowing as the Pybuses were led into the room.

"The breakfast was fine, but I want to know why we are here and where our children are!" Susan Pybus looked distraught as she spoke, and her husband looked grim.

"But did you not find the breakfast satisfactory?" Kanehara was disconcerted that they seemed not to have noticed the trouble he had gone to ensuring that their regular breakfasts were waiting for them—Susan's coffee and her own bread that he had had brought from their house, and Geoffrey's complicated mix of blueberries, muesli, All-Bran, cranberries, hemp hearts, goji berries, and ground flaxseed, with skim milk. Surely they had been astonished by this attention to their welfare? He had expected some indication of their surprise and pleasure, even gratitude. Not having children himself had made him inattentive to the degree of their likely distress and how it would overwhelm the surprise and gratitude he had expected for the breakfast. He should have thought of this, and rebuked himself.

Kanehara kept one room of his house decorated in a sumptuous western style in which he could meet with non-Japanese visitors. "Please, take a seat," he gestured to the brown leather sofa by the window. Once they had sat, he lowered himself back into his armchair, after which Akira, who had silently accompanied the Pybuses, sat to the side at a small table with a computer.

"Akira," Geoff said, "has told us only his own name, and has told us nothing else. We still know nothing of why we are here. What's going on? When can we go home?"

"As soon as you tell me of your work with Marcos Morata, as I said yesterday in the car. You refuse to tell me and declare, unbelievably, that you do not have any such connection. I need to know what you are doing for him, and what he is doing at the university, at UBC."

"Mark Morata? UBC? I told you, I have met him only once, when we were in a car accident. I haven't seen him since. I'm waiting to get an estimate of the cost of the damage to my car. He said he'd pay for it."

Kanehara waited awhile, puzzled. He thought the night away from their children would have persuaded them to change their story at least a little. Geoff looked at the Japanese, trying to work out what he wanted, what would get them out of here and back into real life. How could Morata fit into this? Taking on the burden of having saved his life was no longer a joke.

"Perhaps you, Dr. Pybus?" Kanehara nodded towards Susan. "Perhaps you can tell me of your dealings with Morata?"

"I don't know what you are talking about. I have never met him. He's someone Geoff was involved in an accident with a couple of weeks ago, as he told you."

"But you know of his business; a business we share? He has spoken to you of his work and UBC?"

"After we met," Geoff responded, "he told me he was in import/exports—he exports salmon, I remember, and he imported executive toys, though I never really understood what he meant by that. But I've no idea about any connection to UBC. He didn't say anything about the university. In fact, he seemed not to know much about it at all."

"So you spoke about it?"

"Only that I worked at one of the universities, and my wife worked at UBC. Look, we haven't the faintest idea what you are talking about, what you want with us. We need to get back to our family." Geoff was sitting forward, and noticed Akira also moved, perhaps ready to prevent Geoff attacking Kanehara.

"Yes, of course. But please help me first ..."

Kanehara stopped speaking. He prided himself on his acuity in analyzing business associates; he could detect a lie from minute cues, which is why he liked Morata as a competitor. Morata never lied. In a business like theirs, it was important not to have to deal with crooks. These two were giving off nothing but convincing innocence. He had had reliable evidence both of Marcos's involvement at UBC and of his interest in Susan Pybus, though his operatives could not discover the nature of the connection. Surely there must be a connection, even if these people did not know it. Was she in some way a key to some market Marcos was after and she was unaware of it? It seemed increasingly improbable.

"Even if I accept for the sake of argument that you are telling me the truth, what is Marcos doing at UBC? You will agree that it is a strange coincidence that he should become involved in the place immediately after meeting you?"

"I can't think why you see any connection at all. Why do you think ... I mean, yes, it's a coincidence if you insist, but certainly nothing I said or heard from him could have anything to do with UBC. Why do you think there is some connection?"

Kanehara sat silently. The hints his operatives had extracted from phone taps suggested there was a connection. It also seemed unlikely that extensive questioning of them would yield some clues he could follow up. A conundrum. He would take time to think about it further.

He could not understand the motivation and thinking of people like these professors. Their concern for their children was universal, but their overt emotion and emotional expressions could only mask something else, he felt sure. The surface never betrays what is within in a civilized person. Perhaps what one saw was what was there: inside and out the same. It seemed inconceivable. Perhaps the poetry might give him some clues to what they understood, and whether they were simply telling him the truth.

Kanehara nodded to Akira who took some papers from a neat file, giving copies to each of the Pybuses. They both looked at the top sheet, further bewildered.

"Please read, the first short haiku," Kanehara nodded to the papers.

The dark air gathers.
The water lily's colour
Fades slowly away.

"Tell me, please. What do you think of this, professors?"

Geoff looked at Susan, and she looked back, both clearly thinking they had entered a madhouse that was frightening because of their uncertainty about the children and whether refusing to comply with their Japanese captor might be dangerous to them all. And now they were expected to provide literary criticism. Or was it a test of some kind? Clearly Kanehara was serious, even if mad.

"I suppose I have had some exposure to haiku, as a part of my reading during building the Japanese garden," said Geoff. "But I really know very little. I'm sure your knowledge is much greater than mine."

"Yes, but what do you think of it?"

"Well, I don't know really. If you told me it was a classic sixteenth or seventeenth-century haiku translated into English, I would believe you. It seems to have all the requisite qualities, and rather nicely leads into that kind of calm and silence of the mind that is achieved by the best haiku."

"That is good. Thank you. Yes, very good. Now please read the next poem."

Unrequited love
And is she thinking of me now?
And the answer is no, She is thinking of her children by another
man,
And they are thinking of, the oldest, a hamster, the next, riding
a dragon,
And, three, the youngest, angry revenge.

"What is your opinion of it, please?"

Susan sighed heavily and leaned forward, elbows on knees looking down at the verse. "The language is undistinguished. I suppose the last line adds something interesting to it, or it could be interesting. But it is simply a small riff on the old joke, or witticism, by Alice Thomas Ellis."

"Joke?" Kanehara looked bewildered.

"Yes," Susan said. "It goes: there's no reciprocity—men love women, women love children, children love hamsters. Hamsters don't love anyone; it is quite hopeless."

"Ah, yes. That is very good!" Kanehara smiled. Geoff noticed that Akira did not smile.

"Maybe it's just the first verse of something to come? Look, none of this is making sense. Why are you having us read fifth-rate attempts at poems? Why are you holding us here? What has this to do with our getting back to our family?"

"Yes, yes. I see. I just thought that while you had some time to wait here, you might find the poems diverting, perhaps of interest. That we might talk about them. Perhaps not a good time. May I, though, pass on your comments to Marcos, who is the author? I will, of course, mitigate the critical comments somewhat."

Susan shrugged, looking around the room as though for something that might give her some hint of hope.

"He also sent me a haiku, you can see at the bottom of that first page."

Men poured from God's mould,
Chestnut brown, gleaming ebony,
And some pale as death.

"I should say that this, like his other uses of the haiku form are not really orthodox. They are just too ... well, I'm not quite sure what is the problem. What do you think?

Susan pulled at her hair, half-distracted. "The second line is a syllable, or an 'on,' too long."

"Ah you know the Japanese term? That is impressive."

"Well, it is my job. I was just going to say that this has a striking visual violence that is alien to the traditional haiku, but may be more acceptable today."

"I don't understand his method of composition. I spend many weeks working on a haiku, paring it to the bone, but he now sends me three or four poems a day. When does he find time to write them? He must not revise anything. And the topics he deals with are so varied. My own, I acknowledge, are too tightly constrained to the elements of Japanese gardens—stones, moss, water lilies, cherry blossom, and the human emotions that these elements can capture or hint at.

"Oh dear. I'm not sure how I will convey your criticism to him. Marcos is, I have often thought, a sad man. Though he has a reputation for sudden anger and being dangerous to deal with. And also for quiet charm. He manages to frighten people easily. These contradictions make him interesting, I think. Don't you?"

He paused, smiling as he looked at them.

"I only saw the quiet charm, I guess," Geoff said after he realized it was a question directed at them. Was it an Evelyn Waugh novel this reminded him of? Some sane character is held captive by some madman in a jungle who makes him read Dickens incessantly.

"We have never actually met in person," said Kanehara. "And Marcos is not someone I like to make unhappy. Something went wrong for him, I think, perhaps long ago. I wondered whether the next poem gives a hint of it."

He read it aloud: "'Rain in October in Santiago,' is the title.

'She came into the shop with my friend, both laughing.
I knew immediately she was the one heaven had made for me.
I stood waiting,
Not just for the choir eternal,
Though it was coughing and shuffling,
Ready for her recognition that I was the one heaven had made
    for her.
There was a stop in time as we shook hands.
My friend told me that she was recently married.
I looked down at the hand she had shaken.
She smiled a moment, turned, and something terrible happened to my life.
If this, then nothing need work out well.'

"What do you think?"

"Well, this one is affecting," said Susan, "but again is mostly in pedestrian language. Maybe if it was put it into rhyme, it might help. I like the empty hand indicating the terrible loss that leaves his life bereft. He needs to get it clearer though. The final 'work out well' is too slight to hold the sense of desolation, the discovery that his unconsidered narrative of expected happiness is suddenly, in that moment, destroyed. But the lines lack cadence, any rhythm that might distinguish the piece from prose."

"Have we done enough lit. crit. to see our children now?" Geoff said quietly and firmly. "You do know that kidnapping is a serious criminal offence in Canada, and you might go to prison for this?"

"Oh dear, I hope you don't think of your visit as kidnapping. I confess, I am uncertain now what to do."

"The obvious question is why can't you simply ask your friend Marcos what is going on at UBC, and the fact that you haven't or can't does suggest there is something going on here more than you are telling us, which we know nothing about. If you want our help, it would help us to know what we are helping."

"Yes, a reasonable request, which unfortunately I can't comply with. Apart from other reasons, it might compromise Marcos in some way. Let us continue to assume you are indeed as unknowledgeable—is that a word?—as you claim ... While Marcos and I cooperate in our businesses, we are also competitors. I would like to know what he is doing at UBC. Yes, yes, I recognize that you claim you do not know ..."

Keiichi paused again. Throughout, he had at no point either threatened or inflicted violence on them. And their being separated from their children had not inclined them to talk. And he could see no sign from their behaviour that they were lying. The conclusion: he had indeed kidnapped them. There was some possible irony in coming to the attention of the police for kidnapping after evading them for more than a decade of drug dealing.

"Here is what I shall do. I will indeed phone Marcos and try to sort out what has been going on, and Akira will make renewed efforts at UBC to find out what business Marcos has there. I will endeavour to expedite verification." Kanehara smiled, clearly pleased at that sentence. "You will see that Akira has made a note of it. In my experience that is equivalent to it being done."

Akira nodded almost imperceptibly.

"But when can we go home?"

"I will phone very soon, and Akira will immediately take whatever help he needs to investigate UBC. If all works out as I suspect it will, we will arrange your return home quickly. Akira will show you back to your room. I hope you will join me for dinner?"

"For dinner! You expect us to be here all day?" Susan half stood, as though preparing to throw herself at him or break down the door, looked around wildly. Geoff took her hand, and she subsided, sitting back on the sofa, eyes brimming with tears of anger.

"Please. It is a matter of possibly great importance to me. I will be as speedy as I can. But you must not expect me to put my business at risk."

Kanehara's voice had slowed and lowered, and stunned both Pybuses with a sense of visceral menace. The smiling host gave a quick, perhaps unintended, glimpse of something truly frightening behind the cheerful front. No wonder Akira was so attentive and careful. And if Kanehara talked of Morata as frightening, what grinders have they found themselves between? The Pybuses were eager to get out of the room, away from this suddenly terrifying haiku writer.

Kanehara rose and bowed as they followed Akira back through the house. Kanehara sat down as the door closed, and tried to work out what was going on. After a few minutes, he stood up quickly, irritated. How could one think calmly in a room stuffed with things like this one? And there had been something about the way that woman looked at him that had made him uncomfortable. He walked deliberately back to his own study.

CHAPTER 16

ELISABETH NORLAND ARRIVED LAST IN THE ROOM AND, reluctantly, took the only free seat around the table, next to William Simpson. Since she had arrived in the department five years earlier, she had hardly had a conversation with Simpson in which he hadn't touched her. It no doubt always looked no more or less than friendly—a hand on the arm, or on the back or shoulder, sometimes a hand over her hand and a small squeeze. It was never either so intrusive or so lengthy that she felt able to tell him that she found it always repulsive. Perhaps one day she would vomit on him.

He leaned unnecessarily close to her as she sat, handing her a couple of sheets of paper. The middle finger of his right hand was prominently bandaged over what seemed like a splint.

"The final two referee letters for Susan," he whispered too close to her ear, his sad grey ponytail dropping too close to her arm. Simpson, whose career had begun when he was belatedly a sixties radical in the eighties, liked to be called "Bill," insisting on it still even from students. She longed to tell him that the students called him "Pill."

Elisabeth read the letters quickly, relieved that they were strong and supportive. One from Australia, indicating some international reach, as well as indicating Susan's reputation among people who could distinguish quality from hype. The full committee was gathered around the table. She looked quickly at her colleagues

143

with her usual sense of dismay. Reading the finest literature was promoted as sharpening one's human sensibility, refining one's intellectual acuity, raising one's emotional intelligence, and other virtues. Looking at these inveterate readers of the world's great works seemed an unanswerable counter-argument to such claims. That is, if they actually read them as something other than a job.

"Bill. I have to be out of here by three. Truth is, I have a plane to catch this evening." Cameron Todd, sleeking back his hair, usually began meetings by informing the rest of the attendees that he had to move on quickly to something more important.

"I hope we won't be detained too long by this afternoon's business," said Simpson testily. "We have only the one item; the final vote on Susan Pybus's tenure case. You have now read the final reference letters that have been holding us up. Both letters speak very favourably about Susan's work, I think it fair to say. How would you prefer to proceed? I favour a brief comment from each member of the committee, indicating your likely disposition. If there is no evident disagreement, we might then move rapidly towards the vote. Is that suitable?"

"What happened to your hand, Bill?" asked Hilary Lockett.

"An accident," he said brusquely.

"We didn't suppose you did it on purpose," she replied. "How did you do it?"

"Perhaps we can discuss my hand after the rest of the agenda is dealt with?"

"As you wish. Did this accident have anything to do with our other agenda item?"

Elisabeth controlled a smile; trust Hilary to bring out into the open what they all wanted kept quiet. Simpson's response was to look angry, ashamed, and to blush, and to stroke his beard quickly. Elisabeth's response to his response was also to feel sudden anger and to blush as well. Mark had said that he had bribed and threatened at worst. Had he also tortured?

"Good God, Bill! Did that man attack you physically?" Hilary continued to make explicit what was on all their minds.

"No. It was something else. An accident."

There was silence around the table. Elisabeth keenly wanted to know whether Mark had damaged Simpson's finger, but she, like the others, had reasons for remaining quiet.

"Let us continue with our first statements on this case, with an indication of the reasons for our position. Perhaps we can go counter-clockwise, as Elisabeth was the last to arrive and may need a few extra moments." He turned towards her with a rather sickly, and, to her, sickening, leer, which was no doubt intended as a charming smile.

Olwen Greenwood removed her discoloured plastic retainer and put it down on the table. Olwen had given up on her body and anything beyond the most basic attempts at hygiene and concern with her appearance. Her lank brown hair seemed always in need of a good combing, her eyes looked deeply tired, embedded in crumpled brown-grey caves of wrinkles, and her face had in the last couple of years begun to gain unwanted fat that sagged sadly around her mouth. What was her problem? She was clever, witty at times, energetic about most aspects of her life, but seemed unable to keep up with her workload. Did she drink? No evidence of it. Had she some secret life that sapped her energy? Was being ugly so hard? In Elisabeth's observation, ugly people seemed to have fewer problems managing their lives than the beautiful; less of the intrusive expectations of others to deal with.

"I think the letters make a good case that Susan's work is of a very high quality, even if not extensive in quantity. But we knew that already. I see no reason to change from my earlier straw vote, that Susan not be granted tenure. No doubt we will give every consideration to keeping her on in a lecturer position, or some such."

She sat back in her chair, and reinserted the retainer over her teeth, signalling only too clearly that she had nothing else to say. There was a moment of silence as the others reflected on the meaning of the negative vote.

"Thank you. One 'No' vote. Of course, we are concerned only with the tenure decision and not implications that might follow from our vote. Cameron?"

"Well, to tell you the truth, I've concluded we were too precipitous earlier. The letters give further support to the view that the quality of Susan's work and her extraordinary teaching and service components, more than compensate for the exigu ... er ... few publications." He paused; rarely one to say little when he could say much. "That's it."

"I'll go along with that," was Kate Colebrook's brief contribution.

"Hilary?"

"Oh, I don't care. I voted 'No' earlier, and I do so again. Clearly some of you have undergone a conversion experience, influenced by someone who, I can predict, has calculated there will be a clear positive majority."

This was followed by another stiff silence, though none but Hilary could know that her sharply angry tone was fuelled by the stupid gesture that had cost her $20,000, and had not resulted in his getting in touch with her again. Still, she had cleared a week next month and booked herself into a hotel in the centre of Verona.

"Ken?"

Kenneth Gissing was not a favourite of Elisabeth's. Small and intense, struggling to be some kind of reincarnation of George Gissing, except for the talent, he did as little as possible in service to the department and students. His interest was Kenneth Gissing and what he had been heard to describe as his "career." To Elisabeth's disgust, his selfishness seemed to pay off time and again in the university. While the institution constantly claimed to value service to the community and teaching, it constantly betrayed such claims by rewarding with promotion, tenure, and chairs those who had attended most assiduously to their own

careers by publication and grants gained—however vacuous the
work involved. And who needed yet another Kenneth Gissing
book on George Gissing?

"I have reread the pieces that Susan submitted, and have been
persuaded that they have a resonance and insight I underestimated on first reading. I'm inclined to go along with those of my
colleagues who have voted 'Yes.'"

Elisabeth wondered about the various inducements Mark had
used to reap the positive results. Surely he wouldn't have used
violence? And surely Pill Simpson would not have held out to the
point of finger-smashing? It wasn't credible. Perhaps it really had
been an accident.

"Elisabeth?" Simpson leered again.

"Yes."

"Your vote?"

"That's what I was saying 'Yes' to." She felt distressed that
the others might be imagining how she had been coerced, and
what inducements she had accepted in exchange for her vote. She
wanted to, but couldn't, point out that her case was different.

"Ah. Thank you. I myself will go along with the positive
majority."

The room was silent again; shamefully silent, Elisabeth felt.
Gissing, Colebrook, and Todd began closing their folders and
sliding towards Simpson the copies of the reference letters. The
others sat, as though something needed to be said, but no one was
willing to be the sayer. No doubt in other minds around the table
the formidable image of Mark Morata was lodged, but perhaps
in none with the surprising affection Elisabeth felt each time she
reflected on their meetings, which was frequently.

"I will record our vote and pass our recommendation for Susan
Pybus's tenure to Ian Carbonell, who will make an independent
judgement before passing it on to the senior appointments committee. Thank you. I should maybe, if it is the will of the committee,

add to Ian our very strong recommendation that should he or a higher committee vote against Susan's tenure, the department should make every effort to retain her services in some other untenured position, perhaps as a senior sessional lecturer. I recognize that this would only be advisory, as we have no remit to require such a result."

"If we tie up a salary in a non-tenured position," said Kate Colebrook, "we lose the ability to hire a visible minority person, to do something about the lack of diversity we white middle-class folk keep claiming we want to correct in the department. So I'd recommend leaving our vote as it is, and not tie our hands if the final disposition is other than we have voted for."

Silence greeted this.

"I strongly agree with that. Scrub the face-saving addendum," said Hilary.

Mumbles of agreement led Simpson to nod. "Okay. I'll just forward the vote to Ian."

Elisabeth wondered how independent Carbonell's judgement would be, if her persuasive friend had already reached him. She was determined to find out how Simpson's finger had been damaged, but realized for the first time that she had no means to contact Mark.

CHAPTER 17

THERE WAS A SEAL! AND ANOTHER OVER TO THE LEFT. THE near one kept its muzzle and large liquid black eyes out of the water, watching Ian as he urged his kayak quietly towards it. Carbonell came within ten feet before it dived leisurely and was gone. He pushed his right foot forward in the kayak, turning the rudder to take him further out into the bay and towards the tankers and cargo ships anchored there waiting to enter the docks to unload.

It was a perfect day for kayaking. No perceptible wind, and the bay was without waves but resting in slowly shifting low hills and shallow valleys of water. Some optimistic sailors had come out and sat becalmed. The unusually smooth surface was a delight, with the strange sensation of sinking into a heaving valley and then up a minute later onto a rounded ridge. He had never seen the bay quite like this. But one of the surprising discoveries of kayaking was that the water was never the same from day to day.

He pulled forward, aiming for the four-craned cargo ship about, he calculated, twenty minutes ahead of him. One of the other pleasures of kayaking in the bay was slowly paddling round these massive ships that were like small cities. He would go up one side then curve around the bow and come back down the other. Often some sailor would look over the edge and try a greeting in a facsimile of English. Voices carried easily on the water and he'd had conversations with many Eastern European sailors, many Chinese, Filipinos, some South Americans.

Shit! A powerful speedboat curved round the cargo ship and was making for him. He hated speedboats. When they roared by they often sent a wave of water over the top of his kayak, threatening to capsize him. And this one was getting closer every second.

Carbonell turned and paddled hard for a couple of minutes, intending to move sufficiently clear of the boat's path that its wake would be only a minor nuisance. As he moved, the boat seemed to be turning synchronously, aiming directly at him. Carbonell turned right around, facing the opposite shore and leaned into it, feeling his strong arms and shoulders drive the sleek boat forward. What a pain! The damn thing was ruining the pleasure of this beautiful slowly shifting water.

Irritation was quickly turning to fear as the boat continued to alter its course as though aiming at him. This was ridiculous. Some idiot drifting around, not looking where he was going. But it kept coming. It was no more than half a minute away. Carbonell kept paddling as fast as he could, now breathing hard with sweat beginning to dribble down his ribs and his forehead. But the boat kept coming at him. He tried another rapid turn, left foot slamming against the rudder mechanism, but the speedboat just shifted its course too.

"Look out! Stop!" he shrieked as the big boat roared at him. Terrified, he grabbed at the front of the spray skirt so he could get out if he was capsized or hit. But the boat was on him too fast. His mind went blank. He sat with his mouth open, eyes closed, helpless, waiting for the impact.

Which didn't come. He opened his eyes as the kayak was thrown around by the boat's wake, and slapped the water with his paddle blade to prevent himself tipping over. As he got the kayak under control, he realized that the boat had slowed and was coming back towards him. It kicked into reverse for a few seconds, to come to a stop alongside the bobbing kayak.

Carbonell couldn't find his voice as he looked up intending to shout. His heart was pounding, and his mouth felt completely dry. Water was dripping through the spray skirt onto his legs. A man leaned on the rail of the boat above him, looking down casually.

"What the hell do you think you're doing?" Carbonell managed to croak.

"Oh, just havin' a bit o' fun." He had a strong Scottish accent.

"Are you mad?" He couldn't believe the man could be so casual, but he couldn't think of anything else to say. It was too crazy.

"How far can you swim?"

"What are you talking about?" Carbonell was trying to turn the kayak back towards Burrard Inlet, but as he began to paddle in that direction, the boat kept alongside him. Carbonell was looking around, for someone who might help, but the nearest becalmed sailboat was more than half a mile away and nothing else was nearer.

"Could you swim from here to the shore, say?"

What was the lunatic on about? The Scotsman had something in his hand. It was a gun! And he seemed to be screwing a silencer onto the barrel.

"I was thinking, if I was to put a hole in that wee boat o' yourn, do you think you'd make it to shore? Or would you go doon wi' the ship?"

Carbonell kept paddling hard. The Scot fired into the front of the kayak, creating a neat hole in the Kevlar hull. Carbonell recoiled with shock, slamming his knees against the inside of the kayak as the paddle shot into the air and out of his hands. He lurched sideways, then back, barely keeping upright.

"I suppose that'll be letting water in a bit, eh? I didn't want to make too much noise, see." He pointed at the silencer. "Noise carries over the water a long way, ye ken?"

"What do you want? What do you want me to do?" Carbonell helplessly watched his paddle float away. "This is a rented boat," he said pathetically. Even through his panic he hoped the Scotsman didn't realize that kayaks were built in three watertight compartments. The hole would let water into the front one only, and he would still be able to stay afloat with the other two. But already he could feel the nose of the kayak dipping a little as the water entered.

"Don't you think it's daft to come out here in the middle of the bay, further than you can swim back? The water's cold. You'll catch your death. You look like a big lad, but I'd put serious money on your not making it to shore without your wee boat."

As he spoke, Alan Wilkie casually turned the gun to the rear of the kayak and sent another bullet through it.

"For Christ's sake! What do you want? Who are you? What do you want with me? Look, I think this is a mistake. Do you know who I am? Perhaps you think I'm someone else."

"Ah no. I think you're you. Who do you think you are?"

"I'm just an English professor, from the university." Carbonell pointed vaguely behind him in the direction of the campus out on the point.

"You know, the lad I'm after is an English professor too. Not likely a mistake then, eh?"

"Why? For God's sake, why are you doing this?" The boat was settling lower in the water. "I'm going down," he said plaintively.

"Well, I suppose you'd better come aboard then." Mr. Wilkie kicked over a short rope ladder. Uncertainly, Carbonell pulled the spray skirt from around the rim of the kayak, and brought one foot forward. He leaned over, took hold of the rope ladder, and pushed up from the centre of the kayak. Within a couple of minutes he had climbed over the rail and stepped out of the spray skirt. Alan Wilkie was standing to the side with the gun pointing at him.

"Let's go inside."

Alan indicated with the gun barrel that Carbonell was to pre-
cede him down the steps from the rear deck into the main cabin.
On the cabin door, there was a sign that read "Know schews." He
looked at it for a moment, feeling that he had suddenly entered a
mad world where nothing made sense.

"Take your shoes off."

"Oh. I see."

Carbonell kicked off his runners, and hesitantly pushed open
the door. He entered a luxurious room, with deep piled carpet and
a rich beige leather sofa with matching armchairs. Another man
was sitting in one of the armchairs, leaning forward examining
papers on a low table. He was without a jacket, with shirt sleeves
unfastened and rolled up. The room was pleasantly warm.

"Dr. Carbonell. How kind of you to give up the pleasures of
your paddle to join us." Mark Morata leaned back and indicated
that Carbonell should sit in the armchair next to his. Alan sat on
the sofa across from them, gun at the ready.

"I've got a rented kayak sinking outside. What's supposed to
happen to that?"

"My boat, my agenda," said Mark. "First, I want to invite you
to consider some of the documents I have here."

"What…?" Carbonell paused. "You have a copy of my book."

"Yes, on the differences between Wordsworth's 1805 and 1850
versions of *The Prelude*. It is a topic I was once interested in, but
I must confess … Well, my opinion of your book is of no matter."

"You nearly drown me, shoot my kayak from under me, and
now you are criticizing my book!" Carbonell was increasingly
distraught.

"You will recall Chapter Six? I wanted to draw your attention to
this paper, written by one of your students three years prior to the
publication of your book. And also, consider Chapter Nine and this
thesis written by another of your students four years earlier. Both

the students have written these letters, in which they detail their relationship to you and the ways in which you plagiarized their work. You criticized their work and then, with minor changes, used it in your book. I have three other student papers, and my research assistant located a thesis written at Cornell University twelve years ago, that establishes most of what makes up your Chapters Three and Four. I suspect a little more searching would disinter all the sources from which you compiled this book."

"That is ridiculous!" Carbonell was still disoriented, and had begun to sweat, particularly in a band below his nose, which was with him a sign of distressed anger. He hastily pulled his hand across the line of sweat.

"The debt you say I owe to the students is the other way. They were my ideas, freely given in my classes, which these young ladies used in their writing. I think their thanks would be more appropriate than these absurd claims. And what, anyway, has this to do with anything?"

"Perhaps I could direct your attention to this other letter. It describes a series of occasions on which you made it clear that Miss Diane Mayberry would be able to successfully complete and defend her thesis only if she 'came across,' is the phrase she claims you used. You required a sexual return for your academic favour."

"That is nonsense!"

"Well, there is attached a further two letters from Mr. Colin Lee and Miss Jane Schwartz, who are prepared to give evidence that they mistakenly entered her apartment, finding you in a state of undress and shouting at Miss Mayberry … well, the details of what they heard are in their letter. I have a number of documents making similar accusations from eight other women."

"Would you mind telling me what all this is about?" Carbonell was disoriented by the madness of the past ten minutes, and this raking up of what he had assumed were buried indiscretions and successfully survived risks.

"Perhaps I might also mention this letter by a previous secretary of yours, Greta Anderson. She claims that while she was on probation you drew her attention to her status each time you asked for favours that were no part of her job."

"I never touched her!"

"Indeed, no. The concern here was your requiring her to type up screenplays for your girlfriend at the time. I gather the university administration does not approve of its resources being deployed on such private enterprise. And there are a number of other items. Of particular interest to your academic colleagues is the fact that two articles you have in your Curriculum Vitae, are not in fact in the prestigious journals you cite. Also your own Ph.D. thesis on Coleridge bears an uncanny likeness to one written at Berkeley twenty-three years earlier."

"What do you want?"

"Within the next week you have to make an independent decision with regard to the tenure case of Susan Pybus. Your departmental committee has, to everyone's surprise, I gather, delivered a positive recommendation. You will concur with that positive decision, and send it forward to the university tenure committee."

"Is that all? Is that what this has all been about? You are the guy who put pressure on the committee members? Why all this background research, and why the kayak and ..." he waved a hand around "... all this?"

"I put someone onto the research early on, just to collect a little information. Quite quickly, my researcher began to turn up hints of these items, and I authorized a more intensive look into the rumours. It became clear that you are what I believe is called a scumbag. As for the kayak; merely a coincidence. I wanted to follow you this afternoon for a brief discussion. When you rented the kayak, I thought it would be amusing to meet you on the water. The earlier entertainment was, I'm afraid, the result of my Scottish colleague's Scottish sense of humour. Now, if you do not produce a positive judgement in Dr. Pybus's case, this portfolio will find its way to your university president, vice-presidents, your dean, and the local newspapers."

Carbonell looked as though his mind was working overtime, but couldn't manage to focus. "Now, look … I mean some of this looks … I mean Mayberry, for example …"

"I'm afraid I'm a little busy. No time for extended discussions. Time for you to leave. Remember your responsibility with regard to this case. I'm still not entirely sure what to do about all this." Mark swept his hand across the papers on the table. "But if you should fail to give a positive recommendation about the Pybus case, my friend will pay you a more aggressive visit."

Alan indicated with his gun that Ian Carbonell was to rise and leave the cabin. Outside he slipped into his running shoes and they went on deck. Carbonell was surprised to see that they had come in close to shore, entering the run under the bridge to the docks.

"What am I to do about the kayak?" he asked Alan. "They take an impress of a credit card, and will charge me the replacement costs."

"Ye should ha' thought about that afore ye let me sink it."

Alan led him to the low rail where he had climbed into the boat.

"Now, Carbonell. Before ye leave us. You probably don't care that I was brought up in Glasgow, in the Gorbals, before they came down. It made me what you'd perhaps call a bit o' a psychopath. I've even heard a few say—famous last words, like—that I'm a homicidal maniac. Well, this should be of interest to you because my friend in there gave you some instructions, and I'm to see you carry them out. D'ye see? If you fail, or whisper a word of what's happened here … Well, as they say, I know where you live. Y'understand?"

Carbonell nodded. There were a few people on the shore path: a group of joggers, a couple of mothers pushing prams, two or three men in business attire striding purposefully. One or two looked round in surprise as a man seemed to have fallen from the deck of a passing boat into the water. But it was none of their business. And the man was swimming to shore, so wasn't in danger of drowning.

CHAPTER 18

"AS YOU SAID, MARCOS, IT BECAME QUICKLY APPARENT that the Pybuses had no idea about our business. Some of my younger colleagues did indeed want to pursue their traditional methods of verifying this, but I was able to restrain them. Your English appears to be as good as people say, and I trust the books I left do adequately reflect your taste?" Keiichi watched the water falling into his pond, conscious that Marcos would hear it and perhaps wonder where he was phoning from.

"Yes, certainly. I am most grateful. I have in mind a small set of books that I would like to give you in return. And I will add a piece of information, about the movement of cocaine in Xi'an."

There was brief silence. Mark thought he heard the quietest intake of breath. "How very kind. This is what I have spent some time and not a few lives trying to discover. And in return?"

"Just to show my appreciation for your release of the Pybuses unharmed. Mr. Pybus saved my life. Well, I may not have been in mortal danger, but he risked his life to save me. I owe a debt, and I am trying to help his wife at the university. Nothing to do with business. You have my word."

"That is quite enough for me. In our business circle, Marcos, it has been assumed by more than me, I'm afraid, that you have a business interest in the university. One of my young men was followed by some of our Vietnamese business rivals and they seemed to have made incorrect inferences about our both having interests in the English department. And while I think of it, we might sometime soon discuss what we should do about Jimmy Phan, who is becoming irksome."

"I think Mr. Phan is going to fade away, but if he fails to do so, I'll be in touch to discuss alternatives."

"Excellent. Also I envy you having had the opportunity to converse with so many professors of English. Once I cleared up the confusion with the Pybuses, we had a number of most engaging discussions. Marred, I fear, by their incarceration and consequent anxieties."

Mark felt that Keiichi was working very hard at his English. They both used the language in somewhat stilted ways, he was aware, catching in Keiichi's early twentieth-century elaborate correctness an echo of his own English, shaped by the literary contexts in which they had learned it.

"Perhaps we can arrange an exchange as soon as is convenient for you. I will have Mr. Wilkie phone later and make arrangements. Perhaps tonight?"

"Yes. Reluctant though I am to lose their company, I am quite eager to see what books you have for me, and the information about Xi'an would permit immediate benefits to my organization."

"Good. I look forward to our next conversation."

"As do I."

Mark clicked the disconnect button, continuing to look across the water at the North Shore Mountains. He climbed out of the Tesla, walked to the edge of the beach, and sat on a log, wondering how he might bring order back into his increasingly chaotic life.

CHAPTER 19

PROFESSOR XAVIER O'HIGGINS CLIMBED UP THE STEPS OF the swimming pool, pulled off his goggles, wiggled his feet into a pair of plastic sandals, and walked towards the glass door to the changing rooms. Mark gave him a minute or so, then followed.

O'Higgins was under a shower, pouring conditioner onto his thinning and greying hair. Mark turned on another shower and slipped off his shorts, letting the hot water carry away the residue of chlorine from the pool. He followed O'Higgins into the changing room, and they both stood towelling themselves.

"Nice to have a pool almost to oneself," said Mark.

"Yes. A pool of one's own and $200,000 a year would suit me well. But it's usually like that at lunchtimes during the week. I haven't seen you here before." O'Higgins had an Irish accent.

"First time. I used to swim at the Aquatic Centre downtown."

"I've been there when this place is closed for cleaning. Here I swim in the fast lane. Down there, with all the gleaming young athletes, I started in the fast lane, and then gradually was pushed across the pool to the slowest lane."

Mark doubted that O'Higgins had to go far from the fast lane. He was lean and muscular, with a body that looked as though it was largely unchanged since his late teens, except for a small layer of fat above the hips and a slight thickening around the belly. He was maybe five inches shorter than Mark.

"You have mostly a regular group here each day?" Mark asked.

"Yes." O'Higgins had one foot on the bench, drying his testicles with that curious look of abstracted contemplation that was common with men during this brief and delicate operation. He looked at the clock. "We are a little early, but in a while the old guys for the Aquafit exercises will arrive. A good workout in the water, and it's gentle on the joints, and I think they enjoy ogling the attractive young woman who is the instructor. Probably pumps the blood that bit harder, inducing heart attacks in some and warding off Alzheimer's in others."

"And do you work nearby? Is this your lunch hour?" asked Mark, pulling on his underpants and reached into the locker for his shirt, pleased that O'Higgins was so genially talkative. A shower went on around the corner. One of the two other men in the pool had followed them out. Clearly not the one with the walker. It must be the other, whom Mark had noticed earlier; stout, much grey hair over his body, white on top, and with a smiling and benign face like a contented abbot.

"No, I'm ashamed to say I'm an academic. I work at home when I can, and come here every day I get to work at home."

"What do you do? At UBC?"

"Yes, I'm at UBC in the math department."

"Ah, I ..."

O'Higgins laughed as his head emerged from the sweater he was putting on. "I know, you've always been hopeless with numbers. It's the bane of the mathematician's life. Mention your job and people feel a need to apologize and confess how they could never understand anything beyond the simplest math."

"Well, I was going to say that I have always had an odd gift for numbers, which I've never been able to understand."

"Oh, sorry. How interesting! And what form does this gift take?"

They both paused for a moment, as the old guy in the shower began to sing in a worn voice. But then he seemed to forget the words and trailed away, da, da, da-ing the tune.

"I sometimes think this place is as close to paradise as I'm likely to find on earth," O'Higgins said. "There is no anxiety, no one is in competition with anyone else. The unforced friendliness astonishes me every day. Old Bob will be out in a while. He's the one with the walking frame by the poolside. When he gets dressed, which is a slow business, he can manage everything except getting on his right sock. Some injury. He just can't reach it. But the regulars, old or young, Black or white or Asian, just take it for granted that someone will notice when Bob is ready for the right sock and will put it on for him quite casually. All those monks in their monasteries, dreaming of heaven as a garden or green fields with flowering trees. But here it is: a swimming pool changing room. Sorry, you were going to tell me about your gift for numbers."

"Well," said Mark, amused by the easy digressions, "I don't usually have to calculate. I see the numbers, somehow. My work involves sometimes quite complex calculations, but I rarely need to rely on the people I hire to do my books. It can be convenient. It's as though the solution just takes the place of the numbers that need to be calculated. I'm not aware of doing anything. If I try to calculate, I can do so only a little better than most people."

"How interesting! That's very rare. Less rare among professional mathematicians, but not that common even then. How's your chess?"

"Pretty good."

O'Higgins was putting his towel and swimsuit into a plastic carrier bag, and stopped. "This is quite a coincidence. I've been involved with a colleague in our Education faculty, doing research on people with unusual math abilities. We're looking for ways to improve math education, which is generally grotesquely bad, as you no doubt know. I wonder would you be willing to be a subject in our experiments? The hardest part we've had is finding subjects with such a gift, as you might imagine."

"Of course. I'd be interested, if only to discover something more about why it works that way for me. Look, I was just going to get lunch on 41st Avenue. Would you care to join me?"

"I would, indeed."

As the two men walked down the corridor beside the pool, Mark said, "I have a friend who works at the university, and I've recently met through her a few people in the English department. They seem to be constantly caught up with committees, and wouldn't be able to take lunchtime swims."

"Well, I try hard to keep mornings free for my research. But that's going to be disrupted soon. I'm chair of a committee whose work becomes quite onerous next week."

"What's that?"

"Oh, boring university rituals. It's called the university tenure committee. We have to deal with all the cases of tenure and promotion from around the university. To guarantee an angelic justice in decisions across the different faculties and departments. Where were you thinking of for lunch?"

"Well, I hadn't thought of it too much. I noticed a few restaurants. Any one would do. You are the local. Do you have a favourite?"

"I like to go to the Pastry Club Cafe. It's a couple of blocks down. You mentioned that your job required complex calculations. What kind of work?"

Mark told him about the legitimate import/export business, as they walked together past the shops. They exchanged names as they entered the small cafe and took a table by the window. Their fellow diners were mostly elderly women enjoying lunch out with friends, chatting amiably and quietly, creating a pleasant and undisturbing buzz. Mark and Xavier ordered smoked salmon sandwiches on French bread with soup.

"But you do have some academic background?" O'Higgins asked.

"Only an undergraduate degree in English literature, in Santiago. But the working of universities interests me. I have a friend whose wife has been involved with some tenure decision, and I have been quite astonished at the complexity and time that have gone into making judgements. In the business world, we tend to be simpler and cruder in making such decisions."

"And possibly no worse for it. In universities people try to defend against bias and nepotism of one form or another, and this cumbersome machinery does provide some defence against many forms of corruption and stupidity."

"Tell me, Xavier, in the work of your tenure committee, if a case comes to you that has the unanimous support of the departmental committee and of the head of the department, would it not likely be supported by your committee automatically? How could you as a mathematician question a decision about, say, an English professor when the English department committee, who are expert in the field, judges the person meriting tenure?"

"Yes, such a case would normally go through more or less automatically. Unless there was something anomalous about it."

"Such as inadequate publications?"

"Such as inadequate publications." O'Higgins smiled, and they sat back as the food was put in front of them. "Now you will forgive me for saying it, I hope, but I think you are not being entirely straightforward with me, Mark."

"Why do you say that?"

"Oh, I may be quite wrong, but I am beginning to feel that this is all too neat. You have a particular interest in the tenure committee's deliberations? This is not a chance meeting, or a chance invitation to lunch to discuss my research and your possible role in it?"

Mark looked at the slender face opposite him, into the dark blue eyes, and felt some surprise that his ruse, or Frank's rather, had been uncovered so easily, and that the Irishman seemed quite unperturbed.

"I'm ashamed to admit that you are right. I have an interest in the case of a Professor Pybus from the English department."

"Mm. Haven't seen it yet, so I can't really help."

"Well, I suppose I should ask your advice. She has done lots of service work, has outstanding teaching, but has few, though good, publications."

"A book?"

"No. Just a few papers; three or four, I think. Two before she began her contract. She does apparently have a book manuscript somewhere being looked at by a publisher, but she has heard nothing from them. The department supported her case, committee and chairman, and I am eager for it to go forward, for reasons of my own. I may perhaps mention that I have never met her. My interest is a little complicated."

"The best of motives, I'm sure. So you are looking for my judgement about how it is likely to go?"

"Well, yes. And I wondered if I might persuade you to support it too."

O'Higgins looked up at Mark, nodded, and muttered something, a kind of grunt in his throat, as he took a few mouthfuls of soup. At the table next to them, four women had stood and were gathering coats and gloves, smiling apologetically as they manoeuvred in the small space.

"Hard to know. The committee will be expecting to vote in favour as it comes with no dissenting voice. And that will help. But with so few publications, it might well seem anomalous. We will probably want the advice of the English department person on the committee. What's his name? Conrad Smith. And then you said you wanted to persuade me. I do have the feeling you didn't mean only by pressing on me the merits of Dr. Pybus's publications?"

"I did have in mind ... Well, I don't know. I am a simple businessman, and I had assumed that I should deal with this tenure business the way I am accustomed. Actually, my work ..." Mark paused. "But I have another friend in the English department who is intent on persuading me that I should not use such methods."

"Bribery and threats?" O'Higgins took a bite out of his smoked salmon sandwich, apparently treating their discussion as of purely intellectual interest. "The other inference I am perhaps improperly making is that this case has not reached my committee without some input from you. Is that right?"

Mark took the last spoonful of his soup, and pondered how to deal with this Irishman's acute intuitions.

"I mean," added O'Higgins, "the case as you describe it would be unlikely to arrive with unanimous support. Now the problem you face, of course, is that your continuing work on behalf of Dr. Pybus is likely to hinder her rather than help."

"Why so?" Mark was surprised and disturbed by this observation.

"Because while I might have been inclined to take the previous support as favourable evidence, I now know that I should scrutinize the case with some suspicion, and discount those earlier votes."

As O'Higgins was speaking, Mark noticed a tall, dark-haired beauty collecting a cake box from the counter. After paying for it, she turned and eyed Mark coolly then stopped and seemed almost to gasp seeing O'Higgins. She moved between the small tables to stand beside them.

"Dr. O'Higgins. Margaret Amundsen. I took ..."

"Of course. You are not so easily forgotten as you seem to assume. How are you doing?" O'Higgins stood briefly, shook hands, and sat again.

"Your letter to Waterloo ... you wrote a reference ..."

The young woman blushed as she spoke. Mark was fascinated at her adulatory attention to O'Higgins, and his calm politeness in response. She stood as if in front of something holy, in a kind of awe, smiling timidly, oozing dewy-eyed affection. After a few minutes, she bowed to him awkwardly a couple of times, nodded apologies to Mark while not really seeing him, and left.

"One of the perks, or temptations, of the job?" Mark asked.

"Ah, no, no ... It's ..." O'Higgins seemed to be lost for words for a moment.

"She seemed to look at you with something like love."

"Ah well, I am their favourite uncle, who is a priest. It is the stance I try to take. Occasionally I will shake hands, but otherwise ... You know Aristotle's *Poetics*? He charts the different kinds of plots plays can follow, and, it has seemed to me that life follows similar plots. For these young women this particular plot is usually a comedy. A comedy is when, in the course of everyday life, an incident occurs that, in the end, leaves the protagonist better or happier than before. So this plot usually runs: student meets elderly professor; student falls in love with elderly professor; student comes to her senses. Unfortunately, this play seems commonly to have a tragic corollary. That plot goes: student meets elderly professor; elderly professor falls in love with student; student comes to her senses. One learns to accept the catastrophes with apparent imperturbability. I suspect they damage my chances for longevity."

"My sympathy."

O'Higgins accepted it with a brief wave of the hand and a smile.

"Sympathy accepted. This no-touch priestly uncle routine does have odd effects sometimes, though. I find myself chairing meetings, assiduously taking notes, I assume my colleagues assume. But I find after the meeting is closed that I have written four or five closely packed pages that read 'Margaret, Margaret, Margaret, Margaret ...'"

"I'm not sure I believe that last bit. You would not write pages of Margarets."

O'Higgins looked Mark in the eye for a second or two. "Very astute of you. That was poetic licence, I suppose. But we males all do various forms of tortuous emotional damage to ourselves, ensuring women's greater longevity."

"Well, what would you advise in my damaging pursuit of tenure for Dr. Pybus? I am supposed not to use bribes or threats, or *plata o plomo*, but, at the same time, it is very important to me that she gets tenure. I also think, incidentally, that she merits tenure. What am I to do?"

"I'd have thought there's nothing much you can do. Leave it with me. If I think she merits tenure, she'll get it."

"But you are only one vote, even if the chair. Perhaps I should meet with this Professor Smith you mentioned. The member of your committee from the English department. What is he like?"

"Large, overweight, scruffy-bearded, lazy, self-pitying, self-justifying, weak, petulant, vindictive, and without much I can discern in the way of compensating qualities."

"And you will rely on his judgement of the case?"

"Oh, don't worry. As I said, I'll ensure she gets tenure if she merits it. I can be persuasive."

"And if you conclude she doesn't merit tenure?"

"She won't get it."

"Are you perhaps a little overconfident?"

"No. Realistic. Based on a fair amount of experience. I can deal with committees the way you deal with numbers."

"So I should resort to *plata o plomo* with you?"

"I thought you'd sworn off them."

"Only if I can't find some other way. I will accept no other result except Dr. Pybus getting tenure."

"Well I don't know how to advise you. If you threaten me, I shall just announce I have an interest in the case and withdraw myself."

"But presumably if my threats were credible, that is one of the things I would require you not to do."

"Ah yes. I hadn't thought of that. Of course. Mm. What can we do then?"

"When I mentioned *plata o plomo*, it was because I was associated, when I was a very young man, with Pablo Escobar, whose name you might know." O'Higgins nodded. "I am in the same business. My interest in this case should be taken very seriously, by you."

The two men sat silently for a minute, until the waitress asked could she move their dishes.

"Coffee?" she added.

They both looked up at her distractedly, then at each other.

"Not for me," said O'Higgins. "You, Mark?"

"Do you do cappuccino?"

"Yes."

"I think I'd like one."

As the waitress went to get the coffee, O'Higgins stood up. He put fifteen dollars on the table.

"That'll cover my share, and a tip."

"No, no," said Mark. "I invited you."

"But in the circumstances, I can't give the impression that I might have been bribed, can I?" He smiled easily. Mark wondered whether he really believed this was real, or whether he treated all reality like this, saving his sense of the serious for his world of numbers.

"Please—an odd request perhaps." O'Higgins cocked his head on one side, and sat down again. "I have led an academic life from the beginning, it sometimes seems. Ivory towers all the way up, or down. Tell me something of your life, your drug business, if that's what you meant. Any single event, or adventure, or person you dealt with. Whatever comes to mind. I'm a voyeur of others' lives, I fear."

Mark thought for a moment, bemused by the manner of the request. Not the high drama stuff; something of his past everyday life.

"Too many scenes occur. Well, randomly ... I worked for a few months for a wealthy lawyer, much of his money inherited, but more of it accumulated by his wits. I was—it is complicated—but you might say on loan to him, from my patrone, Felix. A tall thin man, the lawyer loved the things his money could buy, which drew him into the world of drug dealing. Nothing else could allow him to accumulate a dozen or a hundred times as much as his law practice. He began to invest his substantial profits in Martinique, where he bought land and built a palace near the sea.

"I was good with numbers. Not as good as I suggested earlier, maybe. That was a scenario invented by a friend of mine that was supposed to lead into a conversation about gaining your support in the Pybus business. But I have always been good enough. He decided on the place in Martinique, and I was the one he put in charge of getting the plans converted from paper into concrete, steel, and glass on his chosen site.

"I had rented a small house, just a block back from the beach. From the upstairs bedroom I could see the building site. This was a little way to the north of the Bay of St. Pierre. Do you know Martinique?"

"No. Never been there."

"A lovely setting, mountains behind, clear sea, good beaches. The lawyer, Gabriel, would come and stay, perhaps twice a month, usually for just a couple of days. Always with a different girl, or nearly always. One I saw four or five times. Unlike most of the successful people in the cocaine business, he was also a consumer. And the girls were often high.

"I mostly worked in the main living room downstairs, a side window onto a strip of bamboo that blocked out the neighbour's house, and the front window looked down on the unpaved street. The girls complained that it was a nuisance walking to the beach. One visit, I was trying to work on designing the garden. Gabriel had said he wanted a classical French garden built, and I had looked at various designs. He had approved the sketch I had made for the space available, and having calculated the quantities of stones and gravel and sod and plants we would need, I was trying to talk to a supplier and arrange delivery.

"Gabriel was at the bank—I think he had accounts all over the place, the big money in Switzerland, but smaller deposits in a dozen places he might have to run to. The current girl, perhaps sixteen, was in a bikini, perched on my desk, high on cocaine, and wanting attention. I was trying to set up a new Excel document on my computer, and intermittently also trying to phone two young men at Cornell University, who we used as mules for some of the cocaine that arrived in Miami. After their spring break, when they were guaranteed a good time aided by cocaine at parties on the beaches of Florida, supplied by our people based in the hotels, these, and dozens of others, would carry astonishing amounts of the powder to their campuses up the east coast. And I was supposed to be coordinating that as well. I'm sorry. This is maybe going on too long, and not what you were interested in?"

"No, no—exactly what I had hoped for."

"'Well, these guys will be more fun!' the girl said suddenly. She slid off my desk and headed for the door. A dark green Peugeot, an old 404, I remember, had pulled up in front of the house, and two guys in dark suits were moving slowly up the path. I panicked. I assumed Gabriel must have been caught trying to cheat Pablo, or perhaps they just suspected that he might be cheating—that would have been enough. Enough to have got us all wiped out. Standard procedure, you might say. I shouted to the girl to hide, but she was laughing and working at the locks on the door. I knew, from the slow progress they were making up the path, that to run out the back door would get me killed immediately. Again, standard procedure. If the guys coming to the front of the house were to make the hit, they would have arrived fast with heavy ordinance, and would have shot the house to pieces before we'd seen them. If they come slowly up the path, that means there are guys already waiting behind the house. As soon as you open the back door, you are dead.

"What I am trying to convey is in part the intensity of daily experience in my job, and the inescapable risk of imminent death. In my job, unlike yours, you cannot be sure at any moment whether someone, for reasons you might not understand, or by means you do not suspect, may kill you. One can take precautions, of course, but this element is incessant, and has been a vivid part of my experience since adolescence."

"But what happened in Martinique?"

"Oh, nothing. I ran upstairs, checked the side windows, but could see none of the expected gunmen. Then I heard the girl laughing. I realized it wasn't a hit, just business. I can't even remember what they wanted—something to do with getting Gabriel to change euros into dollars, or the other way round."

"Bit of an anticlimax. I was expecting pyrotechnics and blood all over the place."

"Oh I have such stories, but you just asked for a random slice of daily life."

"Yes. It has its vividness. Thank you. Perhaps we can have the other stories some other time, but I'll need preparation. Anyway, I've got to go."

He held out his hand, and Mark shook it. "Got some papers I need to get through this afternoon. I've really enjoyed our talk. Perhaps you can let me know when you decide if you'd like to do something further about this case? I don't think bribes or threats are likely to work with me, though I shouldn't say that, of course. I suppose that would depend on how big either one was."

"I assure you I would make either as big as necessary."

O'Higgins, to Mark's slight discomfiture, laughed in response. "You will remember St. Teresa of Ávila's caution that more tears are shed as a result of prayers answered than those unanswered. Consider that you might not be doing Dr. Pybus a favour."

The Irishman waved in the friendliest way as he left the cafe. Mark considered whether he would go after him and try to take back control of the situation, which had clearly escaped him.

"Would you like something with the coffee?" the waitress asked.

"I was resisting asking for one of those chocolate pastry things, but you've broken down my good intentions."

"Good. They're delicious. I'll get you one. Or two?"

"One, thank you."

So what next? O'Higgins would no doubt respond to sufficient threats. Perhaps to his family, his computer—whatever it took. But Mark lacked the heart for it. Elisabeth's voice talking about ends and means kept trying to push its way into his head. But he couldn't simply give up now. It was a matter of what he had called honour—shorthand for this odd compulsion to repay something of his debt to Geoffrey Pybus. He wasn't clear what was driving the compulsion. There were a further six members of the university committee to persuade, which only filled him with dreary foreboding. And he was running out of time. The decision was due in a week, and the Peruvian shipment needed attention now that it was being divided into smaller quantities ready for transportation to Denver then on to Chicago and south to Atlanta.

CHAPTER 20

MARK FELT THE TIME WAS RIPE FOR A TALK WITH CONRAD Smith, the English department's representative on the university tenure committee. He had phoned to make an appointment, to be told that Dr. Smith was this morning meeting with the executive director of Simon Fraser University Downtown, UBC's rival to the east of the city, with a major branch in the downtown core. This was inconvenient.

"It is extremely urgent that I see Dr. Smith this morning. Is he returning to the UBC campus later?" he asked the English department secretary.

"I don't know. He might be going home, or somewhere else. Just let me check … his meeting at SFU ends at 11:30 a.m. and, if your business was urgent, maybe you could try to make an appointment to see him at the SFU facility then. Do you know it? It's at 515 West Hastings Street. They are to meet in the executive director's office. Through the main doors from the street, up the escalator from the central concourse, and it's straight ahead on the second floor. Can't miss it. I'll try to leave a message for him. Perhaps you have his cell phone number? You do, good. If we both try, you'll likely be able to arrange something. Can I say whose name I should leave with the director's secretary?"

"Thank you. Yes. It's Professor Andrew Petter." Petter, Mark knew, either was or had been SFU's president. If Smith was trying to set up something with SFU, then that name might grab his attention.

Mark drove downtown, trying to phone Smith's mobile a few times, just going to straight to voice mail. As he crawled through the downtown traffic, slowed by construction sites, he had to keep moving back the likely time of his arrival. He left his car in a parkade beside the main university building, which was housed in the lower floors of the massive Harbour Centre. He entered through the front glass doors, wondering how to deal with Smith. If he turned out to be another O'Higgins, his job would be increasingly difficult. It was bad enough as a result of his own growing ambivalence about whether he should be trying to deal with these people at all. He kept his head down, walked quickly, and was wearing a hat, thinking it might provide some disguise when he had been expecting to meet Smith on the UBC campus where too many people now might recognize him.

He looked up, hearing a splintering of glass ahead. And what sounded like gunfire. It was muted, inside the building, but as he heard more shots, unmistakable. He began to run. What the hell was going on? And whatever it was, he felt, it was probably his fault. Academics were not known for casual gunfights in the corridors.

Ahead he could see the broad escalator, and heard shouting. A stocky guy in a white shirt with some kind of shoulder pads and black trousers, who looked like security, was jumping rapidly down the up-escalator, waving his arms and calling for help from an office to the left of the concourse. Mark ran towards the escalator, but the security guard held his arms out to prevent him.

"Can't go up, mate! Some lunatics shooting!"

Support for this claim came with further crackles of gun-fire, and the sounds of large-scale smashing glass and screaming, and further shouting in one or more languages Mark couldn't understand. A second security guard arrived and reinforced the first blocking the escalator. Over to his right Mark saw a sign to elevators, and decided the direct route up the stairs was likely high-risk, apart from having to power through the no doubt resistant guards. He ran to the corridor and down between classrooms. Fortunately the elevators had no one queuing. He pushed the button as the glass shattering mayhem above got louder. A door opened immediately, and he prepared to pull out his gun as he moved upward, realizing this slow moving box was hardly a less risky option than the escalator.

The gunfire became more distinct as he rose. Mark urged the elevator on. As it juddered to a halt, he put one hand up as though to push the doors apart. As they opened, immediately ahead of him a Vietnamese gangster was firing back along the corridor. The man turned, saw Mark, and spun round moved his gun at him.

"Morata!" he shouted. Mark had been too slow levelling his gun; as it came out from the holster he knew he would be too late. He dived sideways, tensed for the hit. As he fell, the Vietnamese gunman jerked, his gun flew into the air, and he began to crumple. Blood seeped from him onto the carpet.

As Mark pushed onto his knees, gun forward and ready, a dark-suited yakuza stuck a foot into the elevator as it began to close. His gun was on Mark. Instead of shooting, he lowered his weapon and bowed.

"Mr. Morata. A thousand apologies. It was our carelessness allowed these pigs to discover you would be here. Mr. Kanehara sends profound apologies. We were sent to keep you safe from harm. The three are now dead. We must leave quickly. Are you all right, sir?"

"Yes. I am all right. Thank you, and thanks to Mr. Kanehara." Mark realized grimly that his new friend and protector, Keiichi, would likely have had this yakuza kill him without blinking if that had proved convenient.

"How could you know I would be here?"

"I will thank Mr. Kanehara for you. Your phone, sir, is no longer as secure as it once was, and also those of the UBC English department. Our fault. Jimmy Phan also gained access. A thousand apologies."

The young man bowed again, and then ran towards the rear stairs. Mark came carefully out of the elevator, stepping over the dead body, astonished at the mayhem facing him. Three other yakuza stood by the stairway exit, guns out. One after another they peeled off and headed down at a run. The glass wall that secured the executive director's office was shattered, glittering shards everywhere. Screams from inside the office, a few heads peeking fearfully above desks.

Mark calculated that he had maybe five minutes before the police would arrive, and the campus security guys had not seemed keen to enter the fray. The first gunfire he had heard had been little more than three minutes ago. The yakuza must have been already in place and prepared for the Vietnamese. Three dead in minutes and the yakuza were already leaving the building, no doubt ambling now towards their pickup car. Mark crunched over glass to the reception desk. A young woman was cowering under it.

"It's all right. I think they have gone now," he tried to reassure her. But she stayed down, arms over her head.

"Can you please tell me where Dr. Smith is, and the director's office?"

She looked up at him, blank faced, numbed by the bullets and shattering glass.

"Dr. Smith, please."

"He's in the director's small meeting room, down there," she said hollowly, pointing behind her.

"Thank you."

Mark crunched past her, and turned into the corridor she'd indicated. The place was oddly silent, still in shock, with only an occasional voice in the distance. With luck, it might be only now that someone was calling the police. Why didn't they have some alarm howling? Within five minutes he needed to be ambling away from the building looking professorial. There was a second body at the bend into the corridor. He stepped over it quickly. As he came round towards the couple of smaller meeting rooms, he saw the third body sprawled against a doorway. The floor was littered with spent cartridges, and the walls and some doors scored and splintered by bullets. Mark knocked on the only closed meeting room door.

Silence. He knocked again. Had Smith already run from the chaos? More likely cowering inside. Mark tried the doorknob, but it was locked.

"Dr. Smith! It's all over. They have gone. It's Andrew Petter. I arranged to meet with you now."

He waited. A muffled voice inside.

"I can't hear you!" Mark called. "Will you please open the door!"

The door wasn't opening, but someone opened another along the corridor, saw the dead gunman, shrieked, and slammed it closed again.

"Can't we do this some other time?" Smith spoke from just inside the door.

"I'm sorry. I must see you now. I need to make arrangements for your contract."

After a hesitant few more seconds, the doorknob began to turn, and Smith's eye appeared in the narrow slit he permitted it to open.

"You aren't Petter. I've met Petter before. Are you Morata? They were asking for Morata."

"Yes. I think it was something of a confusion. A rather costly one," he said, looking back at the crumpled corpse. "May I come in?"

The door slowly opened a little further, and a puzzled Smith backed away as Mark pushed forward. Smith was nearly as tall as he was, but, as O'Higgins had put it so starkly, he was "large, overweight, scruffy-bearded." Despite Smith's reluctant, half-aggressive, half-aggrieved posture he was forced further towards the table by Mark's entry and closing of the door. As he slumped backwards there was evidence of the rest of O'Higgins's characterization of him as "lazy, self-pitying, self-justifying, weak, petulant, vindictive, and without much in the way of compensating qualities."

"You were meeting with the executive director. Where is he?"

Smith was clearly in shock, eyes not well focused, and having some difficulty working out who Mark was and what he was asking.

"Him? He left when the gunfire started. Had to secure his staff, he said. Told me to keep the door locked."

"Now Professor Smith … Please sit." Smith obediently fell back into the first chair at one side of the small table, and Mark took the one opposite.

"Is this about drugs?" Smith asked gruffly.

"Drugs? What a strange confusion! Why would you imagine that?"

"That's what he"—Smith gestured in the direction of the body in the corridor—"was shouting about. And he mentioned Morata. Is that your name? It started with two of them kicking this door asking where you were."

"How extraordinary. I can only imagine some remarkable confusion. Anyway, I don't have long, and I am sure you are a very busy man. My business concerns your position on the university tenure committee."

"What about it?"

"May I ask you your initial judgement in the case of Dr. Pybus?"

"No, you may not." There was the petulance. "What are you talking about? There are dead bodies here, and all kinds of chaos!"

Mark leaned towards him, looking calmly into his eyes, till he felt Smith's fear begin.

"Tell me what your vote would be, based on what you know of the case."

"I don't see how this is any of your business. What is going on
in this place? Guns and people killed in the corridors and now
this. What is going on?"

Mark sighed. "I just don't have the time or patience to try
to explain. You represent the English faculty on the university
tenure committee. They will pay heed to your judgement in the
case. The department and its head have all voted in favour of Dr.
Pybus because they recognise her teaching and service are of the
highest quality and her publications, though few, are superlative.
I expect you to reach the same conclusion and to make this view
known in the university tenure committee. Do you understand
what you are to do?"

"Are you mad? You can't come here and ..."

"Don't tell me I can't do what I am doing, you fool. I'm becoming impatient." Mark reached for his gun and took it out. Smith
stood fearfully, pushing the chair backwards, and stepped onto
its wheeled base trying to get away from Mark. He leaned a hand
down to steady himself, but missed the moving arm of the chair
and fell against the seat, slipping heavily to hit the floor with his
bottom.

Mark was momentarily surprised at something like a déjà-vu,
but realized he was recalling his recent visit to Simpson's office.
Mark leaned his elbows on his knees, letting the gun hang loose.
Here again he was back doing precisely what Elisabeth had told
him he shouldn't do. But what else could he do? He slipped the
gun back into its underarm holster and stood up. He looked at the
sprawled Smith, preparing to reiterate what he had to do, but then
wearily concluded that the end maybe didn't justify these means.
He also had not been able to rid his mind of O'Higgins's suggestion that he might not be doing Susan Pybus a favour anyway. He
walked out of the room, closed the door behind him, and moved
fast around the corpse, through the cartridges and splattered plaster and concrete dust and splintered door jambs, and followed the

route the yakuza had taken down the rear stairs. As he came to the main floor concourse, he heard sirens outside, and saw the security guards finally heading up the escalator. There would soon be a mass of cops here. He grabbed a student newspaper from a chair in the concourse, and began reading in an absorbed manner that he assumed was appropriately professorial. He ambled through the front door of the building, stepping aside and holding the door for four policemen rushing in.

Mark felt that his strategy had come apart. Trying to persuade Smith just seemed futile. But he had learned long ago, when bad things happened, one spent no time bewailing the fact; one simply began constructing a different strategy. Susan Pybus would get tenure.

CHAPTER 21

MARK HAPPILY RESPONDED TO THE INVITATION TO MAKE himself at home by taking off his shoes and resting his feet on the footstool Elisabeth had provided. He had noticed before that each chair in her apartment living room had a footstool nearby, which seemed to him a very civilized convention. He wanted to get as comfortable as possible in preparation for what he realized was not going to be a comfortable conversation.

He had admired the directness with which she had asked him at a previous meeting whether he had broken Simpson's finger to persuade him to vote for Susan Pybus's promotion. She had expressed delighted relief when he denied responsibility for the finger. No need to explain it had been the work of Keiichi's overzealous yakuza.

Since their meeting at his place a week ago, interrupted by Keiichi's alarmingly presented gifts, they had met five times. The three most recent of those times had been in this comfortable apartment. When it was past the hour when he should have left, he said that he had observed that there were times when he was with her and times when he was not with her, and had concluded that he preferred the former. And, as they wordlessly considered this, he did not leave until the next morning when their rather different jobs required their attention. Their night together had so shocked them with its delectable wonder that they repeated it the next night, and again last night. But today was their time for truth-telling, which they both increasingly feared.

She was dressed in a simple blue skirt and a high-collared yellow blouse, making coffee in the kitchen area of her apartment. She had invited him here again, claiming that she was confident it was less likely to be an arena for munitions activity than any place he lived. But he suspected they were here because she wanted to be on home turf for her agenda.

She earlier asked him if he had heard about the explosion of violence at SFU's downtown campus. He said he had caught a brief description on the news. They agreed there was clearly an epidemic of mayhem spreading across campuses, and agreed the SFU body count and gunfire far exceeded anything at UBC. She seemed to accept the initial claim by the police that it had been caused by rival gangs carrying their east-side turf wars into shockingly new territory. The victims, it was claimed, were well known to the police. Either she didn't think of this as related to Mark, or she wanted to leave any question about that possibility dormant for now.

They sat across a low table with their coffees cooling and a glass plate with exotic chocolate cookies between them. He liked the room. It was clean and tidy, but not meticulously so. There were books here and there, few but attractive ornaments, and a friendly smell.

"Well, who goes first?" she asked, nibbling a cookie.

"Should we toss for it? Or some other way?" He looked around the room, noticing a small fish tank on her bookcase. "Perhaps the one both of your fish turn toward next?" Mark watched the two tiny fish moving seemingly randomly in a small glass box. It had colourful stones in the bottom, a water snail, a plant providing oxygen, and a tiny hole in the top for feeding.

"I would like to point out that I didn't buy that. My nephew gave it to me as a birthday present, so I don't feel I can liberate them."

"How about which of us the cat goes to?" she suggested, as a luxuriant Persian disdainfully entered the room.

"That doesn't seem an equal bet."

"Especially as she's a terrible flirt and always goes to men." She laughed as the cat made directly for Mark and rubbed itself against his leg. He jigged it behind the ears, and it set up an astonishingly loud purr.

"See the bird on your balcony rail? If it flies away within fifteen seconds, you go first; if it stays longer, I go first."

"Done."

Mark began to count slowly as they both watched the bird. It was a chickadee, preening itself, looking around rapidly, taking little hops, seeming about to fly, then settling for a further second, dipping a quick beak among its chest feathers. At ten it did a funny leap into the air, flapped its wings, turned right around to face them, but then kept its footing on the rail. At that point the cat saw it, and moved towards the glass doors, and in response, at fourteen, the bird took off and dived down out of sight. Elisabeth groaned.

"Good cat," said Mark, and thus encouraged, it returned for further stroking. "So, let us parade our reluctant words."

"Mine are simple, though 'reluctant' is the right word, and 'confused' is another." Elisabeth took a large gulp of coffee and a significant bite of cookie, chewing in silence for a few seconds. "I … well, I think I'm not wrong in thinking we share some growing affection for each other."

"After the past week, I hope we agree to that." Mark smiled.

"But it is complicated for me because there is another man in my life. That's the simple complication."

"Ah." Mark's disappointment was so palpable that she quickly and nervously laughed.

"Well, it is more confused because, even if you had not come into my life, there were difficulties with the other man. I had thought of him … There are some problems with it."

"With *it*?" Mark asked cautiously, puzzled. "Should I perhaps not ask what the problem is, or who he is?"

"No, no, of course. It is entirely your right. The same response, though, answers both questions. I mean the problem and who and what he is. He's a bishop."

Mark nearly spilled his coffee, putting the trembling saucer back on the table. A bishop? Bishops are old, fat men who wear mitres, vestments, walk in processions with crosiers, whose rings you genuflect to kiss. When Mark was a young man, the one bishop he saw most often was saintly, but seemed always to be trailing some vestment not put on properly, or to have lost his glasses, or to have forgotten what he was supposed to be doing in a ceremony.

Was this a joke? Certainly it was as crazy as her question about his gun being licensed. He was torn among the desire to laugh again, total bewilderment, and the struggle to realize that Anglican bishops did indeed marry and had, consequently, to marry someone, and who more desirable than an apparently active and attractive Anglican woman. Looked at that way, it made a kind of sense. But surely, it couldn't be true?

"A bishop?" What was he trying to express? "Are you sure?"

"What do you mean? Of course I'm sure."

"No, sorry. It's just that with a Catholic background ... I mean, Catholic women could not expect to see a bishop in these terms. Bishops, even more than priests, are sexless. Like angels," he added with an attempt at a smile in the face of her frown.

He realized how little he knew her, and how little he knew of her. He had created for himself a simple image of her, as beautiful and intelligent, even if with an edge whose depth he didn't know, nor what drove it into action. He hadn't considered that she might not in reality even fit his image, and might not fit it in disturbing ways. His mind was thrown into confusion, trying to bring the sexual desire for a bishop into the realms of the plausible. Could

this be an identified sexual perversion—wanting to strip vestments off a cleric? What was he thinking!

"So, if bishops can marry, where has been your problem?"

"He is already married."

Mark looked at her closely, for a twitch around the mouth, for
a hint of a sparkle in the eyes—for some sign that she was joking.
But either she was infinitely skilled at dissembling, or she was
telling him the literal truth. Her eyes, indeed, were moistening
as she waited for his response.

"Is he the local bishop?"

"No. Very distant. A diocese north of Oslo."

Between the astonishment Mark was trying to deal with,
and his distress in discovering that Elisabeth was perhaps not
available anyway—but then what of the past nights?—now he
found himself pleased with the small consolation that confessing to being a drug lord somehow seemed much less outrageous.
A married bishop was hard enough for him to imagine, but an
adulterous Norwegian bishop was incomprehensible. He felt
suddenly the urge to laugh again, but suppressed it immediately,
keeping a frown of concern on his face.

"Can a bishop get a divorce? I suppose if he can marry ..."

"It is hardly something that would be edifying to members of
his diocese. He has said he would sound out that possibility, but
I think it is impossible. I wouldn't let him."

"And does Mrs. Bishop know about you?"

"Yes. I mean, I know her quite well, but she doesn't know her
husband declares his love for me, if that's what you mean."

"Yes. I meant that. But, how ... in Norway?"

"We met some years ago. I mentioned the other evening that I
have a lot of family in Norway, and visit at least once a year. Then
I became closer to him when I spent some months there about
three years ago. I was working on the historicity of the Norwegian
Codex Regius Eddur, well, Eddas, Norwegian myth stories, with

colleagues at the University of Oslo. We got a large EU Erasmus program grant—Norway is an 'associated country' of the EU for such purposes—and that paid for my stay. Then we flew to and fro a few times, which was hardly satisfactory. For the past year he has lived in the Lower Mainland. The ecumenical movements of the last decades supported exchanges between different communions, and he arranged a year-long exchange with a bishop from New Westminster. So that's part of the 'how.'"

They sat silent for a few moments.

"It is always for a moment difficult when we discover the world is more strange and diverse than we had imagined," Mark said. "But if I think of him as a professor rather than a bishop, it might be easier for me. Have you told him you are usually an atheist, even if an Anglican one?"

She paused. "No, I haven't. I have ... made sceptical comments occasionally, but I don't think he has seen that as more than everyday doubts."

Mark felt some relief that she had told him something she had not told her bishop.

"He is Norwegian? And would expect you to live there?"

"Well, you can see why this hasn't been an easy business, and for many other reasons as well I was reaching the conclusion that it could not work. Not least my sense ... and I suspect his sense too, brought on by the strains on the relationship, that maybe we weren't ideally suited personalities anyway.

"So, there's my confession on the table. And, added to all that, everything has been confused further because you have come along when I was concluding that I should withdraw from his life, and ... well, I think he's taking it harder and has asked for breathing space before final decisions are made. That's why he's looking into divorce, and why I've told him I don't think that's a real option in his position ... And what's the imp on your back?"

"The imp on my back?"

"The thing you have to tell me about."

"Ah. My turn." Mark paused, considering how to begin.

"Connected to the gun," she suggested. "Clearly something you do is dangerous. I wondered whether you were a secret service agent or a spy." Her voice became easier and almost cheerful as she moved the discussion to him. "I suppose you have to have a gun for self-protection?"

"Ah, not really. It is to shoot people with." Perhaps this was too direct an approach he decided, looking at her shocked expression. "Well, not that I go around shooting people. But I think one shouldn't take very seriously the idea that guns are for self-protection. They are for killing people, and that's what people do with guns. Once a bullet emerges, it is not protecting you so much as it is going to do damage to someone else." What kind of drivel was he talking? That made no sense, but he wanted just to keep talking, fearing and expecting that his confession would be the abrupt end of their relationship.

"Oh, by the way ..." She stood up quickly and walked around the kitchen area into the bedroom that served as her study. She came back with a folder. "I got you the forms you need to license the gun. They're available on the internet."

Mark flipped through the eight or ten pages she handed him. The top one was headed "Royal Canadian Mounted Police," and announced itself as an "Information Sheet: Application for a Possession and Acquisition Licence Under the *Firearms Act* (for Individuals Aged 18 and Over)," followed by some pages of description of the requirement to be met and then a four page application form.

"Thank you. That was thoughtful. Even after I laughed at your concern."

"Perhaps you could explain what was so funny. I have thought a lot about it, but I just haven't been able to imagine what made you laugh."

"I have been most contrite. That's a good Catholic word. I have felt very badly that I might have offended you, laughing at what was your considerateness. I am ashamed."

"But what was funny?"

"Well, the gun is a tool of my trade, in a way. Like you, I am at the stage of withdrawing from a relationship, of a kind. Who I was, in terms of my job or role, will soon be quite different from what it was when I met you. This is a time of transition for me. A major transition. In fact, I am beginning to feel a little uncertain of myself. Something I am not familiar with. And some of the responsibility I think rests with you. I do feel ... I agreed with what you said about an affection growing. I have felt ... I have found myself thinking of you very much, very fondly."

"And the gun licence? What was funny?"

"Yes. My job. My job, you see, has been ... has been ... dangerous. I have needed a gun for self-defence."

"You just said ..."

Mark lowered his head and banged his forehead with his fists.

"From my youth I have been involved in the drug trade. I have been one of the major importers of cocaine into North America. I am what you might call a drug lord. Or you might if it wasn't such a silly name."

He watched her face closely.

"You are joking!"

"You think it is worse that wanting to marry a bishop?"

"What are you talking about? What ... You said you imported toys and exported salmon."

"That is true, but they are merely—well, not so merely—masks and laundering devices for the drug money. But I can quit the drug business, and may keep up only the legitimate business. I may soon be exactly what I told you I was. But for the moment, I am indeed a drug lord." He spoke the last two words in a hollow, portentous voice.

Elisabeth sat looking at him in silence. No doubt searching his face for clues, as he had hers, about whether he was joking or telling the incomprehensible truth.

"I can't believe it. How can someone ... who loves Hardy be a drug dealer?"

"How can a beautiful professor want to marry a bishop?"

"I really don't think the two cases are remotely comparable,"

"You're right, of course. I mean only that they seem to each of us comparably incomprehensible."

"I don't believe what I'm hearing." Elisabeth stood up, but seemed uncertain of what to do next. Mark stood opposite her.

"Dealing drugs is the most immoral thing ... well, among the most immoral things. How can you do that? It kills innocent people, causes endless crime, ruins lives. How can you do that? I don't believe you!"

"I am afraid it's true. But I deal only in cocaine, and some marijuana. I will not trade in heroin. Though heroin is also a wonderful drug for various medical purposes. The things you describe; they are mostly caused by heroin addiction, and other psychotropic and potentially lethal drugs. Cocaine is not so bad a drug if taken responsibly; it has all kinds of uses and benefits ... as long as you stay away from crack and other adulterants in the market. It is much less addictive than nicotine and much less damaging to health than alcohol. It is the stupidity of legislators that creates the crime."

"I don't want to discuss this. I don't know ... what to think." Elisabeth raised both hands, pushing up the hair on each side of her head and then holding her head as though she feared it might explode.

"Since my youth, I have thought of cocaine as mostly a good drug. But here all drugs are lumped together, and alcohol and nicotine are not considered as like cocaine. Yet, I think they are worse drugs. When I was young, I was going to say, I loved to read. Many of those I knew in the trade ..."

"Do you take cocaine yourself? I mean a lot?"

"Never. That is what I was going to say. I think cocaine is good for people who have no imagination. That is what it helps. The unimaginative to pretend for a little while that they have imaginations. It is a drug for those who never really learned to read properly. Who never developed their imagination. And I think that is not such a bad thing for a drug."

"That is just rationalizing."

"No. I think ... Perhaps I can explain. Yes, perhaps I have been much involved in rationalizing. Perhaps we need time to absorb what we have heard. Please, as you think of my confession—and I could have not told you—remember that I am leaving that life behind. And I prefer Larkin to Hardy, in general. Well, some of Larkin and some of Hardy ..."

"Yes. Larkin." She looked at him blankly. "You should go now. Thank you for being so frank."

Mark bowed, feeling like one of the yakuza, and made for the door. Elisabeth watched him go, tears welling in her eyes. She was moving her affections from a married bishop to a drug lord. What was wrong with her?

CHAPTER
22

MARK SAT WITH ALAN WILKIE IN THE BACK OF THE LIMousine. Alan affectionately nursed an M16 combat rifle across his knees, fingering the dimples around its muzzle. They travelled slowly and in silence through Queen Elizabeth Park. It was approaching 2 a.m.

"We shouldn't have a problem tonight, Alan. It is a simple exchange."

"You know your business, Mr. Morata. I know mine."

"Yes. But we do have a wider problem."

Alan Wilkie looked a little surprised. Mark rarely discussed his strategy or plans, and he was clearly trying to work out how to say more.

"I was in Thailand recently, you remember. On business."

"Aye, I recall."

"One morning, I decided to do some sightseeing. No appointments till the evening. A complicated set of confusions, but a German businessman and I had both ordered cars and guides, and … well, it turned out we had only the one car and the one guide but we both had been planning similar tours, around some temples and to the floating market, so we decided to go together."

Mark shifted, looked round at Alan Wilkie's impassive profile, and then looked forward at the curving road lit by the big car's headlights. The driver, one of Alan's people, kept to within the twenty-five kilometre an hour speed limit.

"We took one of those zipospeeds, or whatever they call them— narrow very swift boats with a powerful outboard motor. Well, that is neither here nor there. But we were talking about business. He was the representative of a machine tool company, and was there to bid on a large contract. I wished him luck. 'Oh, I won't get the contract,' he said. I asked why not. He told me that the products of his companies' factories in Germany were superior to those of the Japanese company that was his main rival. 'Was his price too high?' I asked. No. The pricing would be competitive with the Japanese products. While he was here enjoying the trip up the river to the market, he said, his competitor's representatives would be in their room at the hotel all day, a team of six of them, as they had been yesterday and would be tomorrow before their meeting with the Thai officials. They would be planning their strategy. They would have done research on each of the Thai decision-makers, and would have planned how each was to be approached and rewarded, they would have made a dozen phone calls to the members of their team back in Japan, who would be faxing further details and statistics. My German companion said he was the only representative of his company in Southeast Asia, whereas his Japanese competitor had separate teams for each market segment.

"What is my point, you are no doubt wondering. Our friend Mr. Kanehara is part of a company of yakuza. He is an 'underboss,' a waka gashira, of the Yamaguchi-gumi group. They are about 26,000 strong. They have determined that they want the market that I have gained and added to over a number of years. I have concluded that there is nothing I can do to stop them, or, at least, nothing that won't carry a very high price to our people."

Alan Wilkie turned again in surprise.

"We can take these fellas easy, any day, Mr. Morata."

"Well, today you can take them, and tomorrow. But they will simply bring in more and more people till we can't sustain the costs. Well, maybe we could but I'm not sure I want to. Mr. Kanehara is an unusual waka gashira and prefers accommodation and agreement and openness. But he can be no less ruthless than any of his colleagues. Indeed, I suspect much more. He will, sometime in the future, likely be leader of the whole crime syndicate. We have been in a period of accommodation with him, but the pressure is on him to start easing us out, so he will do that."

The car was turning sharply, headed up towards the geodesic dome at the top of the park. They sat in silence for a few seconds.

"Wha're you saying, Mr. Morata? You're getting out of the business?"

"Vancouver will go to the Japanese, and they will take over the lines to the east and the States. The Vietnamese gangs, and the Mexicans, will make a nasty fight of it, but they too will be squeezed out. They may hold onto some segments, but the bulk of it will be run by Kanehara. Though we also have the motorcycle gangs trying to move in, but they will be quickly crushed by the Asian groups, and will retire badly mauled.

"I am considering negotiations with Kanehara so that we can maximise our profits from the assets we have currently in the supply line, and other assets, and to ensure no trouble for our people in the period of withdrawal. You know I have been somewhat preoccupied recently with some new supplies from Peru."

"Yeah, I do. You've mentioned that."

"Well, it isn't simply an extra supply source, but it is potentially bigger than anything else we have done so far. Kanehara knows nothing about it. I have completely new supply lines, distribution networks, down to deals with front-end sales people. I could move in a day to Denver and run everything from there."

"I'm gobsmacked."

"Time for choices. Kanehara is moderately patient, and we have some weeks to make decisions. You can stay here in Vancouver, if you wish. I will ensure a large retirement package for you. And some legitimate business to run. Or the Denver option might appeal. Or I could even sell the Peruvian and Denver operation to Kanehara as well, though I calculate he'd need to borrow heavily from his Yamaguchi-gumi bosses, which he'd prefer not to do. But that's his business. I am sorry, Alan. These might not be choices you want to make just now."

"I dunno. I'll tell ye, I'm taken aback. So you've told Kanehara he can take over?"

"Not quite that. He is beginning to suspect that some deal might be arranged, or that I've got some kind of offer for him. He's uncertain enough not to fight for anything just now, and our accommodation is adequate for him for a while, in which we can make choices. If he hadn't had my hints that he might get what he wants without a fight, I think we might all be dead by now, or soon. But he's also not sure that I might not be bluffing or double-bluffing. I need to keep him uncertain for a while. We need a couple of weeks, to complete movement along that new Denver route and see actual sales to end-users. The first shipment will clear more profit than we have made in a year. The next few days will be crucial."

The car turned sharply again and moved slowly up the narrow slip-road to the parking lot that covered the reservoir. As they emerged from among the bordering trees and shrubs, the car slowed further and Mark and Alan both scanned the car park ahead. The tall lights surrounding the reservoir provided limited visibility.

"They're all here," Alan said.

To their right, engine running and no lights on, was their other car with four of Alan's Scottish gunmen. It had been arranged that it should have arrived five minutes ago. One of the Scots stood at the open passenger door with an AK-47 pointing alertly forward. About fifty feet ahead was one of the yakuza stretch limousines, with, probably six men. It, too, had a point man at an open door, gun visibly at the ready, and it, too, would have been there for five minutes. Twenty feet to its left sat their other stretch BMW, it was dark and silent, and should contain Keiichi Kanehara.

"I hope the bastards try something," said Alan as he opened his door and climbed out, the M16 swinging casually. Mark felt perhaps unjustified security with Alan close by. The yakuza feared him, knowing his reputation for frightening speed, deadly accuracy, and an impassive ruthlessness that was legendary even among the ruthless. He was only medium sized, with a bad back and bad knees, but had a strange relish for violent combat, in the midst of which he remained cool and almost disengaged. His son was one of the best, and most feared, soccer players Mark had ever seen, bringing the same qualities to the game that his father displayed in his part-time work, and probably displayed at the autobody shop where he practised his other part-time job.

Both rear doors of Kanehara's car opened. A young yakuza emerged from one and Keiichi Kanehara from the other. Mark opened his door as his driver picked up a gun from the seat beside him.

Mark walked toward Keiichi. At the same moment, Alan walked away from the car as did the yakuza from the stretch BMW—allowing both of them a clear line of fire towards the other that would not endanger their employers.

"Good evening, Mark. How good of you to come."

"The pleasure is mine, Keiichi. It is good to talk face to face at last."

They shook hands and both bowed slightly.

"A pleasant evening. But we should not delay. Our friends are no doubt more nervous about this meeting than we are, or they should be," said Keiichi. "I have what you asked for, and you have something for me, you said."

"A small set of books, in return for those you so kindly gave to me. Would you like me to tell you what the books are, or would you like the surprise?"

"Perhaps you could tell me about one of them."

"Well, I managed to find an Edo period rice paper printing of Matsuo Basho's *Zoku Sarumino* of 1698, and relatedly a Meiji woodblock of his 1694 *Oku no Hosomichi*. I hope you will enjoy them."

"How exquisite. Really, Mark, I am deeply grateful. For the rest, I must enjoy the pleasure of opening your gift and discovering them myself."

"And inside the front cover of *Zoku Sarumino* is a detailed description of the transfer of white goods in Xi'an. Places, names, method."

Keiichi paused in surprise, and looked up at Mark.

"Ah, Mark, you are more generous than you need to be."

"Not really. I do not have the resources in that theatre to take proper advantage of the knowledge. And you would have found it out yourself quite soon."

"You will want something further in return? I think I should insist."

"I will ask for something further, but not, I suspect, something you will be reluctant to give."

"You remain mysterious."

"No, I am not mysterious. Just that all the pieces are not yet in place. It will become transparent soon I hope. I think you will consider it a good bargain for you."

"Oh, and I have another small present, which I am reluctant to give because it is so worthless. A small privately printed book of my haiku. As you know, I am entirely unsure of their literary value, but I enjoy working on them, and I give them as a token of hopes for future friendship. Dr. Pybus will bring the small gift with him."

"Thank you so much. How very thoughtful. I will be delighted to read them. I did actually also include with my small package a computer memory stick with my poems on. You will see some new ones. I have begun trying to write prose/poems, which I suspect means only that I have given up on mangling rhyme and rhythm. These new ones concentrate on developing an image or an idea in an image. Maybe I'll try to make them into poems later."

"How interesting. You will see, coincidentally perhaps, that the last few pages of my small book include attempts at more modern poetic forms." Keiichi laughed quickly. "A breakout from the prison of the haiku. Very liberating, I must say."

Keiichi turned and waved towards the BMW. A further yakuza emerged, unarmed, from the rear, walked forward and opened the front passenger door and stood back. Susan Pybus slid out, followed by her husband. The yakuza pointed them towards Mark's car.

"Dr. Pybus," Mark called. "Please come this way. Climb into my car. You will be quite safe. I'm taking you home."

Mark waved at his other car and one of the Scotsmen emerged carrying a cardboard box. He passed the Pybuses and handed the box to the yakuza by the BMW. The yakuza lowered the box into the BMW's capacious trunk. He passed over it an instrument that looked like a large cell phone, LED lights flickering on and off along its top. Satisfied, the yakuza then opened the box and checked its contents carefully. He stood up and nodded to Kanehara.

Mark and Keiichi shook hands again.

"They think this is the most dangerous part," Keiichi said with a smile. "We should have dinner sometime, Mark."

Mark nodded, and they parted with a brief bow and a wave, returning to their cars. Mark watched the trunk of the BMW slam over the precious books. At least, he knew where they'd be if this gentlemanly game ended without gentlemanly agreement. They were in a delicate balance that would take little to tip into murderous conflict, with high-stakes.

The Pybuses approached his car, uncertainly, looking at him, clearly in some way their rescuer, but also bewildered by the array of cars, the guns. Geoffrey Pybus, carrying the promised book of Keiichi Kanehara's poems, was looking at Mark, mouth slightly open.

"Thank you ..." he called out.

Mark smiled and waved him towards the rear passenger door of his car.

Alan Wilkie slowly curved back in front of them, guiding them into the second row of seats of the car, and climbing into the rear seat after Mark had returned to his. The other Scotsmen and the yakuza re-entered their cars. For a moment the four cars remained still, each warily eyeing the others. Then Mark's limousine and the stretch BMW began slowly moving towards opposite ends of the parking lot. Mark's other car fell in behind him. They left by the entrance while the two stretch limousines left by the exit. As Mark's cars turned onto the road, they could see Kanehara's two limousines moving at speed down from the park headed east. Mark's cars kept within the park's speed limit and turned west, towards Kerrisdale and the Pybuses' house.

Susan Pybus turned towards Mark. She looked tired and unsurprisingly somewhat distraught.

"Where are our children?"

Geoffrey Pybus was looking at Mark with astonishment. He reached over to shake his hand, grabbing Mark's arm with his other hand, relief and bewilderment overwhelming him.

"You saved us from the Japanese guy!" Then he paused. "Didn't you? I guess we've no idea what is going on, why we're here, why we were there. Our last two days have made no sense to us."

"First, your children are safe and asleep. Mrs. Wilkie and her daughter—and this is Mr. Wilkie—have been looking after them today, and for the two days before that they were very considerately looked after by some young women friends of Mr. Kanehara. I think they would have spoiled the children completely if we'd let them stay any longer. Your children think you had to go on a sudden visit to Geoffrey's sick sister, and they have received loving email messages from you twice a day. Which I composed myself. I think you will find the children in good shape."

The cars picked up speed leaving the park.

"May I recommend that we save the explanations till tomorrow," Mark said, thinking that would give him a bit more time to come up with plausible answers to their questions. "It's all over now. You are entirely safe. What has happened to you is entirely due to an absurd confusion, which I regret to say is in part my fault."

Geoff sat back. "He read us your poems."

"He did what? Was that his idea of torturing you to give information?"

"No, no. He seemed to think they were good. He read one of his own haiku."

"Keiichi is an interesting man."

They drove for a while in silence. The Pybuses were dropped at their front door, and Mrs. Wilkie and her daughter emerged to let them into the house. The Pybuses, disoriented and tired, shook hands with the Wilkies as they passed in the front porch. The women exchanged some information about the children, then Mrs. Wilkie and her daughter took the Pybuses' places in the limousine.

As the car headed east towards the Wilkies' house, Mark was not ready to cover all the explanatory ground he would have to take Alan Wilkie across. And maybe it was all to no avail in winning Elisabeth, he thought grimly. And also wondered whether he was really ready to give up the magnificent organization that he had created centred in Denver. He still felt a thrill from the

meeting with Kanehara and all the intricacies of maybe selling his Vancouver operation to him; it was so deliciously vivid
that he wasn't convinced, now that he was away from Elisabeth's
allure, that he could give up the business. What would he do as a
househusband?

"Perhaps we can meet tomorrow, Alan, and I will outline my
strategy with the Japanese, particularly as it will affect you and
your colleagues."

"Aye, Mr. Morata. Whatever you say."

CHAPTER 23

MARK STOOD AT THE WINDOW OF HIS DOWNTOWN FLAT, phone by his ear, looking again at the tankers on English Bay, all facing the same direction into the strong wind that was roughing the water into angry whitecaps. Two cruise ships were heading up towards the Inside Passage to Alaska, one approaching Howe Sound. Just a couple of weeks earlier he had been close to death on the road that skirted the Sound, and had since become burdened and enriched in this peculiar project to get his rescuer's wife tenure. A half hour behind, the second palatial cruise ship was coming out of the harbour and following the first floating confection. Sun and the shadow of small fast-moving clouds played on the North Shore Mountains. He was waiting to hear whether the Dominicans with whom he had a contract for carrying his truckload of cocaine to Chicago were on time, with the money, and in the force they had promised. When his agent, Antonio Ruis, assured him all was well, he would authorize release of the drugs.

He wondered whether his extra precautions dealing with the gang from the Dominican Republic were due simply to their name, and his childhood preference for the Franciscans over the Dominican friars. St. Dominic had always seemed to him a much less sympathetic figure than St. Francis; he was hardly alone in thinking so, especially because of the Dominicans' energetic engagement in the Inquisition. But these gang members from the Dominican Republic would hardly find the coincidence of their name an adequate explanation for this added layer of close oversight of the transaction.

"Marcos," Antonio said on the phone. "They have arrived in the warehouse. I am in touch with my men who are now talking with them."

"Where are you?"

"Okay. I am just outside. We have a parked van, just checking what cover they have. We have three cars along the possible routes to the warehouse. The Dominicans came alone, as promised. I'm getting a text … Just a minute. Okay, the money is good. All good; everything clean. We go?"

"Thanks, Antonio. Yes. Send the truck in."

"Okay, Marcos. I'll let you know when we have the money and are clear away. I'll keep this phone open."

Marcos could hear him speaking into another phone: "It's a go."

That would trigger his truck to move the four blocks to the warehouse in the Industrial Park in the northeast of Denver. Mark listened to the breathing and occasional engine noises on the open phone line, while he watched the floating white palace move along the north shore. The loud engine passing close to Antonio's car was no doubt the truck approaching its destination at the warehouse he had rented. Antonio's car engine started, and he would be pulling in behind the truck. The Dominicans would test random packages; it wouldn't be a perfunctory check, but Marcos had a solid reputation and they would anticipate finding exactly what had been promised. Now he could hear voices, footsteps, and the rear of the truck sliding open. Then the sounds of Antonio climbing out of his car in the warehouse.

The Dominicans were well organized and generally reliable. He had dealt with their distribution cell before in Houston. Everyone was a little wary, as this was the first shipment of sizable quantities of cocaine to come in by the new route. They were more used to the traffic that came across the Mexican border for distribution in Los Angeles. And no one was used to these quantities. More talking, footsteps, engines picking up, and tires squealing.

"Marcos. We are out. Money good. My men say we have clear roads into the city. The money will be in your account later today."

"Antonio, thank you. Always reliable. I will be sending the remaining payment for you and your men, and the rental on the warehouse," they laughed, "by the end of the day. Plus a small celebratory bonus. Nice work, Antonio. As you know, this is likely the first of many."

"Thank you, Marcos. We will be in touch."

Mark turned back into the room, tossed his phone into the armchair, and pumped the air with his fists. "Ha!" It had all worked! From the plants grown in the highlands in Peru, to the slow drive to the laboratory in Cajamarca, to the port at Pacasmayo, to San Francisco, Sacramento, Denver, and now off his hands and into cash that had infinite liquidity. And the route could be used again and again. He had arranged every step, dealing with growers, negotiating with carriers, removing threats, planning shipping times, from leaf to user on the streets of Chicago and New York. He walked round the room, then back to the window. He could buy one of those cruise ships with spare change. What most delighted him was the organizational and management structure he had created. All those people, growers, pickers, transporters, dock handling and deceptions, dealing with the informer on the ship, the problems at the San Francisco docks, the trucks, the routes to Sacramento, the deals with the Dominicans. He felt a surge of triumph. He was good at this. The new supply line could grow into a profit of further billions.

He leaned against the side frame of the window, counting the tankers waiting on the bay to enter the harbour for unloading. They would each be racking up fees for waiting, and lost income from the delay, and he calculated, given the value of each ship's cargos, the accumulated losses he was witnessing for the nine ships was approaching a million dollars a day. But the triumph had nothing to do with the drugs. He had long since realized that he avoided thinking about the effects of the drugs, of their use. He had phrases that were a part of his avoidance procedure when his mind began to move in that direction—cocaine was a drug for people who lacked imagination; it did not do significant harm, like heroin; it was the politicians' stupid laws that caused the trouble; and so on. But what really kept him engaged was the excitement of organizing such a complicated business, from plant to user, and keeping it going, making increasing profits.

He did have some of the same pleasure from his success with the legitimate side of his business interest, but that was easy, and without any of the risks that made the drug trade always exciting. Would it be possible for him to get the same kick of pleasure from running a legitimate business? He smiled as he thought he could go into founding and running universities. What would it take to set up a string of outstanding private universities? He might be able to create for himself a job as a professor of literature.

Absurd, he thought, pushing himself upright and turning into the room. Yet, if he were to give up the drug business, he could still set about some new enterprise and seek the same rewards of triumphant pleasure in calibrating all the complex parts to fit neatly together to make it work so finely that no one could imagine the world without it. Maybe Elisabeth would be less perturbed at the idea of being married to a university lord if she couldn't deal with his being a drug lord?

He was tempted to open the bottle of Krug Grande Cuvée and the jar of caviar, though he had been planning to do so when Elisabeth next visited. But he could always get more Krug and caviar. He turned towards the kitchen as his phone rang.

"Mark. It's me," said Elisabeth.

"Hello you. I was just thinking of you. In the context of champagne and caviar."

"I can't go on with this, Mark." She sounded distraught, perhaps crying, her voice deeper than usual. He waited a moment. "I mean, I have been thinking a lot about it, about nothing else," she said. "The idea of a long-term relationship with a drug dealer is simply impossible for me. And I have to say too that I can't at all condone your using improper ways of getting Susan Pybus tenure. There, I've said it."

Mark sat down on the sofa. He had been excited to hear her voice. Then he felt as though he had been kicked in the stomach, winded, emptied, violently shifting his euphoria at the new supply chain working to a sense of it all being for nothing. He clearly loved her, he thought, feeling a fool that he had to say it explicitly to himself.

"But I have started arrangement to get out of the business. I could soon have no connection to drugs."

A part of his mind was astonished to hear himself say this. Had he really been preparing for this? His ploys with Kanehara only made sense, of course, as preparation for a total withdrawal. He really must love her.

"But the kind of life you have led, it will always be with you. You have been involved in violence all your life. You must have killed people. I can't live with that. You can't simply make a confession and become someone else."

"I think I have been becoming someone else for some time now."

"I have thought ... well, silly things, because I have no idea ... but I thought if we have a plumber in to fix something and he tries to cheat you, will we have corpses in the driveway? If someone crosses you, will there be Tommy guns firing?"

Mark was for a moment distracted—the shift from his pleasure to dread at what she was saying, and the antique reference to Tommy guns.

Elisabeth continued, "Or a nasty neighbour—will their house blow up around them or their car explode? I know, I know. That's silly. But I will never know how you will deal with everyday life after the life you have led."

"I don't think that is silly. I don't know myself, I suppose. But I am generally a peaceful person in everyday life. And I think, for peace, I will overpay the crooked plumber and ..."

"That's another thing—I can't live on the money you have made from drug dealing. I would feel sordid whenever I bought anything. I would be thinking of the lives that have been destroyed by the drugs, and the people who have been killed in creating that wealth. I just couldn't do it. I can't do it."

She was no longer trying to disguise her crying.

"I will give away the money I made from drugs. We would live on the money from my legitimate business, though I am considering giving that away too. I was just thinking of other things I could do, imagining setting up—now you will think I am silly—a private university, or two, or ten."

"You would give the drug money away?"

"Yes. I will do that for you. I am trying to strip away from myself everything that the drug business has made me. And I had hoped you would help me."

She was silent for a moment."But if you set up a university ..."

"That's just one thing I could do, in remaking myself."

"But if someone came up for tenure, would you smash up departments if you don't like the decisions?"

"Of course not. I think what appeals to me is not the violence, but organizing things and making them happen. It just happened that the drug business was the available option for me."

"I don't know. I was phoning to break it off with you, and now you ... What about Susan? Will you stop interfering with her tenure case?"

"Ah, I can try to withdraw from that ... but I increasingly think an injustice will happen if I stop."

"The ends do not justify the means."

"Well, I can adapt my means perhaps."

"I think you have no right to interfere at all. I think you should withdraw from this whole business. And ..." there was a catch in her voice "... from me as well."

"I'd rather not do that. I am trying to change everything in my life to make it the kind of life you could live with, within. I can't change my past, but I can perhaps revert to the me who existed apart from the drug business."

"The Pybuses were kidnapped!"

"But I didn't do that."

"But you did. It was all due to you and your ... acquaintances, rivals, whatever. When in the future might they emerge to start shooting up houses or ... wherever we might live? I couldn't survive like that. Until I met you, I had anxieties about what my future with my previous ... prospective partner might have been like, worried about meeting members of his diocese, or disapproving glances and pursed lips. And now I have graduated to anxieties about being blown up and children kidnapped and gun battles in the garden. I know, I know ... I just can't see how it could work."

"The mayhem of the past week has occurred because of confusions about what I was doing at the university. Once I am out of the business, everyone will know. I will be of no interest to those people then. I have been of interest only because of my market share. When that is zero, which it will be very soon, they will have zero interest in me."

"Oh, I would like to believe that. But none of us can slide so cleanly out of our past. And your past ... I can't see it not haunting you and coming with you in terrible ways."

"Give me a bit of time. Well, I recall that's what your bishop asked for. You are accumulating men on hold. But let me deal with the next week when I will get myself out of this business, giving it, well, selling it, to a rival. You will see that I can slide away more easily than you think is possible. I have been preparing to do so for a while, as I told you."

"But I can't live on the money you make from selling your drug business; that's the same as living off the drug deals themselves."

"I will give it away."

"All of it? All the money you will make from selling your business? All the drug money?"

"Yes."

"I don't know what to think."

"Give me a week, and then we can think together about what might then be possible."

"Very well ... oh, I'm exhausted. I think it is simply impossible."

They held their phones to their ears in silence for about five long seconds, then Mark heard the click of hers disconnecting.

He sat looking across at the shelves of rare books he had for a time collected enthusiastically. He felt come over him a largely lost image of a dream he had frequently had in early childhood. He was standing as though on a high ledge and in front of him the space suddenly opened out vast and terrible, a scale that was unknowable, so big and cold and threatening that he was nothing within it, just a small bag of fear. Now he could only capture a vague memory of the image and how he had felt—that sense of irrepressible terror at the vastness before him and his frightened self. He had described it once to Josefina in Santiago over coffee in her apartment looking out the window into the jacaranda trees and their lavender flowers. "A birth trauma," she had said casually. Maybe so. It had never been frequent enough that he feared to go to sleep, but the sense of the ungraspable vastness of the world that opened before him had never left him, nor had the fear it had generated in him when he was a small boy.

And then his heart gave another lurch, speeded up for ten seconds, thumped hard, then settled back to its usual rhythm. He felt breathless. Either he needed to see the doctor or to sort out what he should be doing with his life. That he had sacrificed too much for his spectacularly successful business was becoming sadly clear to him. Here he was in the middle of his life, suddenly looking up and wondering if he was lost. Faust was becoming too familiar a companion, and his mid-life disorientation felt like going astray in Dante's gloomy wood—much too literary for a convincing drug dealer, he thought. But now he had to rise and disburse himself of a business, distribute many dollars, and get Pybus tenure without violence. He wasn't sure he could manage all three to Elisabeth's satisfaction, but he would try. And then what?

CHAPTER
24

SUSAN AND GEOFFREY PYBUS SAT TOGETHER AT THE breakfast table. Each had a section of the newspaper open and they were working on the remains of a pot of dark coffee and some toast.

"Another drug bust, it says," Susan muttered. "Fifty kilos of cocaine picked from a boat in the harbour."

"That would supply someone's habit for a while."

"Didn't you find it a bit disappointing that the children took our absence so casually?" She smiled and lowered the paper. "They went off to school as though nothing had happened."

"No doubt a tribute to their security. Long may it last."

The doorbell rang, and they looked at each other with some foreboding.

"I guess that'll be Mark Morata. I'll get it," said Geoff.

"Bring him into the living room. I'll just put these in the dishwasher and join you."

Mark entered a little uncertainly. He should have rehearsed what he would say, but his mind had been bouncing between Elisabeth and how he could, if he decided he would, dissolve the business and his money. He had only the vaguest notion of how he might explain to the Pybuses what had happened to them, and why he was the one to rescue them. He had considered the truth, but decided that that was one of the more incredible of the various narratives he might try.

"Would you care for a coffee?" Geoff asked.

"No, thank you. I have to be at a meeting quite soon, so shouldn't delay. And I'm sure you have some catching up to do."

Susan Pybus came into the room and held out her hand. She looked him in the eye as his powerful hand enveloped hers, and as she held his eye for more than a moment she could see why the fearsome Kanehara might find him frightening. He was entirely pleasant, smiling, and polite, but she would not like to be between him and something he wanted. He reminded her of a tank. Though a tank that was improbably trying to write poetry—an image that didn't make sense in the way she thought he didn't make sense. Elisabeth had spoken to her about him, and about her feelings for him. She'd also said that some parts of his diverse personality seemed not well integrated with others, and the separate parts seemed liable to burst into war at any time. She hoped Elisabeth knew what she was doing.

"Thank you for whatever it was you did," she said.

"Oh, I'm not really deserving thanks. It seems your kidnapping was due to a mistake, a confusion, and I just happened to be the one who, by chance, was able to sort it out. Appropriately, as I was also involved in its happening."

They all sat down. Mark looked out the window at a splendid ornamental cherry tree, which was beginning to come into flower. In a few days that window would be a mass of pink.

"But why us?" she asked. "Why would anyone want to kidnap us? And who was ... I mean is ... Mr. Kanehara? We concluded he was an outlaw of some kind. His house was guarded by young men with guns. You couldn't see a road from the house. We don't even know where we were. He had us blindfolded, you know, going to and coming from that place."

"The house is in Ioco, quite near to the park. Well, the confusion. Mr. Kanehara thought you were someone else. I am not so much the hero of the story for you, as the cause of the problem. You will recall that I paid for the fixing of your car? Mr. Kanehara is a business rival of mine, though he also has activities that are unquestionably illegal. It seems he assumed that we—you and I, Geoff—were partners of some kind, because I paid for your car. He also seems to have assumed you worked for me. And he seems to have assumed further, because of my extensive imports from Colombia and other South American countries, that I might be, like him, involved in the drug trade. So he seems to have added one assumption on top of another, and yet further assumed that he could learn from you what role you had in my drug operation and so what my operation was."

"Yes, he began asking us about drugs and shipments and deliveries and whatnot in the car," said Geoff. "But how did you discover he had kidnapped us?"

"The simplest method. He phoned and told me. He said he had obviously made a mistake in capturing you, because you obviously had no idea what he was talking about, and clearly knew nothing about drugs. I assured him that my trade was in Indigenous handicrafts, and that I was not a competitor in his business.

"But Elisabeth Norland tells me that I have grounds to congratulate you, Dr. Pybus. I gather you have been recommended for tenure by your department and by its head. That's wonderful. Congratulations."

"Thank you. Something of a surprise. I only learned it from my email yesterday. I may have been the beneficiary of some sympathy votes, I suspect. How did you come to know Elisabeth?"

"Oh, we met at the cathedral."

"Ah," said Susan with a puzzled air, as though something else didn't quite fit. "But I think the tenure business has benefited from luck so far, or perhaps some other kind of intervention."

"Divine?" Mark joked.

There was an uncomfortable silence.

"By the way, Elisabeth tells me you now face yet another committee deciding on your case?" He made it a question to lead her away from the further questions he feared she might ask.

"Yes. Well, my reading of the university committee and its chair is that I may not be so lucky at the next step."

"Surely they won't disagree with the two previous positive judgements? How could they disagree with the people who best know your work and qualities?"

"The university committee, at least while it has been chaired by Professor O'Higgins, is quite ready to disagree with all previous judgements. I think he sees himself as a guardian of standards among faculties across the university. He is a stickler for research productivity. And that's where I fall down."

"But Elisabeth speaks very highly of your work."

"That's kind of her, and maybe it was her advocacy and eloquence helped me with the vote of the faculty committee. No, I have only a few articles, and Dr. O'Higgins will think them quite inadequate, I'm afraid."

Susan Pybus's voice faded slightly towards the end of the sentence.

"Susan has also written a book," Geoff interrupted, "which I think is excellent. But she's heard nothing from the publisher in months, well, nearly a year. If the book came through, if the publisher offered a contract, then matters would be quite different."

"Why doesn't the publisher let you know? Why can't you go and ask what is going on with them?"

Susan showed no inclination to answer, though Mark addressed the question to her. Instead Geoff replied for her.

"Two reasons. The first is that it isn't generally a good idea to harass publishers. You always feel they might decide against publication because they think you might keep harrying them all the time until publication of the book and beyond. And Susan is perhaps too diffident, and unwilling to ask them."

"And the second reason?"

"The publisher is the university press in Oxford, England. Not easy just to pop in and ask what's going on. And if you telephone you get a hopeless rigmarole. They have systems to avoid authors. We are so many, and we are all desperate to have our work published. Authors seem the least important people in the production of books."

Mark sat in silence, suddenly struck by his stupidity. What a fool he was; he had been active in the wrong place! He could have saved himself endless trouble by going first to the publisher and making them the offer they couldn't refuse to publish the book! What an idiot!

"Why did you have all those men with guns with you last night?" Susan asked.

"Well, the men were employees of mine. Kanehara, when he phoned, told me that he would bring you to Queen Elizabeth Park and that he would have armed colleagues from his drug business with him in case I wasn't just who I said I was. 'For insurance,' he said. I supposed I needed insurance too. Mr. Wilkie knew someone who had access to guns, so I authorized him to borrow them for the evening if possible."

"But it all seemed almost choreographed," Geoff said.

"Yes, I thought that,' said Mark. "I was nervous that it might not go well."

"You didn't seem nervous," said Susan.

"Well, fearful is perhaps better than nervous. For how I felt, I mean. But it all worked out."

They sat in silence for a few moments. Clearly he had not satisfied the Pybuses, but neither did they want to pursue questioning him about what still made little sense to them.

"I should leave you," Mark said. "Perhaps we will have a chance to meet at greater leisure soon. Perhaps with Elisabeth." His voice gave way, which he covered with a small cough.

"We look forward to that with real pleasure," Geoff added.

They saw him out, both standing at the door as he walked down the steps to the sidewalk. Mark felt irritated that he had been unable to think of more reassuring answers to the Pybuses' questions, and even more irritated that he had been such a fool as not to start with the publisher she had submitted her book to. He crossed the road to his car, noting that Frank and a couple of his Italians, and Alan Wilkie, and another of the Scots in another car, were parked at various points along the block. It had been risky coming here. Jimmy Phan and the Vietnamese were searching for him, and they might have picked up some clue about the Pybuses. He should have dealt more harshly with Phan; just undercutting his business was clearly not pointed enough for him to get the message.

Alan would stay around during the day, as some insurance for the Pybus family. Mark settled behind the wheel of the Tesla and pulled slowly into the road. Now that the Peruvian cocaine had reached its destination, he had no urgent calls on his attention. The routine business would turn over without him. He was reluctant to go to his condo or to either apartment. All seemed potentially insecure. Mark waved casually as he passed his various employees, who were no doubt glad of a morning's well-paid easy work, and he headed for the airport, perhaps still not too late to compensate for his past stupid strategy in trying to get Susan Pybus tenure.

CHAPTER 25

HE HAD HARDLY SLEPT ON THE FLIGHT, HAD BEEN PER-
suaded to take a bus from Heathrow to Oxford as the easiest
method of travel, then woke at four in the morning in his room
at the Randolph Hotel. He couldn't get back to sleep, so got up
at 4:30 a.m. and decided to walk around the town and observe its
colleges in what light there was.

Before heading out he strapped, as was his long habit, the gun
under his arm, recognizing that this was the kind of habit that
Elisabeth feared. In Vancouver he had left the Tesla in long-term
parking, put his gun in the trunk, and carried into the terminal the
packed bag he kept there ready for an emergency. He had phoned
Francisco, an old acquaintance from Colombia, Gabriel Pentata's
cousin, and their conduit for cocaine into Britain. A gun identical
to the one he had left behind was waiting for him in a locker at
Heathrow, the key to which he had picked up from a cashier at the
W.H. Smith newsagent in Terminal 2. This was all routine to him,
and, he reflected, something else he would have to leave behind
for Elisabeth, if that too was not already lost.

Turning from the steps of the hotel, where the porter nodded as
though transatlantic night-walkers were familiar in his experience,
Mark turned right and across the empty street. The colleges were
locked like defensive castles. To keep people in or out, or both?
No doubt the defences were required centuries ago, but did the

massive dark-creamy-gold walls have equal utility today? Looking up at the "dreaming spires," which seemed an appropriate description for this time before the beginning day, began to provide some balm to his growing disorientation.

He stood on the cobbles, surprised at the round Radcliffe Camera, and the church opposite, and the college walls on the other sides. He arrived there as the first pale hints of light from the sun were beginning to offer some help to the street lamps. He marvelled that this miracle was available every morning, but there was no one to enjoy it with him. And, following that thought, the quick sense that he wished Elisabeth was there with him. What should have been a happy thought now left him troubled.

He sat under a lamp on the steps to the Bodleian Library and took out his notebook, looking over the poem he had worked on at the airport and during the flight. It had been stimulated by his thinking of the odd conversation with which his relationship with Elisabeth had begun, when he'd weirdly talked about the view of the world being upside down, which had led him on to thinking about the planet's place in a wandering galaxy. And then mixing that up with his visit some months earlier to a friend's place on Galiano Island.

As we sway and turn
at the edge of this galaxy,
our dead grey moon
is a tethered drag
on our blue earth.
The grey moon is insensible
to what it does between these northern islands
during a late afternoon like today's.
You can look through the dark trees
at an immense weight of water
being dragged swirling below,

carrying fish
which seals harvest,
hauling them half-eaten
onto the rocks,
and what we know of this
is the fish smell
that curls and lingers around the cemetery
here on the bluffs.
It will fade in the morning
when fresh tides clean the seals' tables —
our bright galaxy is insensible
to what it carries and drags on our journey.

He needed a title for it—maybe "Fish swim in galaxies" was a bit too precious. And did he need to hammer home his point with those last two lines?—though they seemed to him needed to pull it back to echo the opening and its galactic scale. Though more troubling was the sense that the lines lacked music, cadence, rhythm—which Keiichi had reported, with much apology, had been Susan Pybus's comment on some pieces she had been forced to read during her captivity.

He looked at the words in his tight script in the notebook. How was he supposed to know whether he'd got it right? He had been pleased with the poem as he wrote it, and more so when he revised and cut out the bits that didn't fit. But seeing them from the perspective of the everyday world that was waking around him, what did it amount to?—just an idle frippery, perhaps pleasant, but it was a lightweight packet of words, which amounted to nothing much. Auden was right; poetry made nothing happen. He was too distracted to do anything with it now.

As the town began to come to life, he returned to the hotel, and lay down, catching perhaps an hour of sleep before again lying too wide awake, staring at the moulded ceiling. He must have slept with his mouth open; it felt as though a flock of moths had flown in and decayed there. He brushed his teeth energetically; showered; dressed; breakfasted among assertive luxury and loud, plummy English voices; and asked at the desk for directions to the university press, which turned out to be just a short walk.

Strolling along the crowded sidewalk he found himself worrying about Elisabeth's disapproval at his method of trying to get Susan Pybus tenure. Her veto was eating at his resolve. He still felt compelled to ensure Susan got tenure, yet at the same time wanted not to use compulsion in the process. So why the elaborately procured gun? He shrugged, grimaced; and realized he was becoming one of those people who failed to censor their inner lives as they walk along the street. Soon people would be looking at him, and then it would be the men in white coats, he smiled ruefully—doing it again.

His exasperation at his accumulating dilemmas and collapsing confidence added a little to the pressure he brought to bear on those at the press building who assured him that he would be unable to see the managing editor in charge of academic submissions of the kind he described. Mark's quiet insistence that he see him, and see him now, resulted in some hasty phone calls, and an eventual surly agreement that he would be able to have a few minutes of the valuable time and attention of Mr. Dylan Madoc-Jones.

Madoc-Jones met Mark at the door of his office, to which Mark had been brought by an immensely tall young woman from reception. Perhaps the range of males she was willing to consider was limited? But why so, he reflected, and was somehow pleased to notice a wedding ring as she introduced him to the Welshman.

Madoc-Jones, right arm in plaster and in a sling, greeted Mark with a warm upside-down left-handed handshake and an invitation to come into the office and sit down.

"What a surprising building," Mark said. "It is more like a college, with that central quadrangle, than a set of offices."

"True. If you prefer honeyed Cotswold stone colleges to modern plastic and glass confections, this is the place. But I'm not so sure. Anyway, you are following up a manuscript submission, I gather. Not something we encourage … But here you are."

"What did you do to the arm?"

"Ask not what I did to the arm, but what the arm did for me. I fell while struggling to hold the stars in place." This claim was reinforced with a swing of the good arm towards the ceiling, completing its circle by sweeping though his disarrayed hair. "Their disturbing movements seem to have had something to do with a quantity of a single malt whisky, which I had never sampled before, and about which a considered and expert judgement was being requested. The only way to accumulate the appropriate expertise in the short time available, I concluded, was to sample as much as possible. It was this dedication that led to my downfall. As the stars veered sideways, I tried to stop them with my arm, which apparently broke my fall, but broke itself in the process … Anyway, clearly meriting a Croix de Guerre, with bar, or whatever distilleries bestow for heroic conduct in the face of allies … Perhaps you could tell me what you want?"

"A friend in Canada submitted a manuscript to you and has heard nothing for many months. I was going to be in Oxford, and so said I would call in and see what I could find out for her. I'm sure you will want to publish it."

"Are you?"

"Yes. Quite sure."

Madoc-Jones was about to say more, but paused as he looked at Mark.

"Very good of you to take the trouble on his—or her?—behalf."

Mark nodded at the interrogative "her."

"Her name or the title?"

"It isn't good of me, as the matter touches my interest. Apart from other reasons, my friend is being considered for tenure at her university. Acceptance of the book could make all the difference. Her name is Susan Pybus."

"Rings a distant bell. But these days most things do."

He tapped at his computer.

"Yes. Here it is. The manuscript was given to the tender care of …" he clicked clumsily a couple of times manipulating the mouse awkwardly with his left hand, "… oh dear, Runciman."

Madoc-Jones sat back and pushed his free hand another couple of times through his hair. Then rubbed his face hard, making a sound like a small irregular motor interrupting a large dog attacking its food, finishing with a satisfied grunt.

"You mean this lady hasn't heard anything? At all? For months?"

"Correct."

"Please come with me, and I shall introduce you to the scale of our immediate problem. Welcome, incidentally to academentia; our homage to the great God of Drivel."

Mark rose and followed the swaying editor along the broad corridor, through whose windows on one side the lawn shone dazzlingly wide. On the other were mostly open doors into offices. Madoc-Jones greeted everyone he passed with abusive remarks, or elaborate jokes, shouting into open office doors such observations as "Stop wanking, Rudrum, and edit something!" "That travel book you are editing, Polly, isn't going anywhere." "We need to get that football book out before the cup final, Janice, and remember, football is like chess, except for the dice." "Readers contaminate the pure spirit of your poetry books, Arnham, but you won't need to worry about that." All expressed in the cheeriest of tones, which were accepted by each visible victim with a smile, and some rolling of eyes. He veered round a corner, good arm out simulating an airplane, pulled out a key, and entered the second office along.

Mark's disorientation lurched a further dimension beyond what the accumulation of this unplanned visit, unfamiliar sense

of incompetence, jet lag, and the gut-undermining residue of
Elisabeth's last tearful phone call had already delivered to his brain,
which resembled at the moment Madoc-Jones's description of his
swirling stars. From his years at university in faraway Santiago
the image of Oxford University's shield with the three crowns
and "Dominus illuminatio mea" stood for a kind of unassailable
intellectual authority when it appeared on the cover of a book.
How could this pleasant clown be a senior editor and his non-stop
jokes—about Polly's going-nowhere travel book, and Rudrum's
wanking, and football being like chess except for the dice—all be
part of what sustained that authority?

Flicking on a light and also going round a book-piled table
to open the blinds, Madoc-Jones then pushed the start button
on Runciman's computer on his desk. Mark was astonished at
the masses of paper piled on the desk, on chairs, in stacks on the
floor, on the lower bookshelves. The higher shelves were filled with
neatly packed books, mostly in three or four copies of each title.
He assumed these were the set Runciman had been responsible for
shepherding through to publication. The crowded shelves filling
one side of the office gave witness to a long career.

"Believe it or not, Runciman is superbly well organized. Mind
you, he refuses to update this antique computer. I just want to
check where things stand with the manuscript. We've been trying
to locate all his … Ah, here we are. Suzanne … er?"

"Susan Pybus. P—Y—B—U—S."

"Quite. Okay. Here we go. Okay. Manuscript received … oh
dear, May of last year. We do like to move things along faster than
that, of course. Sent out for reviews in fairly short order. Well,
must have passed muster with Runciman for him to send it out.
One review back in June. Ah, here's a problem. The other reviewer.
Here's three, four letters. Let's just see … I feared so. Asking for
the review or, failing that, the manuscript back. September. Then

he sent it out to someone else. Then a letter to her in late October. Another in … oh dear, what a dreary lot of idle farts academics are. Ah, sorry. Are you…?

"No."

"Good. Good. And here's another a month ago. And then nothing."

"Where is Mr. Runciman?"

"Up in the John Radcliffe. The hospital. Stroke. Some weeks ago. That's why we're … Now, where did he keep recent correspondence? I mean, if he'd had a reply. If he had got a review from this lady, she'd have sent it in on hard copy, with the manuscript. That's what we require. Trouble is that Mrs. Sherman, Runciman's secretary, is home on stress leave. Worked here with him for twenty-seven years. She found him stroked. Went a bit troppo. She came in for a few days after, but she mainly just cried all day, so I sent her home. Anyway, it's been a bit difficult even sorting out how we might begin to sort it all out. I don't like to phone her, as it just starts her off again."

Madoc-Jones reverted to shoving his hand through the thicket on his head, then rubbing his face and making peculiar sounds.

"I know it looks chaotic." Madoc-Jones swept his arm with the cast heavily around the room. "But Runciman has a system. I mean, every place in the room represents a state of the manuscripts in it, in their process towards publication or review. He hated filing cabinets for some reason. It's just that only he and Mrs. Sherman know the system. I could get a couple of people in to try to locate the manuscript. It might take some time."

Mark looked around the room. "How many books is he responsible for?"

"Well, it's not the books so much as the manuscripts that are submitted. We get gazillions. Every senior academic thinks he, or she, has earned the right to an OUP book, and every junior thinks that it will make her or his career. Anyway, it seems like every bloody academic in the English-speaking world ships us their manuscripts first. When we turn them down they get more realistic. But we have to look at them all in greater or lesser degree. Runciman handles a large proportion of them. He's very conscientious. Likes everyone to have a fair shot.

"Shit. What a buggering mess! It'll take us months to sort through this bloody shambles. Look, I'm sorry. I just hoped there'd be something on his computer that would tell us what had happened. Nearly everyone's manuscript gets rejected. I thought there might be the rejection letter in his rejects file."

"But there isn't?"

"True, but that likely means only that he hadn't got round to writing it."

"Perhaps you could just write an acceptance letter to Dr. Pybus, and publish the manuscript when you find it?"

"In a pig's arse, I could."

"Why not? It's a good book. And even if it wasn't, one dud here or there would hardly matter to you."

Mark looked intently at Madoc-Jones, trying to impress a little fear into him. But the Welshman either didn't notice or didn't care.

"I've often thought the same. Slip in some deliberate piece of absolute stinking garbage, dripping with jargon and every pretentious cliché, arguing patent nonsense. I actually once started writing such a desirable book. But then I come to my senses, and realized that clichéd garbage describes much of what we put out anyway."

"So, why not another one? It would make Dr. Pybus happy, get her tenure, and, more important immediately, make me and you happy."

"If only I could make myself happy by doing something so simple. Look, I can see you're serious. It's a no go, I'm afraid. I can't authorize a manuscript just like that. Needs to go to the bloody syndics, or Sin Dicks, as I prefer to call them. Has to have the reviewers' letters attached. All the steps of the process documented. Sales estimates. Marketing twerps' comments. Well, the whole boiling. Sorry." He said it as though he really meant it.

"But you could fake all that."

"I could but I won't. Sorry. Nice of you to try so hard for your friend."

"If I were to offer you £50,000?"

"One of my favourite numbers. Come on. I've got to get back to my current pile of shit."

Madoc-Jones stood and trod carefully around the piles of manuscript as he made for the door. Mark remained seated. Somewhere in this mess is the potential solution to his nagging compulsion. Should he compel Madoc-Jones to write the letter? He felt a great weariness, realizing his simple impulse was to do exactly what Elisabeth had tried to forbid, and feared would remain his habit for the rest of his life. No doubt jet lag, but this quixotic impulse seemed to be increasingly entangled in moral confusion and emotional dread. And this man whom he had travelled so far to negotiate with, Mark knew, was beyond negotiation. He played the clown, but had something he was honest to. Mark looked up at the editor holding the door open for him.

"You're a great disappointment to me, Mr. Madoc-Jones."

"To you? Get in line! If you want to see disappointment in me that dwarfs yours as does the Great Australian desert Runciman's desk surface, you should consider my wife's. And then, continent scale, her mother's. And galaxies further, my very own." He said it with a smile.

Mark smiled in return.

"Please close the door, Mr. Madoc-Jones. I did have a further point to make."

As Madoc-Jones closed the door and came a few steps back into the room, Mark removed the gun from the holster under his arm. He screwed on the silencer while motioning the Welshman back towards Runciman's desk.

"You can't be serious. I suspect you are, if I am speaking such clichés. What do ..."

"Now, the other arm, or a leg, or two? What will it take?"

"What will what take, for God's sake? Bit out of proportion, don't you think?"

"No. Entirely proportionate, I'd say. You have been unimpressed with my first offer, which was therefore obviously out of proportion. So I am moving up to a threat that I hope will be greater than your resistance to doing what I want. And I am unwilling to accept no for an answer. Now please return to the computer and write your standard acceptance letter, inserting Dr. Pybus's name, and all the other details that would be normal. Then print it out and sign it."

"And if I continue to refuse?"

"I will shoot you, in various limbs to begin with, and then dead if necessary. Then I will find someone else who will do what I want."

"And I thought you were a pleasant and intelligent chap."

Madoc-Jones sat at the computer and pecked inefficiently with the one hand.

"You could have done this yourself, you know, without leaving Canada. I mean, download the OUP crest from our website, paste it onto your word processor, and compose your own letter. Wouldn't perhaps have looked quite as authentic as this, but who'd know?"

Mark tried not to show the impact on him of Madoc-Jones's simple point. Of course he could! What a howling idiotic incompetent he was! Frank could have put together a convincing package of letter and referees comments, sales projections, whatever was needed.

"I really don't need further convincing about how incompetently I am going about this. I am sorry; I must be a big disappointment to you too."

"I was going to say that, but thought you might have shot me, in one or more of my limbs. I was going to invite you for a drink."

Madoc-Jones sounded regretful and resentful together as he pecked away at the keys. After a few minutes, the letter was printed, and he signed it painfully, dragging his bandaged arm sideways, and handed it to Mark.

"I suppose I should have accepted the £50,000."

"You wouldn't have. I'll send you a present later."

"I don't want anything for this. You realize that we'll deny accepting the book as soon as anyone inquires. And what will happen to your friend's tenure when the book fails to appear?"

"Don't worry. This will suffice for now. One step at a time. If it becomes necessary for you to publish the book, you will publish the book."

CHAPTER 26

OVER ICELAND, THE CAPTAIN ANNOUNCED THAT THERE was nothing to be alarmed about, and that everything in the plane was behaving perfectly normally. He immediately had everyone's complete attention. It was just one of those regulations they had to follow, he assured them. A red light had gone on among the cockpit controls and they had to return to Heathrow to check it out and get another plane ready. These things happen every now and then. There are so many backup safety checks built in, it just takes a light bulb burning out or a small error in one of the computers. He encouraged them also to ignore all the fire engines that would be lined up on the runway for their return. Just routine precautions. Those fellows have so little to do that they love to come roaring out at the slightest excuse.

Mark exchanged shrugs and grimaces with the cream-suited young woman in the seat next to him in the first-class cabin.

"That's the second time for me in two days!" she said in exasperation. "Yesterday they couldn't withdraw the landing gear leaving Cairo, so we had to go back. Why they couldn't have gone on and dealt with it at Heathrow I don't understand. I had to spend most of the night in the airport till they could get another plane to take us to Heathrow. Then this was the first flight they could get me onto. It's going to take me three days to get from Cairo to Calgary!"

Mark made sympathetic noises, wondering why she would want to go from Cairo to Calgary, as she didn't look like an oil executive and did look as though she had just come directly from a dressing room at her expensive couturier. But she had sat absorbed to lip-biting intensity in what, as far as he could tell from occasional glances, was the most salacious pornography. She had the look of a potential or actual customer for his cocaine.

He was already tired; frustrated by the futility of his attempt to influence Madoc-Jones at Oxford University Press and the dubious victory embodied in the letter he carried in his jacket pocket. How could he not have thought of the obvious possibility of producing such a letter in Vancouver? He was trying to focus on too many things, and managing none of them well, especially getting Pybus a tenure she might not benefit from in the long run; echoes of O'Higgins and St. Teresa's admonition to be careful what you wish for.

It was after midnight before they took off again. Mark managed to sleep intermittently, seeing at each momentary waking his immaculate neighbour in the pool of light from her overhead console hunched over her dirty book. They arrived in Vancouver in the middle of the night, and walked through a ghostly airport. His seat companion strode with a sprightly step, though she was facing another long wait here before picking up her connection to Calgary. He, who had dozed unsatisfactorily during much of the flight, was entirely unrefreshed. Perhaps he should have asked if she'd had another volume he might borrow.

Now in his home city his telephones were suspect, and his condo and apartments might be being watched. He was fairly sure that only Kanehara was aware of the West End apartment, and he was for the time being more committed to protecting Mark than threatening his safety. But if Kanehara had located it, Jimmy Phan could have done so as well. Mark went to the bank of phones inside the terminal and booked himself into a room at a nearby motel, retrieved his car from the long-stay parking lot—resisting the temptation to check under the hood after his experience with the other Tesla, and once in the motel room, immediately fell asleep.

A rainy morning. He rolled sideways to look at the bedside clock, and sprung awake. It was after 10 a.m. He needed a shave, and this place, unlike the Randolph in Oxford, wouldn't be likely to supply its guests with free razors, combs, toothbrushes and paste. He dialled Elisabeth's office number, and was surprised at how he felt at home with the sound of her voice, how he took comfort in it.

"Elisabeth. Good morning. It's Mark."

"Where have you been? I've been phoning the numbers you gave me and getting only recorded messages?"

"Sorry. I should have told you. I left the country briefly, unplanned really."

"Are you all right? Was there some danger?"

Was she as concerned as she sounded, he wondered with satisfaction.

"No, no danger. I foolishly decided to visit Susan Pybus's publisher in Oxford, to see what was happening with her manuscript."

"You did what? You just went to England ... What did you find out?"

"Little, I'm afraid. Except that publishing seems not the best organized of the world's businesses. Mind you, I did get a letter from them accepting the manuscript."

"Were you aware that the university committee is meeting soon to review her case? What do you mean you got a letter from them? Did they ..."

"I'll explain later. I didn't know about the committee meeting. When is it?"

"Eleven o'clock. In the administration building offices. Second floor. There's a conference room at the back. Turn right at the top of the stairs. Look, I've been thinking about what you said. About the injustice of Susan not getting tenure when people like ... like most of the tenured faculty have it. I think you are right that sometimes the procedures we invent to ensure justice can become very inefficient and yield injustice. There's nothing sacred about the tenure procedures, especially when they deny someone like Susan tenure."

She talked very fast, in a way Mark had not heard before. As though she had been storing the words and they were now unstoppered: "I'm sorry. Yesterday was a hard day. Susan had had some kind of conversation with O'Higgins, and she interpreted something he said as indicating her publications just couldn't support a positive vote. Then Conrad Smith came by my office. Closed the door behind him. Started accusing me of trying to organize terrorists—I think he meant you—to get Susan tenure. He just kept at me. He stood close. He uses his bulk to intimidate: leaned over while I sat at my desk. I thought he was going to hit me, or something worse. I hate it when someone makes me cry. Said he could see no virtue in her case. That we were part of a feminist cabal. He also had the nerve to tell me I'd better not mention his visit to anyone, the fool. Then he said that the Colombian drug runner was going to get his comeuppance. I don't know what he meant. I do hope you will be careful."

Elisabeth's voice was beginning to thicken, as she started to cry. Mark was concerned both for her and for the fact that Smith could know about him, and about the Vietnamese threats to him. "I mean, I think it would be no bad thing to use your influence with these people, and make them give Susan tenure. These old farts got tenure in the days when everyone got it, just as long as you were the right sort of old boy, and they all supported each other. Chummy and corrupt, and now they demand that Susan, and young women in particular, publish reams more than some of them have published in their whole useless careers ... Are you still there?"

"Yes. Oh yes. I am so sorry that you have been bullied by Smith. Perhaps I should have a word with him."

"No. Please. That would be pointless. But you might want to do something about the committee meeting."

"I am … I had begun to think that you were right and that I should let matters take their course. The Oxford visit … I thought if the manuscript was in their process, I could hurry it along, or even persuade them … I really didn't think what I was doing. And the editor I saw in Oxford quoted St. Teresa of Ávila at me, or, no, that was O'Higgins, to the effect that when we try to shape the world and people's lives, even with the best intentions, we often cause more unhappiness than good. And that perhaps Susan would make a better life for herself outside the university."

He could hear Elisabeth sobbing.

"Please … I am sorry to make matters worse. I can …"

"No. I was laughing and crying together. Just makes a funny sound. Thinking that I'd persuaded you and you'd persuaded me. Do you mean you don't think you should interfere now?"

"It was only your … I don't know what I think. I had intended to take my letter to Dr. O'Higgins, and see what additional suasion I can bring to bear on him. I'd better move fast."

"Good luck. Thank you! O'Higgins, everyone says, is a tough nut."

"I'll take some tough nutcrackers with me. I must move quickly. Talk to you later."

Mark lay back for a few seconds, to gather himself. A habit from his mid-twenties when he had learned that a few thoughtful moments might save his life, or produce a plan that had eluded systematic thought earlier. And that moment, in which the day lies all before one, is a small echo of birth and hope. But he had little time today. He had to be at the university within the hour, and his letter from Oxford might not be enough to persuade O'Higgins. It would be wise to take his tough nut-crackers with him.

He dressed quickly and perched on the side of the bed to decipher the instructions for using the in-room phone.

"Hi Alan. I've been out of the country for a day or so. I wonder if you can spare me a couple of hours now."

"Thank God you called, Mr. Morata. I tell you I wasn't sure what to do."

"What's the trouble?"

"I got a call from one o' those boys of Kanehara's. He said not to go out to the university, or to go with a lot o' muscle. They thought you would be goin' out there today for something, but Jimmy Phan has found out about it, and they've got a dozen lads waitin' on you. Was it that you were callin' about? I'm a bit twitchy, Mr. Morata. Sorry. I mean, thinking you might be walking into something, and getting that call. I don't mind tellin' ya, I dinna appreciate them phonin' me. That means they know where I live. I didn't know what direction you might be comin' from. And I've been phonin' round and can't raise enough of our lads. Frank and his boys went up to Whistler—said you knew all about it. An' I can't raise Brian Carroll or his brother. Brian could get us a dozen fellas, but he's not answering any of his phones. The valley boys are too far away to be here fast, and there's not a peep from Felipe."

"Who do you have?"

"There's just me and Dave. We could pull some of the lads away from the Pybus place. I don't see there's any worries there."

"How many?"

"There's four, if we pull them all."

"That's seven of us against a dozen or more of Jimmy Phan's Vietnamese."

"Aye. I dinna like it. It's not the numbers. But they've had all the advantages, setting up, choosing their spots. Do you know the place we're goin'?"

"Not well. Only where it is. We have to do this quickly, Alan. I don't think adding the four from the Pybus place will make the difference. Can you pick me up? I'm at the Best Western place on Marine Drive, just by the bridge over to the airport."

"I know the one. Goes around the corner. Next to the body shop."

"I didn't notice a body shop. I came in the middle of the night. How soon?"

"I'll be there in about fifteen minutes."

As he checked out, Mark wondered how Jimmy Phan could have found out about the tenure committee meeting. Conrad Smith thought the "Colombian drug runner" was going to get his comeuppance. Mark could only assume that Smith had been visited again, by Phan. That would be how Phan could know when and where the committee was meeting. Conrad Smith and Jimmy Phan would make a good pair; if the cards dealt them in the beginning had been mixed, each might have fitted the slot the other occupied.

As Mark waited on the sidewalk outside the hotel he wondered what had been spun into the dark web on the day of his own birth—was he another English professor manqué for whom the Fates had spun a wrong thread; a wrong time thread, a wrong place thread? He used to believe that stuff about being master of one's fate, captain of one's soul, but more recently he felt he was being demoted from captain to something more like a cabin boy at the mercy of all kinds of people as well as fate.

CHAPTER

27

MARK HOPPED INTO THE BACK OF WILKIE'S CAR AS IT screeched to a halt by the curb.

"Can you go out to the university, Alan, and park by … I'll direct you as we get closer."

Mark flicked up a blue tarpaulin from the floor by the other side of the car.

"Good God, Alan, what're these?"

Alan Wilkie turned round from the driver's seat, and his son Dave grinned broadly.

"D'ya like them?" Alan asked with a smile. "They're the Uzis with the Bowers Vers 9S Silencer. Good little machine if you need to clean a room or take out a bunch o' lads quietly. I thought this might be a discreet kinda job, so Dave put them together. There's one fer you too."

"Thanks, but I think we will need to avoid Phan's guys, if we can."

"Aye, but if we can't, yon Uzis will come in very handy."

Mark directed Alan to keep to the road that bordered the campus, and take an entrance sufficiently distant from the Administration Building that Phan, with only a dozen men, wouldn't have the resources to watch. He'd have to concentrate his dozen quite close to the committee room, with perhaps eight of them around the entrance of the building or even inside. Four or five might be sacrificed to watching the main approaches, armed primarily with cell phones.

They parked the car in the lot by the old Faculty Club.

"There are two approaches," Mark said. "To the north and south of the buildings directly across there. Both will be watched by people who would recognize Alan and me. Now, none of this business is worth anyone here getting hurt, so I want to take it step by step, without any undue risk, and I want to be able to withdraw at any point if it begins to look dangerous."

As he spoke, a student passed close to the car on a bike, and began fastening it to the rails outside the doors to the Faculty Club.

"It would be useful first to get a sense of what we're up against."

Mark climbed out of the car and approached the student, pulling out his wallet and turning to indicate to Dave Wilkie that he should follow.

"Excuse me," Mark addressed the student. "Are you in a hurry?"

The young Asian man smiled, looked at his watch, and shrugged. "Not too much. Why?"

Mark pulled out four fifty-dollar bills, and two twenty-pound notes and handed them to the student with a shrug.

"It's a complicated story, but my young friend here would like to borrow your rain jacket and bag and the books for about ten minutes. You'll get them all back then."

The student shrugged back, still smiling. "They aren't worth that, but sure."

Dave slipped the blue and green rain jacket over his jacket, hoisted the books under his arm, and slipped the small bag over his shoulder.

The student pointed at the club building ahead. "I'm supposed to meet someone in here, okay? I'll be back in a minute."

"Sure."

"Just take a stroll along the path up there, Dave. We're headed for the building with the pointed door, on the left as you look down between the buildings. As much as you can see in a couple of minutes. Play it casual. You could go into the building if it seems easy, take a look inside."

"Sure. No problem."

Dave walked across from the car park and Mark joined Alan in the small cover the car afforded them. As Mark glanced after Dave, and then turned his eyes in the direction he was walking, he saw a familiar figure, head down, no doubt making for the Administration building.

"O'Higgins!" Mark muttered to himself. "Dave," he called. "Back here a minute!"

As Dave leaned down to the car window, Mark gave him the letter from Madoc-Jones accepting the Pybus book.

"See the balding guy? Yes. That one. Can you catch him up, give him this letter. His name's O'Higgins. Professor. Say you were asked to give him the letter by the chair of the English department. The chair. Quick."

Dave turned the corner walking fast after O'Higgins. This might be the easy way, Mark hoped. Alan sat quietly, having pulled one of the Uzis from the rear and slid it under his coat. He was good at calculating risks, and knew that Dave was in no danger, but he was, Mark could feel, more than usually alert.

"I'm sure you will have thought about Denver or getting out of the business, Alan. Any conclusions?"

"This morning helped to make it clearer, funnily enough. I'd decided I didna want to work for Kanehara and I'm not keen on uppin' sticks and movin' to the states. I talked it over with Mrs. Wilkie. We had both been thinking about Dave. Aye, I'm out if you're closing down Vancouver, Mr. Morata. That okay?"

"I'm relieved. We'll arrange a good early retirement package, and a healthy pension."

"We're very grateful, Mr. Morata. Mrs. Wilkie said I was to say so too. But it just all made me twitchy about today. I suppose it's Dave."

"Nothing about this operation is worth endangering Dave, or you. We'll just drive away if it looks risky."

In just a few minutes Dave came back towards the car, carrying, Mark was surprised to see, the opened letter. Why hadn't O'Higgins taken it?

"What happened? Didn't he read the letter?"

"Yeah. He handed it back to me and just said that's irrelevant. Then he looked at me, a bit fierce, and said someone's playing games, and walked off. Not very polite. I took a quick look, like you said, Mr. Morata, down by the entrance to the building you mentioned. It's where that guy I showed the letter to went in. There's about five of them outside, hanging near the door, with the pointy top, trying to look casual, pretending to be having some conversations. There's two at this end of the little roadway, one on either side, sort of back in the shrubs, not well hidden. And I could see one at the other end, probably another there I couldn't see."

"So that leaves three or four. They could be further out wandering up and down the roadway, or perhaps inside the building."

"Could you see what kinds of firepower they were carrying?" asked Alan.

"Nothing big that I could see. Probably all hand stuff. But I couldn't see them all. But no loose coats or anything."

"You know, Mr. Morata," said Alan quietly. "They think you're going to show up unsuspectin' like, and they expect to be able to take you out with handguns before you know what's going on. If we all move in fast, keepin' close to the buildings up there, we can take them all out with the Uzis before they know what's hit them. It'd be quick and easy and quiet. Sure, I know you don't like to move until you've got a massive advantage, but this is easy. These lads aren't too swift either. It's no like takin' on a bunch of Kanehara's boys."

After a pause, as Mark sat silently, Alan added, "You've invested a lot a time in this. Ya don't wanna let it all go, and we'd also kick a hole in Phan's operation. We shouldn't have let him go after the drop in English Bay. You know I think that, eh?"

"Yes. But it really isn't worth it. You wouldn't want to see Dave hurt for something like this. O'Higgins's response to the letter has made me angry, and I don't trust myself planning when I'm angry. If we go as a group, I can't see how we can avoid a gun battle, and when bullets are flying you can't control where they will all land."

Mark spun round quickly, hand moving for his gun, to face the point where there had been a noise against his window. It was the student.

"Can I have my stuff back now?"

Mark nodded to Dave who began peeling off the coat and handing the rest of the stuff back.

"Thanks."

"No worries. Rent's due. Gift from heaven." The student waved as he walked away.

"I've noticed that all the university buildings I've been in have more than one entrance," said Mark.

"Aye, it's the building code."

"They are expecting me to come along one of the roadways, and think I don't know they're expecting me. We must use our advantage. There are two buildings between us and them ..."

Mark opened the window and shouted after the student, "Can I borrow the books for about a half hour? Another hundred."

The student came running back, and handed them through the window. "I'll be inside. You could leave them at the desk. Say Derek Lee will pick them up."

Mark climbed out of the car, indicating that the Wilkies should stay put.

"Stay here, okay? A professor strolling alone through these buildings with books under his arm won't alert any suspicion. Flanked by two guys with loose coats, just might alarm folk."

"Aye. Makes sense. I dinna like it, though," Alan said tightly. He leaned over his seat, saying "You'd be better off if you make it to your committee to have an Uzi."

"I think my Glock will be sufficient. I don't anticipate any of the professors will be packing a piece."

Once out of the car park, which was sheltered by trees and a bus terminal to the east, Mark would be most vulnerable. He had to get across the road and into the first building undetected. If Phan had people walking around the approach roads, someone might appear and see him. He hunched over, the books prominent, head lowered, willing himself to look like a professor late for class. Struck, as he reached the far pavement, that he was not getting the kick of adrenalin, the spark of sheer pleasure, that danger used to give him so liberally. Was this age? Or intimations of a different life that was now possible? Or even catching Alan's anxiety about his son?

He pushed open the glass doors of the building, not daring to look round, as that might be the small mistake that would identify him to anyone watching. The building, he realized as he had approached it, was not classrooms and offices, but a theatre, or at least the ground floor he entered was a theatre foyer.

It wasn't clear how one reached the back of the building. There seemed to be no corridor around the theatre. Perhaps there was a way upstairs, or more easy and quick, he hoped, an exit behind the stage. There was no one in the box-office booths this early in the day, so he pushed through the double doors into the theatre itself.

There were voices, a group of maybe a dozen students on the stage, and an equal number sitting in the first seats of the stalls. As the door thumped closed behind him, the voices stopped, and a few of those in the front seats turned to look at him. The only thing to do was keep moving fast. There were steps up to the stage on the right, but no other evident exit to the rear.

"Excuse me. Can I help you?" said one of the men on the stage challengingly—perhaps a professor.

Mark kept moving fast down towards the stage.

"Sorry?" he said. "I didn't hear you."

"I asked whether I could help you. We're rehearsing."

"Yes. Good." Mark kept moving. He was within a few metres of the steps. He needed to give them something to keep anyone from trying to stop him. After dealing with suspicious police and army in various places in the Americas, this was no problem.

"I got a call about the pastrinders." Mark smiled, slurring the meaningless word. "Said I'd check backstage. Professor Minglestroog," he slurred again as he mounted the steps, smiling at the two students at the side of the stage, and waving casually at the professor as he plunged into the darkness between the curtains. Within seconds he was among the ropes and rows of prop clothing. Ahead was the welcome sight of a red exit sign. He skipped down dimly lighted steps, and turned left towards a door in the rear wall. This led to a narrow corridor. About ten metres to the right was a more substantial door underneath another exit sign, with a release bar that should take him outside.

He paused as the door swung closed behind him. Ahead was a short path between low privet hedges. There was a small, cultivated area between the two buildings, but Mark was acutely aware that this area was open to view from the roadways at both ends of the buildings. He used the same routine as before, books up and prominent under his arm, head low, shoulders hunched, and he moved fast across the short garden, up the steps, and through the glass double doors opposite.

Why did none of these buildings have a simple central corridor from front to back? He walked ahead, along a broad corridor with lockers on either side, with an occasional student grabbing or storing books. The corridor ended at glass doors, with a reception desk and secretary behind it. He pushed open the door, and smiled down at the secretary.

"Good morning. I was trying to find a door leading out towards the administration building?" He made it a question, in the Canadian way.

A plump, brown-haired woman scowled up at him. "You can go to the ends of the corridor, either way—they're exactly the same distance—and then turn that way," she said, pointing over her head.

"Isn't there a door leading directly out that way?" Mark pointed over her head too.

"Not on this level. There's the basement, but you'd have to go round anyway, so you may as well go at this level." But that would take him out at the ends of the building where Phan had men posted.

"And how do I get to the basement level?"

She paused, as though offended that he was refusing to take her directions.

"You'll have to go back the way you came, to the front door, then there's the stairs behind the first door on the right."

"Thank you so much for your helpfulness."

She scowled again, as though suspecting sarcasm. Mark walked fast, aware of time passing, and the fact that the committee meeting was already underway. And it might not take them long to deal with Susan Pybus's case if O'Higgins had decided that it was not viable. He skipped fast down the stairs, turned towards the rear of the building along a broad corridor.

Emerging from the dingy basement door, Mark faced another mini-garden strip between the two buildings, but this one was wider than the last. He stayed within the protection of the slight out-jutting surround of the door, and looked east and west. The only danger that he could see would be if his passage between the buildings should coincide with one of Phan's men walking along the sidewalks of the roads at either end of the buildings, perhaps thirty metres away.

He pushed back against the door as he saw one of the Vietnamese men stroll beyond the end of the administration building to the south. The man was looking in the other direction, towards the pathway opposite, as though expecting Mark to be coming from the direction of the Nitobe Garden where he had met Olwen Greenwood just a couple of unusual weeks ago.

Mark scanned the rear of the red-brick administration building, suddenly despondent. Clearly the same building codes had not been in operation in the 1920s. He could see no door into the rear of the building along its whole length. To get in would involve having to go round to the front after all. Damn! It wasn't worth the risk; he'd just have to retrace his steps and drive away with the Wilkies.

The rear of the administration building had broad wood-framed windows along each of its three floors. Through the window directly across from where he stood, Mark could see a number of women in an office. The next window showed, from his vantage point, a bank of file cabinets, with a shirt-sleeved Asian man flipping through one of them. In the next he could see only a single black woman sitting in the glow of a computer screen.

Worth a chance. He walked quickly across to the window and tapped. The woman looked up from her screen and he heard her voice call "Come in." He tapped on the glass more loudly. She turned, looking surprised, and stood up. Mark smiled, shrugged, and indicated she should raise the window. He heard the click of the lock, and the sash window was raised a sliver.

"What's the problem?" she asked. At least she wasn't a scowler, and, giving him hope, seemed slightly amused by this odd interruption. But he couldn't afford to stay exposed like this for long. He handed his books up towards her, which instinctively she took from him.

"Can I explain when I get in? An irregular entry, I realize, but I loathe Parkinson, who's standing at the front door waiting to invite me and my wife for dinner. And I'm late for a committee meeting upstairs. Do you mind pushing the window up a bit more?"

She laughed and pulled it wide open.

"I've never known anyone go to such trouble to avoid a dinner invitation. It's a bit high. Do you think you can manage?"

Mark crouched, put his hands on the sill, and leaped upwards, dragging one knee up onto the sill. As he balanced himself, he heard what sounded like gunfire. A couple of shots, and then … It could have been a car or motorbike. He was getting too panicky. He pulled the other leg after the first, bent under the window and lowered himself onto the carpet inside.

"Do you prefer dark or milk chocolate?" Mark asked her.

"Oh, don't worry. This has been enough fun for one morning. And I don't need"—she emphasized the word—"chocolate."

"For medicinal purposes only, of course."

"In that case, dark. Will you be coming out this way too?"

"I hope Parkinson will have left by then, but if not, it'll be my pleasure to see you later. Which way to the upstairs?"

"Out the door here, then left at the glass partition, then right and that will take you to the foot of the stairs."

As he left the office, Mark was impressed to read on her door that he had been assisted in this unconventional entry by the Secretary to the Senate. He followed the short corridor and was turning according to her directions, when he heard a shout behind him.

"Excuse me! You forgot your books."

"Oh, thanks so much." He tucked them under his arm.

Mark came to a broad, high-ceilinged corridor, with the foot of the stairs visible just ten metres ahead. As the door closed behind him, there was a slamming and scuffle ahead, and then the unmistakable sound of a silenced machine pistol. Mark dropped the books and ran forward, pulling his gun out as he went.

"Dad!" Dave Wilkie shouted. As Mark came past the end of the corridor wall, he saw Dave drilling the Uzi up the stairs. It chattered with a significant noise despite the suppressor. Alan Wilkie was leaning against the wall, his Uzi held in one hand, also firing upwards. As Mark turned and looked up the stairs, two of Phan's men came tumbling down, guns clattering on the stone steps.

"Alan, how are you?"

"Arm, just a nick. No nice, no bad. I was slow there," he said contemplatively.

"Here, Dave, help me pull these guys out of the way."

They dragged the two from the foot of the stairs and parked them sitting in the gloom of two telephone carrels on the other side of the stairs.

"You're sure you're okay, Alan?"

"Oh sure. More shock than anything."

"There's blood dripping from your hand."

"More came from those two lads. See, right down the stairs. Must have hit an artery on one o' them."

Alan pulled a large handkerchief from his pocket and Dave helped him roll up his sleeve. It took only moments to tie up the wound.

"What happened? Why did you come after me?"

"Ah, it was a mess. Sorry, Mr. Morata. I'll tell it while we go. Where's this meeting?"

"Upstairs. Right, the second room along."

They began to run up the stairs.

"One o' Phan's boys came along towards where we were parked. You were lucky he didn't see you. Came round just as you went inside. I crouched down, but the bugger came round the parking lot checking licence plates. Soon as he saw ours, he was runnin' with his cell phone out. Dave and I got the Uzis and had to get after him. But he was a quick little bastard. We got him up on the top road, dragged him in the bushes before anyone came around. Why so few people around, by the way?"

"Reading week," Mark said. "They're mostly at home preparing for exams, it seems."

"Lucky for us.," said Alan. Well, then they pour around the corner at us with their guns out. These Uzi's are bloody good—we just sprayed them, and down they fell. We left them. Too many, and we thought they might be alerted that you were coming. So we came round the front, and took out another two, and the rest left at high speed across the road into the trees. Along here?"

"Yes, it's that door." Mark pointed with his gun.

"We didn't expect the two inside."

"So we don't have to worry about Phan's people returning?"

"No," said Alan, breathing hard. "We probably only have the local cops to worry about when they find the body count out there. The place will be crawling."

"Okay. Let's sort out what we're to do here."

They were at the back of the building, through which Mark had entered below. The left wall had large windows, coloured shields above them, between which were portraits of past presidents, perhaps. Academic gowned and hooded figures anyway. The three of them paused at the door.

"They'll be round a table," said Mark. "I gather eight of them and a secretary. You could take one side of the table each, staying within ten feet or so of the door. I'll just tell them what we expect, make a show of the weapons, and we'll leave. It should be that simple. A friend gave me a list of who they all are. I just need to make it clear that we know where they live, as you put it so effectively ... in fact, let me give you the list, Alan. When I've finished talking, you can just read their names, wave the paper, and use your line about 'where you live,' adding any flourishes you want. I suspect that will do it, don't you?"

"I think we can make them feel their world is comin' to an end. A quick round from the Uzi into the table, d'ya think?"

"If any of them looks truculent maybe. Last resort, though."

Alan took his disappointment with good grace, showing no sign of the wound to his arm. Mark was feeling more uncertain about this venture than he wanted the Wilkies to see. It was only Elisabeth's conclusion that it was the right thing to do that gave him any confidence now.

"Shall we go in with the tools on show?" asked Dave Wilkie.

Mark looked along the corridor. There were a couple of women reading a paper together by a window at the end, and sounds of footsteps on the stairs. The recent mayhem seemed to have occurred with no visible effects back here. But it could only be minutes before bodies were found downstairs, and shouts and screams began to unravel any security they might still have.

"Keep them hidden till I indicate once we're inside. Ready?"

They nodded. This was simple work for them. Mark pushed the door open and walked into the room, followed immediately by the Wilkies who spread along the walls as he had suggested. The woman's voice that had been arguing at speed trailed away to silence, as everyone stopped and looked at the intruders. O'Higgins had had his head down examining his hands on the table, and looked up as the silence descended.

"Mark!" O'Higgins quickly stood up. "How good of you to come. And your colleagues."

O'Higgins grabbed a set of papers from in front of him and came up the side of the room, passing behind a row of silent, gaping academics.

"But we aren't quite finished with this committee meeting yet." O'Higgins continued speaking loudly and at speed. "My confusion. Got the times wrong. Can we talk in the corridor for a moment? Please forgive me." he said to the table of silent committee members.

O'Higgins made the mistake of trying to urge Alan Wilkie towards the door, putting a hand on his shoulder. Alan whipped his shoulder to throw off the hand with such speed and force that O'Higgin's hand was smashed hard against the wall. He winced with pain.

"Okay. Alan. Dave. Let's discuss this with Dr. O'Higgins outside. Oh, and Alan." Mark pointed at the worried face of Conrad Smith. "Remember him, will you?"

"Aye. I've got him."

In the corridor, O'Higgins was rubbing his battered hand, but seemed entirely calm, as though such intrusions were part of the normal course of events.

"I assume you came to press your arguments about the Susan Pybus case. Rare intuition, eh?" O'Higgins added with a quick smile.

"Yes. I and my colleagues are here to insist, forcefully, that in our opinion a positive decision is only just."

"You might be interested to read this."

O'Higgins proffered the sheaf of papers he had brought out of the room. Mark noticed first the blue crest of Oxford University Press, and looked down the page to see the name at the bottom of the letter. It was signed by Ethyl Sherman, pp. Cedric Runciman. He read quickly. On behalf of the syndics of the University Press … delighted to offer a contract … uniformly high praise from three referees of the highest reputation … a few revisions suggested … requesting a date for delivery of the revised manuscript … details of proposed royalty payments … personal excitement to have such an outstanding work in our list … "Warmest congratulations and very best wishes, Cedric Runciman."

Mark flicked over the page, looking briefly at the referees' letters, catching phases of praise for rigorous scholarship and so on. He handed the sheaf back to O'Higgins.

"It was a unanimous vote in favour of tenure."

"Does Susan Pybus know? I mean about the letter?"

"Of course. It was sent to her. She brought it round this morning. Charming woman. Tough nut, I'd say."

"Please excuse me. This is Mr. Wilkie, father and son, Dr. O'Higgins."

They all shook hands. The Wilkies clearly unsure just what was going on, but clear that they had finished this part of the morning's work.

"Sorry about yer hand. I don't like bein' touched."

"Seems like a sensible policy, in general. My apologies. I just wanted to discourage any unnecessary displays."

"If the case had arrived at your committee with two negative votes from the faculty and its chair, and then you had received this letter, would you have reversed their decisions?" Mark asked.

"Yes."

"So I have been wasting my time all along."

"No, no. Don't blame Ithaca if you find it to be a dull and stony place; coming to it is what gave you the journey. I have admired your, ah, work, and hope we will meet again. Perhaps at the pool some lunchtime?"

"Cavafy. The Ithaca poem."

"Right. Ithaca." O'Higgins smiled, waved casually, and re-entered the committee room.

As they walked down the stairs, Alan Wilkie said, "Yon O'Higgins would be a good fella to have beside you in a firefight. Ice cool. I like that."

"I'm not sure he'd notice the fight."

"I've been to Ithaca, you know," Alan added. "My dad used to read the *Odyssey* to us kids at dinner, when he was not too drunk and not too sober, and I always wanted to go. One o' those things; I don't know why. Before Dave was born, this was."

"And was it disappointing and the journey good?"

"No. Lousy journey, but I loved the place. Made the lousy journey worthwhile."

"I recommend not leaving by the front door, especially toting the Uzis. Just follow me." A woman was coming up the stairs with an armful of files, looking at the bloodstains, perhaps wondering if it really could be blood.

The bodies were still propped in the gloom to the side of the stairs. Mark gathered up Derek Lee's books, entered into the office area followed by the Wilkies, and round to the Secretary to the Senate's room. He tapped on the door.

"That was a short meeting!" she greeted him.

"After all that, cancelled. And Parkinson's still there. He wants to invite my colleagues too. Do you mind if we use the trade entrance again?"

Cheerfully, she unlocked the window and raised it to the full extent of the sash. Mark, followed by Alan and Dave, lowered themselves to the ground, the Wilkies hindered by the Uzis under their jackets and Mark by the books. Within a minute they were into the next building, and within four more Mark had left the books where instructed by Derek Lee, and they were back in the car and leaving the campus, passing four wailing and flashing police cars.

Back in his Broughton Street apartment, looking out over the bay, Mark had stood for a long time dwelling on the futility of all his intervention in this case. He tried to tell himself that he should think of it as his Ithaca, the disappointing place that had justified the wonderful journey. But he could not feel anything in common with Ulysses. And then, suddenly out of nowhere, he recalled the Polish doctor advising him to take up some new activity. Mark heard the distant echo of the heavily accented voice; he had not said "make poetry," but "make pottery."

CHAPTER
23

IT WAS A PERFECT SUNNY LATE SPRING DAY, AFTER DAYS OF rain. The Pybuses' lawn was rich and green, the cherry was covered in white flowers, and the apple trees were coming into bloom. Geoffrey Pybus was at the back pointing to the pump in his newly finished pond that was carrying water up to a biological bog filter, from which it ran down a stream, falling from broad stones back into the pond. The young women loudly admiring it were his wife's students. The Pybus children seemed to be responsible for carrying food and drink around to the thirty or so friends who were there to celebrate Susan Pybus's tenure.

Mark and Elisabeth stood together under the farther apple tree, talking intently.

"What did you do with it? How much was there anyway?"

"A little over four hundred and thirteen million dollars."

Elisabeth's mouth fell open. She had been cheerfully voluble all day, and seemed now stunned.

"I … I had no idea. I thought … I don't know. Thousands perhaps, maybe a million or so if it's from drugs. You gave it all away? I didn't realize. I wouldn't … I couldn't have asked you to …"

"But surely the amount is irrelevant. You said you couldn't live on drug money."

"But I thought … I imagined … four hundred and thirteen million? Million?"

"A bit more. A few hundred thousand more."

"Are you all right, Elisabeth?" Susan Pybus came towards them, her three children in tow. She looked at Elisabeth with some concern, then at Mark.

"Oh, I'm fine. Just a surprise. But all good. What a lovely party, Susan. Thanks for including us, both."

"You belong, and you both did what you could to help, even if not … Oh, I wanted you to meet our children. James, Paula, and William, who has already, despite our best efforts, become Bill. Silly of us to think we could resist it. This is Elisabeth, who works with me, and her friend, Mark, who knows Daddy."

The children solemnly shook hands in turn, then went back to their food delivery duties.

"Who's in the kitchen?" Elisabeth asked.

"My sister," said Susan, "and her new boyfriend, who is a chef at the tea house restaurant. God knows what he makes of all this, but she said he'd love to do the food."

As she spoke, Kathryn Colebrook and Hilary Lockett joined them.

"Verona was lovely," Hilary said to Mark. "Sorry you missed it. Next time I'll be better equipped to enjoy it."

He took a quick glance at Elisabeth's face as she looked sharply at Hilary.

"My loss, no doubt. Oh, and Dr. Colebrook, I've registered for your course in the fall. I have a dozen poems started, and not one finished."

Kate smiled. "Well, I hope we won't have to negotiate your grade. The cruise was great, by the way. Jim asked me to say thanks. Looking forward to the next one."

Susan seemed surprised that Mark knew so many of her colleagues. Or maybe the surprise was rather at what must have seemed their odd comments to him. And the scandalous events on the campus, which had involved serious destruction and homicide, had been represented, largely by the bewildered police, as a further eruption of Asian gang warfare in a surprising location. Some of the university's energy in exploring the causes of the violence had been muted by an anonymous donation directed to covering the costs of repairs and refurbishment. And, a little to Mark's surprise, those in the English department who knew better had remained quiet. Tenure committee members had no wish to expose their own roles, and even Conrad Smith seemed to have weighed the threat of Alan Wilkie against any likely revenge or benefit to himself and stayed silent.

Mark felt a little shamefaced, as he had had to visit each of the tenure committee members for a second time in the past few weeks, clarifying and in some cases apologizing for the futility of his previous attempt to intervene in the Pybus case, and showing evidence that it would have gone the way it had regardless of his visits to them. In each case he had repeated his previous gifts or threats to never mention to the Pybuses anything about his involvement in the case—except that Hilary received the $20,000 this time, and Gissing a new computer to take fuller advantage of his new desk, or workstation, as he preferred to call it.

As he had discussed with each of them the futility of his behaviour with regard to Susan's getting tenure, he just rubbed in further the unfamiliar sense of incompetence that had been dogging him for the past few weeks. He had particularly resented, while recognizing the justice of, those who had given evidence of pity or sympathy for his misdirected efforts.

"Do you know," Susan said to Elisabeth, "I got the nicest note from Conrad Smith, saying he was so pleased, and how well-deserved it was. He was on the university committee, you probably know. I didn't expect that. It was so nice of him. And, maybe I shouldn't mention it, but Ian Carbonell insisted on putting me on a higher step of the associate professor scale than I had expected. Now I really will have to produce the second book. And a lot of others sent emails. I do feel welcomed into the faculty family, more warmly than I had expected somehow. And someone has sent a gorgeous seventeenth-century Chinese galleon. It looks like ivory, but it surely can't be; maybe a ceramic-marble mix. I don't know. It's nearly two feet tall, with tiny figures of sailors. It must be worth a fortune. But there's no indication who it's from, and I can't imagine. Rather disturbing really. You didn't send it Mark?" He shook his head and shrugged, wondering how long before she might suspect Keiichi. "Oh, here comes Cameron with Ian now. I'd better greet them. James! Can you bring a plate for each for the two gentlemen arriving?"

"Gentlemen?" said Mark quietly when Susan had left them.

"What did you do with the money? How can you spend four hundred and thirteen million dollars? Or give it away."

"I had help. I explained to my friend Dr. Xavier O'Higgins that I had received a very large bequest, and that I needed to off-load some of it, donate it to do some good, for complicated tax reasons. Not that he believed me, of course."

"I bet four hundred and thirteen million is a number that even our prodigious mathematician will have balked over."

"He treated it as though I had asked him the time of day. He suggested seven different academic organizations, only two of which were concerned with supporting mathematics research. Three charities, which he knew had low overheads—one of them an organization of women's crisis centres. Some endowed chairs in Canada, and quite large donations to nursery schools, kindergartens, and orphanages in Eastern Europe. That soaked up quite a lot of it. The bulk of it he directed into supporting girls' education in Africa and Asia, which he is quite passionate about. He also knew about some United Nations projects in Africa, which are likely surprised by sudden large gifts. It turned out that we both shared an amateur interest in astronomy, so a number of projects searching for exoplanets can now afford more observatory time. I provided retirement packages for all my employees, and gave the legitimate businesses, the salmon and executive toy pieces, to the Wilkie family. I suspect they might make a good go of it. I'll offer consultancy services, and Alan can hire a lot of his recent colleagues. And there was a variety of other things I've forgotten just now. We went back to O'Higgins's house, and he had the whole thing calculated, and we found addresses from the internet, all in a few hours. It was amazingly easy. I thought there would be endless red tape, but money travels like electronic magic these days, at least away from one. Oh, and O'Higgins suggested a travel bursary, anonymously donated to the university, to support research on Victorian women writers."

"You gave it all away?"

"But you said ..."

Elisabeth couldn't help herself and threw her arms around his neck and kissed him. A few people turned and smiled and turned away.

"A kiss for a mere four hundred and thirteen million?" Mark said, holding her carefully. She had specified the money he had made from his past drug-dealing work, which had not included the potential from the new Peruvian operation, which Keiichi had surprised him by being able to take immediately without needing to negotiate loans. Mark's security blanket in the Zurich bank, which could buy many more kisses at that rate, had been no part of their discussion a few days ago. And the South American real estate could not easily be liquidated. And there was the Verona money, and other accounts, including a big one in Tallinn, and a smaller one from some work he did in Kaliningrad. He worried that he shouldn't deceive her, and that he was adhering to the letter rather than the spirit of their agreement. He should tell her about the nest eggs as well, and see whether she would require that he give that money away too. Though some of it was from his legitimate business. But this was no basis for what seemed like a long-term relationship. He had decided to leave it for a while and worry about it later. You never know when you might need a billion or two, or three.

"I think I'd like to sit down for just a minute. No, no, I'm fine. Perhaps I'll look in on how things are in the kitchen."

But she remained standing beside him.

"What will you live on? Or are you planning to sponge off me for the rest of your life? You didn't think to keep something aside for emergencies? I'm not sure how attractive an unemployed and impoverished ex-drug lord might be."

Her face was moving from quick smiles to small frowns and back in seconds. He supposed it was shock, but the edge was showing again.

"You mean you aren't willing to support me now? You asked me to impoverish myself, and now wonder whether you can live with a poor man."

"Didn't you really keep anything?"

"We will have to sit down and discuss money sometime soon. I haven't been able to liquidate my real estate holdings in South America, for example. My current problems are due to the fact that I was very good at my recent job. And I seem still to have accounts in banks around the place I had largely forgotten about."

"Around which place?"

"The world, I meant. So I won't immediately have to start sponging off you."

"This is too much to take in. I'll be in the kitchen. Head in stove, perhaps."

As she walked away, Olwen Greenwood approached him. She held a nearly empty glass in one hand, and a full glass in the other.

"Unusual at these affairs that one gets such excellent champagne." She sounded as though the alcohol was having a significant impact on her.

"The least I could do. And the House of Krug no doubt needs the money."

As one of the Pybus children walked by, she hurriedly gulped one glass and gave it to the boy, taking yet another full one.

"Men are such fools. You'd be much happier with me over the long run, you know. But, as I tried to warn you during our last little chat, faces and bodies trump voices. I thought you might have had more sense. I almost certainly cook better than Norland too. I suppose you have time to reconsider? Haven't done anything irrevocable yet? Except, of course, everything is irrevocable. Tragic bloody life, isn't it?" She smiled up at him. Mark wondered where she had put her retainer.

"There are more than four items to be considered," he said.

"Four? Four what?"

"Faces, bodies, voices, and cooking."

"Ha. But you'll be bored with her in a year, or two. I would be interesting forever, and more interesting as time goes by. Age will not weary me, nor custom stale my infinite variety. Of course you're just thinking about bed. But you have absolutely no idea what kind of performer I might be. And I'm not given to boasting. I suppose I should just wish you well. Did I mention I approve of the removal of the moustache? And I'll probably still be available when Norland's 'best before' date is passed. I might be willing to consider a contrite reapplication of your suit."

"I'll remember. Sad to discover that I fit into your category of the ninety-five per cent of weak-minded men?"

"How can I conclude otherwise? Indeed, very sad."

"We can only play the game with the variously defective instruments we are given, and fare forward."

"Well, don't expect me to sympathize with the folly you wreak upon yourself with your defective instruments. Ah, look, here's O'Higgins," said Olwen. He strode up the garden and joined them.

"Nearly late. How did I get to be toastmaster, by the way?"

"Universal acclamation, I can only surmise," Olwen said, finishing another of her glasses of Krug and setting off after one of the Pybus children who was carefully carrying a tray of rosé and golden drinks.

"So, Mark. Now that you are a poor man like the rest of us, what do you plan to do?" O'Higgins asked.

"I hope you won't be too surprised if I tell you I have been thinking of an academic career."

"You do surprise me."

"It has become clear to me that I know and care about literature more than many of the people I have been dealing with of late. I thought I might seek a job in the English department."

"That will be a long haul. You'll need a Ph.D."

"My friend Keiichi Kanehara has agreed to supply me with all the requisite certificates—we settled on a Master's degree from Harvard and a D. Phil. from Oxford. He has people in his organization who do very good work in the forgery line."

"But if anyone should check, there will be no record of you having been in those institutions. And, after some of the recent scandals we've seen, it is becoming common to make such checks."

"Keiichi assures me that the university records will also have the appropriate entries, including the courses that I have taken. The task has been given to one of Keiichi's most assiduous aides, a computer hacker of heroic virtuosity. It is a virtual reality. I can almost remember some of the lectures. And in return, Keiichi asks only that he might be invited to give the occasional guest seminar on haiku."

"But ... interviews ... and people here have ... er ... encountered you in the past."

"I thought I'd invite Mr. Wilkie and his son to the interviews. I feel that my reputation at the university is more likely to encourage a positive decision than any alternative, don't you? There's a bit of spare money, and I can anonymously offer to endow a couple of positions in modern English literature. I imagine, in a few years no doubt, a deanship and then president. I think universities are interesting institutions, and need some guidance. I think I could do useful work."

O'Higgins laughed. "Well, I worry what might happen when your tenure case comes to my committee. You are pulling my leg, of course."

"Somewhat, but not entirely, actually. When I joked about it with Keiichi, he did set his hacker to work, and presented me a few days later with my various degrees, fine parchment rolls and rich ribbons. I'm not sure how far he was joking; irony is difficult cross-culturally. But I do now have very fine degree documents. I must have them framed. But the serious part was that I did have a few thoughts about founding a new private university. It would be somewhat experimental in some regards. I think it would be possible to raise the money to get it started. Keiichi offered to donate, when I mentioned it."

"But you would need serious academic cred. To have its degrees recognized. I mean there are so many problems ... quite interesting problems ... creating a new university. You'd need to sign on a bunch of fairly high profile academics early on."

"Yes, I had already given thought to that. Also important to establish the right tone by the choice of the first president."

"True. Did you have anyone in mind?"

"Funny you should ask, Dr. O'Higgins."

Paula Pybus approached, carefully balancing a tray of drinks. The champagne had been poured. When everyone had a glass, a bemused and amused O'Higgins was motioned to the centre of the garden, raised his glass, and said,

"Ladies and gentlemen, boys and girls," he smiled at the Pybus children gathering around their parents under the cherry tree, "It is always a pleasure welcoming a scholar into full membership of our community. And those of you familiar with Dr. Pybus's work will recognise that we are now able to welcome a scholar of such achievement and promise that it seems certain she will become one of the most accomplished among us. So please join me in a toast to Dr. Susan Pybus and," he paused, "to her long and productive tenure!"

ACKNOWLEDGEMENTS

I have mercilessly requested comments on drafts of the manuscript of *Tenure* from family and friends. I am grateful for the responses and many helpful suggestions made by Susanna, Michael, Catherine, and David Egan, and for those of many generous friends who have read some or all of the novel: Pamela Thomas, Stan Kanehara, Isabelle Eaton, Don McLeod, Ann Pearson, Sue Macht, Antonis Parras, Alan Rudrum, Cedric Cullingford, Laurie Anderson, David Nyberg, Patrick Keeney, Pamela Dalziel, Rina Zazkis, Brenda Guild, Hunter and Kristie McEwan, David Nyberg Gordon Pybus, Max Wyman, Tom Gorman, Stuart Richmond, and Gillian Judson. In conclusion I wish to apologize to the hardworking and conscientious members of the English department of the University of British Columbia whom I have replaced with a bunch of layabouts and scoundrels.

ABOUT
THE AUTHOR

KIERAN EGAN WAS BORN IN CLONMEL, TIPPERARY, Ireland, and educated in England, receiving a BA in history. He then went to California to work with IBM Corp. as a consultant while beginning a Ph.D. at Stanford University, which he completed at Cornell University in 1972. His first academic job was at Simon Fraser University, in British Columbia, where he remained till his recent retirement. His academic work dealt with innovative educational theory and detailed practical methods whereby implications of the theory can be applied in everyday classrooms. He focused on the nature and development of imagination, and argued for its centrality in learning and the construction of meaning. There have been about forty translations of his books into around twenty languages. He and his wife have three children and five grandchildren —all, of course, wonderful, and all the children produce books of various kinds. During his academic life he gave talks in most European countries, and throughout Asia, South America, and Australasia. He also writes poetry, and his first book, *Amplified Silence*, was published in 2021 by Silver Bow Publishing. His poems have appeared in many Canadian, British, Irish, and USA magazines. He has an interest in Japanese-style gardens, and built one at the rear of his house, which resulted in a book, *Building My Zen Garden*, (Boston: Houghton Mifflin, 2000), and also a TV program in the *Recreating Eden* series. He was an athlete when younger—quite good at long-jump and triple-jump—but after four operations, he now has metal screws in his knees. He lives in Vancouver, BC.